Her opponent st

Thank God.

He rolled to his back [with] her sprawled across him, breathing hard. Their frosty breath mingled between them. He reached up – slowly – to push up his snow goggles and pull down the knitted tube covering his mouth and nose. Yowza. Hunk alert. He was one of those tanned, smooth-skinned, square-jawed, achingly handsome Nordic types. In the moonlight, his eyes looked silver.

He scowled up at her. "Uncle."

She was too knocked over by how gorgeous he was to do much but nod.

"But I think you'd lose the fight anyway," he said, with a faint Norwegian accent overlaying excellent English.

"Why's that?" she retorted. "You're looking pretty dead to me right now."

"Because my men have defeated all your comrades and they would now turn upon you and defeat you."

Karen looked up. He was right.

Dear Reader,

I started the Medusa series thinking that there are certain missions women could probably do not only as well as men but also better than them. *The Medusa Prophecy* highlights perhaps the most important of these – making contact with indigenous peoples, befriending them and gaining their assistance in completing the assignment.

Over the course of writing the Medusa series, I've learned something about Bombshell women. They're not measured in guns or martial arts moves or superhero powers. They come in all shapes and sizes, backgrounds, vocations and avocations. Women who live their lives with courage and grace in the face of overwhelming odds, women who suffer but go on, women who laugh when there are tears in their hearts – they're all Bombshell women.

My favourite Bombshell character in this book is Naliki, an elderly Sami medicine woman, a rebel in her day for fighting the Nazis and insisting on being trained as a shaman – a traditionally male role among the Samis. Then, in the waning years of her life, she quietly changes the future for an entire people. Now, that's a Bombshell! It's an honour to get to write books about strong women for strong women.

Until we meet again between the pages, happy reading!

Warmly,

Cindy

The Medusa Prophecy

CINDY DEES

MILLS & BOON™
Pure reading pleasure™

*First published in Great Britain 2008
by Harlequin Mills & Boon Limited,
Eton House, 18-24 Paradise Road, Richmond, Surrey TW9 1SR*

© Cynthia Dees 2007

ISBN: 978 0 263 85987 4

46-0808

*Harlequin Mills & Boon policy is to use papers that are
natural, renewable and recyclable products and made from
wood grown in sustainable forests. The logging and
manufacturing processes conform to the legal environmental
regulations of the country of origin.*

*Printed and bound in Spain
by Litografia Rosés S.A., Barcelona*

ABOUT THE AUTHOR

Cindy Dees started flying aeroplanes while sitting in her dad's lap at the age of three and got a pilot's licence before she got a driver's licence. At age fifteen she dropped out of school and left the horse farm in Michigan where she grew up to attend the University of Michigan.

After earning a degree in Russian and East European studies, she joined the US Air Force and became the youngest female pilot in the history of the Air Force. She flew supersonic jets, VIP airlift and the C-5 Galaxy, the world's largest aeroplane. She also worked part-time gathering intelligence. During her military career, she travelled to forty countries on five continents, was detained by the KGB and East German secret police, got shot at, flew in the first Gulf War, met her husband and amassed a lifetime's worth of war stories.

Her hobbies include professional Middle Eastern dancing, Japanese gardening and medieval re-enacting. She started writing on a bet with her mother and was thrilled to win that bet with the publication of her first book in 2001. She loves to hear from readers and can be contacted at www.cindydees.com.

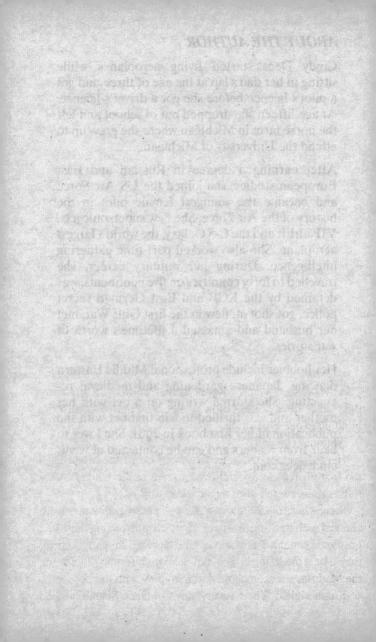

Chapter 1

"Anybody see them?" Karen Turner murmured, scanning the glacier-filled valley below while she squinted against the blinding expanse of white.

Nothing. *Dammit.*

Her teammates, the other five members of the Medusas—the first all-female Special Forces team in the United States military—muttered grim negatives as well.

Somewhere out there was a Norwegian Special Forces team charged with tracking down the Medusas and treating them like hostiles if caught. Translation: if the Norwegians caught them, they'd beat the living crap out of them in the name of teaching the Medusas a lesson about daring to play with the boys.

Karen sighed. Their supervisor, Col. Jack Scatalone, had

warned them this wouldn't be easy. He'd said that foreign Special Forces teams would take grave offense at women trying to do the same job as men. American women soldiers had been allowed into combat in the 1990s and American soldiers had had a decade of getting used to the idea under their belts already. Not so in most other parts of the world.

Problem was, for the Medusas to be effective in the long term, they *had* to be able to work seamlessly with their foreign counterparts when crises arose around the globe. In today's world, Special Forces teams had to pool their resources and work together because almost all security threats crossed international borders.

That meant the Medusas *must* overcome foreign teams' reluctance to work with women. And that meant training with them, or more to the point, sucking up whatever crap teams like this one handed out to the Medusas until they earned the foreign soldiers' respect.

If the Medusas couldn't win over their foreign counterparts, they stood no chance of being combat effective. It was that simple.

Which was why the Medusas had been hiking around out here for twenty-four hours straight. Only about five of it had been in actual daylight and all of it had been in bitter cold. Welcome to February in the Arctic.

The Norwegian team had been on their tails relentlessly the entire time. The bastards had actually laughed during the mission briefing when they'd found out their job would be to track down and capture the Medusas. They'd even offered to give the women a couple hours extra head start.

Of course, the Medusas had declined. It hadn't been until after she and her teammates said no that the Norwegians casually mentioned four of the six men on their team had been

Olympic medalists in biathlon—combined cross-country skiing and target shooting. *Great.*

Her boss, Major Vanessa Blake, asked over the throat mike and earpiece setup they used, "How much longer can you break trail for us before you give out, Python?"

All of the Medusas had a snake nickname and Python was Karen's field handle. She considered Vanessa's question. She was getting dehydrated, and between trying to stay warm and outpace a bunch of damned Olympians, she was way down on calories. It took six thousand a day out here to function. Fortunately, her creeping panic at watching these guys inexorably eat up the gap between themselves and the Medusas could be used for fuel, too.

She replied, "Another hour, I suppose. Two if we don't have to climb any mountains."

The terrain was slashed by steep valleys and deadly crevasses in the permanent snowcap. Someone had to go first and break the crust of snow, generally sinking about waist-deep in the process. They'd each taken their turns at it, but because of her size and strength, she'd been taking double shifts on point.

By her reckoning, they'd covered about twenty miles. She glanced at the sun skating low across the horizon. It would duck down out of sight soon, even though it was barely afternoon.

"Hey, Viper," Karen said. "Did Scat hint at what these guys are planning to do after they catch us and rough us up?"

Major Vanessa Blake, the Medusas' commander, snorted. "He didn't tell me squat. Besides," she added with a hint of laughter in her voice, "we had better things to do than worry about upcoming training."

With Vanessa and Jack both active in Special Operations, he in Detachment Delta and she in the Medusas, their personal relationship had to squeeze in between their missions and training. What her boss saw in Col. Scatalone, Karen couldn't fathom. But then, she had never really forgiven him for calling her oversized and mannish in her initial training. Oh, she knew he'd only been trying to mess with her mind. Nothing personal. Head games were part and parcel of any military training. Still, he'd nailed her Achilles' heel, and the memory of it stung.

"Gee, you mean you don't sit around and talk shop when the two of you manage to get a moment alone?" Karen quipped.

The other women chuckled, although the sound was strained. Everyone was worried these Norwegians would make short work of the Medusas. If that happened, the Medusas stood no chance at all of earning the men's respect. And they all knew what rode on that outcome.

She pulled herself a few more inches forward on her elbows and in the maneuver scooped more snow into the neck of her white thermal windbreaker. It melted slowly, dribbling down the front of her shirt. A blast of wind hit her cheeks above her scarf as she peeked out from behind a rock outcropping. It sprayed her with needle-sharp crystals of snow and made her misery complete. What bad guy in his right mind would operate in an environment like this? It was hard to fathom when in their work the Medusas would ever have need of the ability to work in such a frigid wasteland.

"I smell a rat. Jack's messing with us. There's more to this exercise than a simple chase to the North Pole."

Vanessa laughed. "You're always suspicious of him."

"Yeah, and I'm usually right, too," Karen retorted.

"We'd better get moving. For some reason, I'm happy to delay the moment when these Norwegians catch us."

Karen nodded and shouldered her pitifully small pack of supplies. Jack hadn't let them bring out more than a bare minimum of food or fuel—to use if and when they ever got around to stopping and resting. She headed down the slope, plowing through the waist-deep powder. She hoped the Norwegians were enjoying strolling along the trail she'd made for them.

She scooped up a handful of snow and ate it. The good news was, with her working this hard, eating snow didn't dangerously lower her core body temperature. In fact, it helped keep her from sweating. So what was the crawling sensation along her spine then? It was like beads of sweat rolling up her back and across her shoulders. Not good. She announced reluctantly, "I feel like I'm being watched."

"Check six, team." Vanessa ordered quickly.

The six women dropped flat in the snow, pulled out binoculars, and scanned the valley they'd just crossed.

Katrina Kim, the team's sniper, murmured, "I may have movement at two o'clock, range four hundred yards. Top of that last ridge we crossed."

Four hundred yards? Karen swore under her breath. If the Norwegians were that close, it wouldn't be long until they caught up with the Medusas. She had to admit, these guys were good. They'd picked up the Medusas' trail and closed a gap of several miles in a single day. She moved her field glasses further along the crest of rock. If the Norwegians were on that ridge, they'd fan out to cross it.

For a couple minutes, she saw nothing. But then a faint movement caught her attention. It could've been just a gust of wind stirring up a whorl of snow between those two boulders. Or it could be a soldier in white arctic gear sliding across the wash of snow close to the ground.

Karen reported, "Possible movement. Two hundred feet left of Katrina's siting."

Vanessa ordered under her breath, "Let's put the ridge at our back between us and them. Full stealth mode for crossing the ridgeline. Huddle on the other side."

Karen crawled the last few feet to the top of the ridge and slimed along on her belly, digging through the snow at snail speed. The idea was to tunnel through the snow deeply enough so her profile never rose up above the surface line of the snow. Easier said than done. It involved shoulder-killing shoveling and eating copious quantities of snow. But eventually, Karen panted on the far side of the ridge from their tails.

She surveyed the narrow, rocky valley stretching below her feet while the other women joined her over the course of the next couple minutes.

"Okay, now what?" Misty grunted, grimacing.

Karen felt for her California-born-and-bred teammate, who had to be hating this cold. Nothing sucked quite like frostbiting a good tan. "Take a look down there." She pointed near the bottom of the rift. "See below us where those two long lines of rock outcroppings narrow down like a funnel?"

The others nodded.

"What if we set an ambush at the bottom of that? It's not like we're gonna be able to outrun these guys all the way to our meeting point with Jack. So why not turn and fight now at a place of our choosing instead of theirs?"

Vanessa replied, "We've only got an hour or less of daylight and relative warmth left. They'll have to slow down then."

Karen commented, "Yeah, but so will we."

Vanessa nodded. "True. What did you have in mind?"

"What if we make a big, obvious trail through that funnel and out the other side of it, then we back up and spread out in that open area at the bottom of the funnel and bury ourselves in the snow for an ambush?"

"How do we breathe? It's not like we have snorkels out here," Aleesha asked. She was the team's doctor and an avid scuba diver.

Karen thought fast. They'd need long, hollow tubes of some kind. "What about our tent poles? We could stick them up through the snow and breathe through them."

Aleesha frowned. "They're aluminum. We could freeze our lips to the metal. We'd need to hold them with our hands right above our mouths to prevent cold from traveling down the tube to bare flesh."

Vanessa added, "We'd also need to be able to see the hostiles, and to coordinate when to jump them."

Karen pictured their flexible mini-periscopes. "I think our peek-a-boos are narrow enough to fit down a tent pole. We could stick the lens of one up through the snow and have one of us watch for the tangos to walk into the trap. When they're in position, the lookout could call the attack over our radios."

The others nodded. Aleesha added, "I want radio check-ins every two minutes to make sure nobody accidentally smothers. And we can only bury ourselves under a few inches of snow. The heat from our bodies will melt the snow around us and form a shell of ice. That can't be allowed to get so thick and hard we can't break through it. So, every fifteen minutes, I want us to break through to the surface."

Karen nodded along with the others. Aleesha, a trauma surgeon in her pre-Medusa life, was the resident mother hen in charge of looking out for their health and safety. And she did a great job of it, too, even if her methods were occasionally a bit unorthodox.

In short order, Karen waded right down the center of the natural rock funnel while the others followed. Then, carefully, they backtracked to the ambush point, walking backward the whole way so their footprints wouldn't give them away.

Since this shindig was Karen's idea, she was elected to man the periscope, which was just as well. She was a bit prone to claustrophobia, and burying herself alive in snow wasn't her idea of a great time.

Rigging up the breathing tubes and burying the first several Medusas wasn't hard. Karen was fourth. She blew up a plastic storage bag they used to keep equipment dry and put it in front of her face. Fully inflated, it was roughly the size of a basketball. Once Vanessa and Misty had buried her in a relatively comfortable crouch, she breathed the air out of the bag, deflating it, and leaving an open space in front of her face to maneuver her hands and twist the periscope back and forth in its aluminum tube. One tube in her mouth to breathe, another tube near her eye to peer out the periscope. The arrangement was awkward and uncomfortable, but it worked.

Vanessa's muffled voice came from above. "How's the view?"

Karen took a look. "Tilt the end of the scope up a little more. All I can see are your mukluks."

After a couple more minor adjustments, she could see the clearing for the ambush and the last hundred feet or so of the approach down the mountainside. She watched Vanessa bury Misty and then pull a plastic sheet pre-piled with snow over herself.

"How do I look?" Vanessa asked over the radio.

"Like a snowball," Karen replied.

"Great. Now, we wait." A pause, then Vanessa added, "You do realize, of course, that Jack's going to throttle me. He hates it when we pull stunts like this."

Karen laughed. "You're the dope dating the guy who trains us."

Misty added, "When have we ever held back if someone was in need of a good gotcha?"

The others keyed their mikes to join in ribbing Vanessa. It also served as a radio check. Everyone was transmitting loud and clear. They got down to business and settled into the silence of predators lying in wait. After a few minutes, Karen actually felt warmer. The layer of snow covering her was providing much-needed insulation as the sun set and darkness began to fall, along with the outside temperature.

And as the minutes dragged by, doubts began to creep in along with the cold. Had she mistaken that slowly moving white shape? Were they merely sitting here burning what little lead they had on their pursuers—on nothing more than the strength of her word?

The moon rose, although she couldn't see it. But a wash of pale blue lit the snow, highlighting the false trail they'd laid in sharp shadows. They unburied and reburied themselves four times, marking the passage of an hour.

Where were the Norwegians? Surely they'd made up what little remaining gap there was between the teams. So why hadn't they barged down here into the trap? Were they just cautious bastards, or had her false trail and trap been too obvious? She was blowing this mission, and her teammates were too loyal to her to tell her so.

Humiliation started to send its unwelcome heat through Karen's gut.

"Radio check," Aleesha announced.

Karen waited her turn and duly reported in. Before long, it would be time to break out of their icy shells again. When they all came up to the surface, she was going to suggest they bag the ambush and press on before it got too cold to breathe, let alone hike these steep mountains. Before they blew what little chance of success they had left by going along with one of her stupid ideas.

She was already tasting the crow she was about to eat when, to her vast surprise, she saw movement on the trail leading down to their hiding spots. It wasn't an actual person, but the shadow of one, cast by the rising moon. *Son of a gun.* She gave two clicks on her radio mike to alert everyone.

The stillness around her was intense. She forced herself to exhale normally and not hold her breath as her anticipation climbed sky-high. Everything rode on the next few seconds. Her future. Maybe even the future of the Medusas.

The shadow was replaced by a man. He wore full winter whites—waterproof pants and a hooded parka made of white thermal nylon. He glided across the snow like a ghost. Karen clicked her radio once. One hostile.

And then another man came into view. Another click. And another man. A third click. All in all, there were six men. The entire Norwegian team was traveling together. The tangos' rifles—painted white—were slung over their shoulders. Perfect. That meant hand-to-hand fighting for this ambush.

The Medusas had talked earlier about the most efficient way to convince the boys that the girls knew what they were doing, and they'd all agreed that unarmed combat was the way to go. They'd probably lose to the men, but if the Medusas even held their own a little bit, it ought to impress the hell out of the Norwegians.

The men eased forward in a standard threat formation. The guy in front looked right, the guy behind him scanned left. The third guy looked right and to the side, fourth guy left and to the side. The last guy turned around periodically to scan behind them. And they walked right into the middle of the Medusas like lambs to the slaughter. Karen grinned around the end of her breathing tube. She took immense satisfaction in the idea of showing these guys and Jack Scatalone a thing or two about the Medusas' cunning.

A few more steps…

There. The men were in perfect position to get jumped. The

Medusas had practiced this sort of move so many times there would be no question about who took what target. They'd move as one and leap on the men like wolves.

All she said was a muttered, "Go."

She exploded up out of the snow, taking the rear guard closest to her. The soldier whirled, not nearly as stunned as she could've hoped for, but he barely got his hands up in front of him before Karen was on him. Three things the guy didn't know about her: first, she'd grown up on a pig farm in Iowa and had done heavy manual labor all her life. When she joined the military, she'd taken up power-lifting. Which was to say, she was *really* strong for a woman. Second, she was a marine. And the jarheads cut women no slack at all when it was time for hand-to-hand combat training. Third, she had an ax to grind with the colonel who'd sent these men after her.

She took the offense and charged her target because he wouldn't expect it of a woman. And he didn't. She knocked him over with her shoulder and followed him to the ground, landing on top of him. But from there it got tough. This guy was strong and fast, and he obviously had wrestling training. He put a nifty hold and twist on her left arm that she thought was going to wrench it out of the socket. She rolled with the pain and collapsed on top of him, rapping his temple hard with her forehead. It stung her like crazy, but it had to make him see stars.

He went defensive then, rolling with incredible speed and power to the side and out from under her leg. She dived for him, grabbed his chin from behind, and gave it a very gentle tug to the side. Had this been a real attack, she'd have wrenched his chin sideways with all her might and most likely broken his neck in the process. If—big if—these guys' rules of engagement were to play fair, she'd just put a lethal move on him, and he was honor bound to yield the fight to her.

Her opponent stopped fighting instantly.

Thank God.

He rolled to his back beneath her, leaving her sprawled across him, breathing hard. Their frosty breath mingled between them. He reached up—slowly—to push up his snow goggles and pull down the knit tube covering his mouth and nose. Yowza. Hunk alert. He was one of those tanned, smooth-skinned, square-jawed, achingly handsome Nordic types. In the moonlight, his eyes looked silver.

He scowled up at her. "Uncle."

She was too knocked over by how gorgeous he was to do much but nod.

"But I think you'd lose the fight anyway," he said with a faint Norwegian accent overlaying excellent English.

"Why's that?" she retorted. "You're looking pretty dead to me right now."

"Because my men have defeated all your comrades and they would now turn upon you and defeat you."

Karen looked up. He was right. Her teammates were all lying on their backs with a white figure sitting on top of them or in some way restraining them. The Medusas looked pretty well worked over. But the good news was the Norwegians didn't look much better. Yeah, the Medusas had lost, but the Norwegians were also sporting puffy eyes and red jaws, and were breathing hard. The promised ass-whupping by the Norwegians hadn't been an entirely one-sided affair. Mission accomplished.

Karen shrugged. "You guys walked right into our ambush. Had we used weapons, which we most certainly would have in an actual ambush, you'd all be dead and we wouldn't be having this conversation. However…"

Karen flexed her right wrist, releasing a knife from her forearm sheath. With a quick flip of her hand, it slid down into her palm, and she pressed the razor sharp blade lightly against the side of the guy's neck.

"I'm already dead," he murmured.

She shrugged again. "They don't know that. And just because I broke your neck, that doesn't mean you'd die right away. Question is, would your men jump me anyway, even with my knife at your neck, or would they back off?"

All of a sudden he wasn't amused anymore. He gazed up at her long and hard, assessing her. "You'd really slit my throat, wouldn't you?" he finally bit out.

"Absolutely. I'm a warrior, and killing's part of the job."

Something flickered in his transparent gaze. What it was, she couldn't tell. "Which one of the girl soldiers are you?"

Girl soldiers? This guy had a lot to learn about the Medusas.

Karen pressed up and away from him and jumped lightly to her feet. She stuck a hand down to help him up. His gloved hand took hers, and she gave a sharp tug. Thankfully, when he stood up, he was a couple of inches taller than she was. She hated looking down at attractive men. And at six feet tall, it happened to her a lot.

"My name is Karen Turner. Captain, United States Marine Corps."

"I thought you ladies were army."

"Our team draws from all the armed forces. We just happen to work in an army detachment."

He turned his head carefully, stretching his neck muscles. "Nice move," he commented.

"Thanks. And your name is?"

"Oberstløytnant Anders Larson. Norwegian Defense Special Command."

Karen nodded. And abruptly noticed that all the other men were staring at her.

"You beat *him?*" one of them asked incredulously.

She frowned across the snow. "What's so hard to believe about that? We *are* trained Special Forces operatives. And that does include hand-to-hand combat training."

The guy who was just now climbing carefully off Katrina—a martial arts expert whom even Scatalone engaged with extreme caution—grumbled, "Yeah, I noticed." The guy's nose looked broken and he was spitting out blood.

"What are your orders now?" Vanessa inquired. "Is playtime over and you head out, or do you plan to proceed with us to our rendezvous point?"

"The last bit of your route today involves technical mountain climbing. Your colonel asked us to give you ladies some help with night climbing."

The Medusas already had plenty of night mountain-climbing training, but Vanessa answered smoothly, "We'd be happy to learn anything you gentlemen can teach us."

Karen frowned, but her boss made eye contact with her. And that was enough. The reminder had been relayed. They were here to get along with these guys. To act like the professional soldiers they were and make believers out of the Norwegians. As always, the thought that she was a no-kidding special operator cheered Karen. She'd fought for ten years to be allowed to do this job. It was a dream come true to actually get to do it.

Anders commented, "You ladies moved quickly today. Are you too tired to continue at that pace, or shall we proceed in the same fashion?"

Karen snorted. "Surely, you realize that now we've got no choice but to keep up with whatever pace you set."

Anders grinned. "I was counting on it. I'll take point." He rattled off a marching order that alternated his men and Medusas. Then he glanced over at Karen. "You fall in behind me. You can take point next."

Oslo, Norway, February 26, 5:00 p.m.

In a conference room high above Oslo, Norway, the senior
marketing staff of Omnicom Telecommunications filed in for a
late briefing on the European Union telecom consolidation that
was set to go into effect shortly. They'd been having trouble
syncing up their internal phone-switching systems with the new
trans-European grid, and the senior brass wanted an update on
how the crisis was being resolved and when it would be fixed.

Harried engineers straggled into the briefing. They really
couldn't afford to stop working to put on this dog-and-pony show,
but when the boys upstairs barked, they jumped. They already
were going to have to work late into the night. A few of the lead
engineers had been here for the past three days around the clock.

One of those engineers, Kjell Krag, flopped into a seat. He
tugged at his shirt collar. This room was hot and stuffy, and his
tie, hastily donned for this stupid briefing, felt as though it was
going to choke him. He'd almost had the computer code
repaired in a particularly nasty section of the translation algo-
rithm when these idiots had to go and call a meeting. He had
no idea how long it would take him to reread the code and pick
up his train of thought again.

The CEO, a Danish entrepreneur who'd been brought in to
whip Omnicom back into shape after years of sliding stock
prices, stood up and delivered a fiery monologue about how important this deal was and how he didn't want to hear any
excuses. He wanted results.

What a jerk. One did not yell and fist-shake at Norwegians
and get anywhere. It only made them more stubborn. But ob-

viously this Dane hadn't figured that out. Egad, but it was hot in here. Kjell pulled out his handkerchief and mopped the beads of sweat popping out on his brow.

As the tirade went on and the atmosphere in the room grew more and more tense, Kjell began thinking about ordering out for a bite of supper instead of going back to work right away. In fact, maybe just to needle this guy, he'd step out of the building and go down the street to that little fish place that had just opened up. Although, the way his stomach was rolling all of a sudden, maybe he'd better skip eating.

Must be the little magic pills he'd been popping like candy to help himself stay awake. They were probably responsible for the abrupt tremor in his hands and knees, too. Either that, or the Danish big mouth was really starting to get under his skin.

He glared at the CEO, willing him to shut the fuck up and sit down already. But no. The guy just went on yapping, all holier than thou and yelling at them like a bunch of lazy children who needed a swift kick in the pants. Kjell's face felt like it was on fire. His whole body was tense. So tense he shook with it.

Finally, the Dane shut up and sat down. Kjell dragged in a couple of deep, ragged breaths. But they didn't do a thing to slow the pounding pulse in his neck.

The project leaders all stood up next, obedient lap dogs that they were, and lied through their teeth about how long it would take to bring the Omnicom system on line. The bastards! They were setting up him and the other engineers to take the fall when this thing didn't happen on time!

Kjell threw a furious look at a couple of the other technical engineers, who all rolled their eyes back at him. Pressure built behind his forehead, and with each lie, another ice pick stabbed the back of his eyeballs.

"Mr. Krag!" a sharp voice cut across the room.

The Dane. Kjell lurched, breathing hard. He tried to focus down the table at the source of the voice, but his vision swam. He squinted at the fuzzy double image of the Danish asshole. Would he never shut up already!

"Do you have a problem?" the Dane barked.

Kjell opened his mouth. Tried to form words. But nothing came out except a hoarse sound from the back of his throat. His palms itched to wrap around the Dane's throat. To squeeze until the Dane's tongue turned purple and swelled so big he couldn't talk. Kjell pushed to his feet. Staggered a bit, unbalanced. Steadied himself on a chair back. Focused on the Dane. Made his way through the red haze toward the moron. He stumbled. Banged into a narrow table by the wall. His hand bumped into a tall, narrow vase. Wrapped around the cool, heavy glass.

He continued forward. More voices came at him now. Sound with no meaning. Unbearably bright light. His eyeballs were going to explode! Hands grasped at him, but he shook them off. He tried again to form words, but his mouth wouldn't cooperate. A few more steps, and then he stood over the Dane. Or at least the spinning image of him.

Kjell lifted the vase. Crashed it down on the asshole's head. Beautiful crunching noise of skull and glass breaking. Screaming. Make the noise stop. The Dane toppled out of his chair onto the floor. Kjell scooped up a shard of glass and jumped on the Dane. Two fountains of red. His hand. Dane's face.

Brilliant red. Must have more. Another slash.

And then everything went white and hot. And he *became* Rage. He swung madly at the hands grasping for him. And the haze was painted red.

And then a great weight landed upon him, crushing him flat. The white light spun and he breathed in the rage. Tasted it. And then his entire body went rigid, arching up, throwing off the weight on his chest. His heart clenched in a mighty spasm of the purest fury he'd ever known. His breath caught at its perfection.

And then everything went black.

Northern Norway, February 26, 7:00 p.m.

In a remote corner of northern Norway, so cold and desolate that no human being ought to be there, let alone live there, an old woman huddled in a tiny sod hut. She was a dying breed, one who remembered—and observed—the old ways. For she was a *noaide*. A shaman of the Sami people.

Her ancestors had eked a meager living out of these northern climes since before history began. They hunted and fished and followed the ever-moving reindeer herds across the Arctic lands. And when the great herds were diminished to a fraction of their original size, her people learned to raise their own reindeer. They were survivors, her people. And this was their place, the frozen North. Europeans came and named them Laplanders, but they had always called themselves Sami. And the Sami called her Naliki.

Tonight, Naliki had a problem. Yet again, the modern world had intruded upon her people. Several teenage boys had apparently overdosed on one of the outsiders' recreational drugs. Foul stuff, those drugs.

Except, these overdoses were unlike any she'd seen before. The boys had collapsed in convulsions, and when others had tried to restrain them, the boys had lashed out violently, raising their hands to their own parents without any apparent concern for who they harmed or how badly.

None of her traditional remedies had calmed the boys. It was only when they fell unconscious that they'd subsided. She'd stayed with them for hours, until the rigidity finally left their bodies and they settled into normal rest, she hoped to sleep off the effects of the chemicals in their systems. Then, she'd come here. To her spirit lodge. To ask the gods how to counteract this new and terrible drug.

Her *runebommen,* a traditional Sami drum, throbbed under her fingers in a slow rhythm, more ancient than words. It pulsed deep in her soul, calling her up and out of herself. Forward. Toward the void. Into the spirit world. She tossed a handful of dried herbs on the fire, and pungent smoke swirled around her. She inhaled deeply. Ahh, the green, summer smell brought back many memories. Of her father and brothers tending the reindeer herds. Of her grandfather, walking with her across meadows in the short alpine summer and showing her the rhythms of nature. He was her teacher when she was young. He was her spirit guide now.

She intoned words asking him to show himself, to embrace her spirit and be with her. To give her the answer she sought.

A gust of wind howled outside and the fire burned a little more brightly. The rich, earthen smell of the turf hut grew stronger. The fire flared even higher, and the spinning sensation that marked the beginning of a spirit journey made her faintly dizzy. She spread her gnarled hands wide, grasping at the warmth of the fire with her swollen knuckles and waving the smoke to her nostrils. "Show to me that which you wish me to know," she asked the spirits in the old tongue.

A dream rolled over her, images of gods and goddesses striding forward. One of them, a beautiful blond woman arrayed in armor and bearing a sword and shield, announced in a tongue so ancient that even Naliki barely understood it, "Find the source of this new evil, then take me to it. I shall destroy the sickness that walks among you and prove that I am true. In return I ask but one boon of you."

"Anything, Great One," Naliki breathed.

"The old ways are lost by all but a few. Soon, they will disappear entirely. It is time to restore them."

Naliki stared. Usually her visions dealt with weather and the fertility of the reindeer herds, or making a villager well.

The goddess continued, "Restore your people. Restore your lands. Restore the faith. We come presently, and we are the sign."

The drum beat on, and the smoke swirled thickly, and the goddess slowly faded away. But her message did not. Find the source of the drugs and take the goddess to it.

The task was set. Naliki was the watcher. The one who would mark the coming of the gods and their sign that, at last, her people would be free.

Chapter 2

The last valley the Medusas had to cross to reach their rendezvous point was a great rift gouged out of the earth by the glacier resting at its bottom. It was a sheer cliff down and another sheer cliff up the far side—not a big deal normally—but cold this extreme turned a relatively simple exercise into another game entirely.

The Norwegian Special Forces men stood back and didn't offer the Medusas a lick of help. Which was just fine with Karen. If the Medusas were going to prove their competence to these skeptics, the less help the Norwegians gave them, the better.

She did catch a few raised eyebrows passed back and forth among Larson and his pals. Apparently, they'd expected to have to haul the women up the cliff face to compensate for lack of upper body strength in the Americans. *Not.* The Medusas might avoid carrying a grown man on their back for a hundred miles or pulling the same man up a fifty-foot wall, but they certainly were capable of hauling their own body weight up a cliff.

And even if tonight they weren't capable of the feat, Karen had no doubt every last Medusa would claw her way up that cliff by her fingernails if that's what it took to erase those smug looks from the Norwegians' faces.

The women worked together, helping each other past the difficult sections, spotting for each other, and lending a hand when needed. They all busted their butts to make it up that cliff as fast as humanly possible, and all of them were huffing when they finally flopped over the edge onto their bellies in the snow. If that didn't impress the Norwegians, she gave up. They'd all given the climb everything they had, and then some.

Karen caught her breath enough to lift her head and look around. An open plateau stretched away in front of her. A faint glow in the distance announced the exact location of their meeting point with Scatalone. She gathered her strength and pushed herself to her feet, and immediately sank to her hips in dry powder. Great. Leave it to Scat to make sure this last bit of trek was completely miserable.

Anders murmured something in Norwegian, and his men stopped and dug around in their packs. They pulled out handfuls of aluminum and sinew, and in a few seconds had unfolded and assembled snowshoes.

"Change in marching order," Anders announced in English. "We go first and compact a trail for you ladies. Otherwise, it will take us forever to get to that igloo."

Karen's mouth twitched as she replied lightly, "If you boys are getting cold and want to hurry this along, we understand."

Larson's gaze narrowed, but he continued strapping on his snowshoes. Poor guy. He must be under orders to behave himself and make nice with the girls.

The Medusas fell in behind the men on the path the single-file line of Norwegians made. Karen still sank to her knees with every step, but it was a far sight better than flailing around in the deep stuff.

They reached Jack's igloo in about an hour. Distances were bloody deceptive out here in this white-on-white world. She'd have sworn Jack's shelter was no more than ten or fifteen minutes away.

"Who'd like to do the honors and announce your presence?" Larson asked.

Karen grinned and looked over at her boss. That one was a no-brainer. "Be our guest, Viper."

Vanessa dropped to her knees and crawled into the tunnel that arced down into the snow. Karen heard faint voices from inside. The insulation value of the blocks of snow was really impressive.

In a few moments, Jack Scatalone crawled out of the tunnel, followed by Vanessa, whose cheeks, if Karen wasn't mistaken, were rosy with more than cold. Ahh, true love. She was glad her boss had found it. As for herself, Karen didn't hold out much hope in that department. What man would want an amazon of a woman who could break him in half? Case in point, she was the only Medusa to have defeated her Norwegian opponent in the ambush. How embarrassing was that? As much as she'd love to be petite and feminine and fragile, the fact was she was none of those things. She sighed. And found herself averting her gaze from Anders Larson.

"Welcome, ladies. Took you long enough," Jack said sarcastically.

Larson spoke up. "Your team stopped to set up a little ambush for us."

Jack's eyebrows shot straight up, then lowered ominously. "How'd it go?"

Larson's jaw went tight, but he answered evenly, "Had they used weapons, my team would be dead. As it is, they chose hand-to-hand combat. In that scenario, we'd be delivering them all to you as our prisoners, except for Captain Turner. I'd be dead, and I believe she'd have successfully gotten away."

Scatalone's sharp gaze swung her way. "Well done, Python." Jack turned and stomped away in the snow toward the far side of his shelter. The group trooped after him, and Larson fell in beside her. "Python?" he repeated questioningly.

"My field handle," she mumbled.

"It fits you. Beautiful creatures. Strong. Independent."

Karen gaped. Most people assumed she'd earned the name because she was wreathed in muscles like a python. But Vanessa had specifically given her the name because pythons are beautiful snakes. Karen had earned the name the first time Jack ever called her the ugly names he now used routinely…Butch. She-man. Or her personal favorite, S.O.L. As opposed to its more traditional meaning, shit outta luck, he called her Statue of Liberty, or S.O.L. for short. But she expected he meant the other connotation as well.

The Medusas always told her to shake it off. To ignore him. Logic told her they were right. Despite her pride in her abilities she couldn't ever quite shake her own futile wish to be small. Delicate, even.

Then Jack was talking again. "It's too late to get started on the next leg of your journey tonight. There's some weather moving in, and you need to find shelter before it hits. Best guess is you've got two hours until the harsh stuff gets here. Your tents will not be adequate to protect you. When it lets up, we'll move out. Oberstløytnant Larson, I'm sorry to say your ride out of here tonight has been postponed. Your helicopters are socked in at Nordkapp."

The Norwegian team groaned under its breath, but Larson answered gamely, "No problem. We've got our full comple-ment of gear and we're checked out at Arctic survival."

She bet they were. After all, they lived and worked in snow most of the year. Why anyone did that voluntarily, she had no idea. As for the Medusas, they'd had classroom training on the princi-ples of building an igloo and watched a video of native Alaskans doing it. The Inuit made it look like a piece of cake…which had made Karen highly suspicious. In her experience, anything that looked *that* easy had to be hard as hell to master.

She was right.

The Medusas flailed around for a good hour trying to figure out how to make blocks out of the light, dry, powder snow. It simply wasn't happening. They'd managed to make one pile of snow appropriate for jumping in, but that was about it. They tried putting up one of the tents and partially burying it, but the weight of the snow collapsed the lightweight frame. Besides, a stiff wind would blow away all the powder and leave the tent exposed anyway. If they ended up having to rely on just their tents—assuming they'd even stand in high winds—they were in for a wicked cold night. She had no illusions about spending the night out here. Their situation could get desperate pretty fast.

The Delta Force and the Medusas—whose training mirrored their male counterparts' as much as humanly possible—were all about realistic training. Karen had no doubt Jack would let them sit out here, completely exposed, in a blizzard, in the name of realistic training. He would intervene to prevent one of them from dying or suffering an irreversible injury. But that was about it.

Karen's back ached and frustration burned in her gut before Vanessa finally called a halt to their futile efforts. "This is a waste of time. Anyone got any suggestions?"

Karen glanced over at the Norwegian encampment that was almost finished not far away. Each of the men had built a small, oblong shelter for themselves. "Yeah. Let's ask for help."

Misty piped up. "They're gonna rub it in our faces."

Karen nodded. "If it's a choice between humiliation and freezing, I'm for the humiliation. Besides, part of being a pro is knowing when to ask for help."

Vanessa shrugged. "Works for me. You ask, Python. Oberstløytnant Larson likes you."

Karen blinked. "I beg your pardon?"

"He's impressed that you beat him in a fight."

Karen snorted. "That does *not* constitute liking me. That makes me a circus sideshow."

Vanessa blew out a puff of white breath. "Get over it, Karen."

Karen huffed back. She glanced up at the line of clouds just beginning to scud over the moon. "We're going to lose the moonlight soon, and that storm's getting close. Another hour at most if clouds this far north behave anything like they do back in Iowa."

"Go ask," Vanessa said quietly.

Karen floundered over to the encampment to which the six men—who had scattered a little while before—had just returned. They were emptying bags of black lumps of what looked like rock into piles in front of their igloos.

Larson looked up at her and said with exaggerated politeness, "Can I help you?"

Karen sighed. "We can't figure out how to hold the snow together in blocks so we can build shelters. Is it against the rules for you guys to help us…or at least give us a hint?"

One corner of his mouth turned up in a dry smile. "Our only rule was we had to wait until you asked for help."

Jack Scatalone was such a *jerk!* He wanted to make them grovel, damn him.

Larson interrupted her murderous thoughts. "In conditions like this, the trick is to build small shelters and work with the icy crust of snow at the surface. Come on. We'll show you."

The men trudged over to where the Medusas waited and paired up with the women to demonstrate. It didn't escape Karen that Larson chose to work with her. It took her a few tries to get the hang of cutting and prying up the icy sheets. She showered herself with snow a couple times in the process, which made Larson laugh. He had a great laugh. It was surprisingly friendly, with no malice to it.

He showed her how to stack the sheets of ice on edge, double-thick. She left a six-inch-wide gap between the sheets which he helped her pack with loose snow for insulation. The curving sides of the oblong, one-woman igloo weren't too bad to build once she got the hang of it, but it took the two of them working together to lift the final piece of the roof into the center of her shelter. She'd forgotten snow could be such heavy stuff.

As she heaved on the hunk of ice, she grunted, "Last time I hefted snow like this was when I was a kid and used to build snowmen. Do Norwegian kids do that?"

He grunted back, "Yes, and we make snow angels and forts and have snowball fights. Kids all over the world are pretty much the same when it comes to snow."

They dropped the long capstone into position. Karen

squatted in the darkness, looking upward by flashlight, and Larson did the same beside her in the cramped space. "What are the odds this thing will collapse on me in the middle of the night?" she asked.

"Nil. It's well-built."

"Thanks." And since part of winning over the Norwegians would no doubt include getting along with them, she added, "I couldn't have done it without you."

He nodded and said gruffly, "The last bit is to dig a tunnel entrance. Go down below the level of your floor, then back up to the surface. That will trap the warm air in here, since it rises, but still allow for some circulation so you don't suffocate."

They lay back-to-back and dug the tunnel, using their breath and body heat to soften the snow enough to make it packable. The tunnel was barely big enough for the two of them to squeeze through. She was vividly aware, even through the many layers of insulating clothing, how the powerful muscles in his back and shoulders contracted and stretched as he dug beside her. Was he registering the same thing about her? She sincerely hoped not.

Before long, they'd dug their way back outside. In the past few minutes the temperature had plummeted and the wind was screaming. They had to shout to be heard over its fury.

Larson shouted to her, "If you get too cold tonight, come to my hut."

Uhh, right.

He must have seen skepticism in her eyes because he shouted, "I'm serious. If you get warm all of a sudden and very drowsy, come to my igloo. This is a killer storm. Even trained people perish in these arctic blasts. You may be out here for survival training, but we are not. We have all kinds of gear and supplies to help keep warm. Don't die in the name of proving yourself, all right?"

A perceptive comment. She nodded her reluctant acquiescence to its wisdom.

He pulled something long and thin out of his pack and pounded it into the snow with his climbing hammer. She watched as he tied a nylon cord to the long stake and ran the line over to his hut's entrance tunnel. He secured that end with a long stake as well, then waded back over to her. "It will go to whiteout conditions soon. As long as the string has tension on it, it's safe to follow."

"Got it."

"Are you sweating?" he shouted.

Okay. Not what she'd expected him to say next. "Uhh, yeah, I guess. A little. We worked pretty hard building that shelter."

"Go inside now. Take off all your clothes. Get dry. Don't put anything back on until every last bit of your clothing is dry. Your body heat will build up in the hut and dry the cloth in an hour or two."

Karen stared, slack-jawed. "You want me to get naked in *this?*"

A tremendous gust of wind almost knocked her off her feet and made Larson stagger. "Trust me!" he shouted. His words were torn away by the wind until she barely heard him. "We must take cover now. The storm is here."

No shit, Sherlock. She watched him take the knee-high cord in his hands and grasp it. What was up with that? His shelter was only forty feet or so away. And then another gust of wind tore through, and she lost sight of him completely. Just like that. In an instant. One second he was there, and the next he was gone, swallowed by driving snow. Total whiteout. Wow.

Abruptly, she was so cold she could hardly breathe. Her teeth chattering, she turned around. Thank goodness she was only standing two feet from the entrance to her tunnel. She could barely make it out right there at her feet.

It was quieter inside. A deep chill hung in the air. And the idea of stripping down seemed absolutely ludicrous. One of their instructors had talked about it in their classroom training, and she'd thought it sounded crazy then, too.

She dug in her pack and pulled out the down sleeping bag they'd been issued for this training. It wasn't the warmest thing on the planet because Jack didn't want to make their survival training *too* easy. But the sleeping bag was a far sight better than nothing. She unfolded a fist-sized Mylar blanket into a sheet that covered her whole floor. The plastic would keep her sleeping bag dry. She took off her damp boots and crawled into her sleeping bag, parka and all.

She lay there shivering until she thought she'd shake her teeth loose. If the hut was warming up, she couldn't tell. She felt like she was lying in the anti-hell. The air was so cold it literally pierced her body with knives of pain. She looked at her watch. She'd been in here a grand total of thirty minutes.

Larson's shouted, *Trust me* came back to her as she lay there. What the heck. She wasn't going to last an hour, let alone an entire night, like this.

She crawled out of her sleeping bag and with shaking, clumsy fingers, unzipped her parka and stripped off her clothes. She laid them out on top of her sleeping bag to dry. Then, so cold the pain was starting to give way to encroaching—and dangerous—numbness, she climbed back into her sleeping bag. She pulled it all the way up over her head, and used the drawstring to draw the mummy top shut, leaving only a small hole for her mouth and nose to poke through.

And a strange thing happened. First, her damp skin began to feel dry. And then the sleeping bag warmed up a little. She actually began to regain feeling in her skin. And then she had to clench her teeth against the needle-pricking sensation of returning circulation in her hands and feet. But after ten minutes or so, she actually started to feel reasonably comfortable. Her nose and cheeks even started to feel warm. Son of a gun.

Was Larson naked in his sleeping bag right now, thinking of her?

She fell asleep wondering about it. She woke up some time later, disoriented. She was somewhere dark and confined, and she disliked both intensely. She struggled against the smothering blanket for a moment, and then realized it was her sleeping bag and she was in a hut in a blizzard in the Arctic Circle in the middle of winter.

A single thought leaped into her mind. And she'd *volunteered* for this?

She sat up and unzipped herself far enough to check her clothes. Dry. And the ambient air temperature wasn't half-bad. She could still see her breath, but it was close to freezing. The walls glistened where ice had formed in a thin coating on them. She checked her watch. She'd been asleep for about four hours. Still a lot of night to get through.

She pulled on her high-tech polyester long underwear and the first layer of her clothes, a micro-fleece turtleneck and leggings. Almost immediately, she felt downright cozy. Ahh. That was nice. She pulled out her canteen and had a drink of water—dehydration was a big problem in the middle of all this snow. It took a ton of body energy to eat enough snow to stay properly hydrated—too much to make it worthwhile unless a person was in the middle of exercising vigorously. Maybe once the storm broke they'd have time to rig up a solar heater and melt themselves some more water. The days could get surprisingly warm up here in the blinding glare of the sun.

She went back to sleep, listening to the wind whistling around her.

Her watch said it was nearly four o'clock the next time she
woke up. Her feet were in so much pain she could barely stand
it. She tried to move them and was shocked to realize her
sleeping bag was frozen solid. Panic leaping in her chest, she
tried to sit up. Thankfully, she could do that. She flipped on
her flashlight.

Oh, God, it was freezing in here! What had happened? And
then a gust of wind blasted her and she knew. The wind had
shifted. It was blowing straight in through her tunnel. Even
though the tunnel took a sharp dip, forty-below-zero air was
still being driven into her shelter. Now what? Should she dig
a new tunnel and close off the first one? Her brain was foggy
with sleep and she struggled to remember what they'd said in
her classroom instruction. She couldn't remember any refer-
ences to wind shift. *Think, Karen.*

First order of business was to put on more clothes. She was
still dry in her current clothes, so she could add more. Sitting
on top of her sleeping bag, she awkwardly dressed herself. It
took a long time. Too long. She was so clumsy she could barely
get her parka zipped. And still the cold intensified around her.

She couldn't feel her feet at all. She tried to crouch, to drape
part of the Mylar blanket across the tunnel entrance, but then
she remembered something Larson had said. It was important.
But her brain refused to retrieve it. Oh. Yeah. Suffocation.
Couldn't block the tunnel off.

And then it hit her. She was being way too stupid here. And
way too sleepy. Oops. Maybe time to head for Larson-land. The
Norwegians would no doubt give her hell about wimping out
and not being able to cut it. But a little voice of caution in the
back of her head said to listen to Larson's advice. This was his
area of expertise. And besides, he was cute. Might be nice to
have a slumber party with a hottie like him.

The thought startled her to momentary alertness. Something was definitely wrong with her. She simply didn't have thoughts like that in the middle of a crisis. And a crisis this surely was becoming. Quickly.

She headed out of the tunnel and gasped as the breath was torn right out of her lungs. As she crawled into the full fury of the storm, she had to stop for a moment to stare. She could see nothing but a wall of black, not even her hand in front of her face. Not the huts of her companions, not even the spike she knew to be inches from her face. She reached out. Groped around in the dark. And found the stake. Carefully, she felt for the cord. It was taut against her mitten. Thank God.

She tried to stand up, but collapsed with a yelp of pain as she put weight on her feet. What was wrong with them? She tried again, and collapsed again. The pain pierced her thoughts, which were rapidly turning to mush. *Must. Get. To. Larson.*

And so she crawled on her hands and knees. It was awkward with one hand always on the string, but she struggled along. Far too many long, icy minutes later, she finally felt the second spike. Now all she had to do was find the blasted tunnel entrance. She felt around in front of her and tried to picture the location of his tunnel relative to that second spike.

There. Her hand pressed down into nothingness. She dived head-first into the tunnel. The relief from the wind was immediate. She drew a full breath. Her lungs felt like Popsicles, but oxygen was good.

"Anders," she gasped.

A dark form in the even darker space lurched. "Karen?"

"Yeah. I think I'm in some trouble. I can't stand up."

Suddenly, strong hands were there, hauling her inside by the armpits. His flashlight went on, and the space went golden-yellow.

"Wow. This place is huge. You could fit three or four people in here."

He grinned as he set to work pulling off her boots. "What's twenty-five plus fifty?"

She frowned at him. "Uhh," She thought for a moment. She could do this. One quarter plus two quarters. "Three quarters," she announced triumphantly.

"Spell your name backwards," he ordered.

"Y-o-u-r-n-a-m-e-b-a-c—"

He interrupted her. "Very funny. Karen Turner. Spell it backwards." She made it through R-E-N-R before it struck her as funny. "Renrrr," she rolled off her tongue like a car engine revving. She giggled at how silly it sounded.

"Your toes aren't frostbitten yet. But you didn't miss it by much. We need to warm them—and you—up."

She stared in shock as he scooted forward in a seated position, yanked up his shirt and planted both her feet against his incredibly warm, incredibly hard, incredibly sexy stomach. He sucked in his breath sharply.

"Kinda like ice cubes down your shirt, eh?" She grinned.

He grimaced at her. "Exactly."

"The wind shifted," she explained. "Came in the tunnel. Was nice and cozy till then."

"Ahh. Yes. That will do it. You must dig a deeper tunnel when that happens. Give it a sharper down and up bend."

She nodded slowly. "I figured there must be something I should do about it. But for the life of me I couldn't remember what it was."

"You did the right thing, coming to me."

She wiggled her toes against his stomach and the muscles beneath the soles of her feet contracted hard. "Yeah, but now you're going to think the Medusas can't hack it with the boys."

He frowned and made no reply.

Yup, she was right. Still hadn't made a believer out of the oberstløytnant.

"Karen," he said quietly, "I need you to start talking now. And keep talking until your feet don't hurt anymore."

She frowned at him. The cobwebs were clearing from her brain enough for her to reply, "But my feet don't hurt."

"They're going to soon."

And he wasn't kidding. The agony was so intense it was all she could do not to writhe and moan with it. She'd experienced some pretty harsh pain in her Medusa tour to date, but this was by far the worst she'd ever endured. At one point words failed her and she bit down on the sleeve of her parka, which she shoved into her mouth to keep from screaming.

"Talk to me," he urged her. "Tell me about where you're from."

She gasped, "Iowa. Farm. Pigs."

"Do you have any brothers and sisters?" he asked forcefully.

"No. Only child. Dad wanted a son, though. Raised me to...do boy things."

"Like what?"

"Fishing...arrggh...hunting...play football."

"American football with tackling?"

She nodded, in too much misery at the moment to draw breath. The wave passed. "My cousins and me. We played football."

Larson grinned. "Is that where you learned to tackle like you did to me this afternoon?"

"Yeah."

Over the next few minutes, she told him between gritted teeth about the house she'd grown up in, where she went to school and how to build a birthing pen for a sow to keep her from rolling over on her piglets. Anything to keep her mind off of the fire scorching the skin off her feet, layer by layer. Finally, it began to subside, and eventually, it was no more than an unpleasant itching sensation. She flopped backward onto his sleeping bag, which still held some of his body heat.

"How come your bed's still warm?" she demanded, her mental faculties fully restored.

"Air mattress underneath it. Great insulator, air, you know."

She sat up and peeled back the corner of the down bag. Sure enough, there was a thin, sturdy-looking pad under his bed. On closer inspection, it was, indeed an air mattress, but much thinner than the ones she'd seen floating in swimming pools. "Do you have a heater in here, too?"

"No, but I can build us a fire if you like."

She stared at him. "A fire? With what? There's no wood for miles in any direction!"

He grinned. "Back in a minute. I'll show you." He ducked into the tunnel and crawled back in a few seconds later, carrying several of those black lumps she'd seen his men gathering earlier.

"Okay, I'll bite. What's that?"

"Reindeer…how do you say it? Turds?"

She burst out laughing. "Well, that's one way of putting it. We'd probably call it manure in polite company. But turds works for me."

"No, no. Women are polite company. It is reindeer manure."

This guy's ingrained chauvinism was going to be a bear to overcome. "I gather we're going to burn said manure?"

He nodded. "What direction is the wind blowing from?"

She pointed to the right side of his shelter. The two of them cleared the downwind side of the hut of his gear. He pulled out a metal tube about the diameter of her forearm and maybe eighteen inches long. She watched, bemused, as he poked it through the wall of his igloo at an upward angle and shook out the resulting plug of snow. He placed one of the reindeer chunks beneath the end of it and pulled out matches.

"This stuff lights easily. Contrary to popular belief, arctic climates are really quite dry. This stuff is completely desiccated within a few hours of being…deposited."

Her lips twitched at how delicately he'd put that. Indeed, the black lump was very dry and began to smoke right away. It gave off a small flame in under a minute. Within several minutes, the chunk glowed red, and gave off a ton of heat. Enough that she started stripping off layers of clothes to avoid sweating. She'd learned that lesson already. Sweat equaled wet, and that was mucho bad out here.

He sat back, studying her intently.

"What?" she finally blurted as his continued perusal made her uncomfortable.

"I was trying to figure out if you look more like Lauren Bacall or Ingrid Bergman."

She blinked, startled. She shared both women's wavy hair, light eyes and rather patrician, classic features, but she didn't consider herself anywhere near as beautiful as either actress. "Me? Ingrid Bergman?" she scoffed.

"Yeah," he replied gruffly.

She laughed. "In a Xena, Warrior Princess, sort of way. Put me in green camo paint and I'm the Incredible Hulkette."

He frowned, but said nothing in response. Heat and silence built up inside the igloo. Finally he murmured, "Hungry?"

"No, thanks. I ate earlier. And we're supposed to be surviving with our own supplies out here. As it is, Jack's going to ream me out royally for coming over here to you." A sudden and supremely irritating thought occurred to her. "Does Jack have all this gear, too? Air mattress and subarctic sleeping bag and fire capacity?"

"Of course."

"You're sure?"

"I helped him pack it myself."

Karen's eyes narrowed. "So, while he's all nice and cozy, we're supposed to ride out this storm with the bare minimum gear to stay alive?"

Larson frowned. "He did insist on realistic training. You did the right thing to come to me, though. You were legitimately in trouble. I must say, I think your instructor is expecting far too much of you all to throw you out here in a storm like this."

And then he made the colossal mistake of adding, "After all, you're women."

Chapter 3

Karen froze. Blinked slowly. Said carefully, "Excuse me?"

"Women don't belong out here in an environment as harsh as this. It takes tremendous strength and stamina to survive in the Arctic."

Wrong thing to say to a Medusa. The past twenty-four hours of humping across the Arctic, setting a perfect ambush, and climbing a damned mountain in the dark and cold hadn't made any impression, eh? Karen began yanking on her clothes. Donned her boots and parka. Said stiffly, "Thank you for taking care of my feet and for the suggestion on digging my tunnel deeper."

"Is everything all right?" he asked, frowning.

"Yes, everything's fine. I'll just be heading back to my shelter, now."

"You can stay here if you like. It'll be warmer."

"No, thank you. I'm here to experience Arctic survival. Air mattresses and fireplaces don't qualify, I think."

"Do you want me to walk you back to your hut?"

"No," she answered a little sharply. He didn't get it. He had no idea how seriously he'd just stepped over the line. What in the hell did he mean by that comment? *After all, you're women.* Of course it took tremendous strength and stamina to survive out here! Who the hell did he think the Medusas were? A knitting circle? She'd had no patience with condescension from American soldiers, and it turned out she had no patience for it from a Norwegian, either.

She crawled outside. The storm had abated, at least to the extent that she could make out the other lumps of the Medusas' and other Norwegians' shelters. But then the wind gusted again, and visibility dropped fast. Boy, this weather was changeable! She wasted no time following the guide rope back to her igloo. She crawled inside her tunnel and redug it at a much sharper angle. And sure enough, as she packed snow from the newly dug floor against the ceiling, the wind diminished and finally disappeared.

Just to be safe, she stripped off all her clothes again when she was done with the job to let any hint of moisture evaporate from her skin. And again, she warmed up as soon as she did so. She pulled on her long underwear and crawled back into bed.

Sleep was a long time coming, but, she was reasonably comfortable when it did. Women, indeed. She'd show Anders Larson a thing or two about what women were capable of.

The Arctic Circle, February 27, 10:00 a.m.

Over the next couple of days, Jack summoned them by radio to come out for training whenever the storm let up. Larson and his men taught them how to make solar snow melters out of their Mylar survival blankets and how to cut slits in strips of leather for makeshift sunglasses that would protect their eyes from snow blindness. The incredible glare of the sun off miles and miles of white snow could severely sunburn a human's cornea in a matter of hours.

It was hard to tell what the Norwegians thought of the Medusas. Like most Special Forces operators, they held their cards pretty close to the chest. But Karen thought she detected a certain thawing in their attitude. And they didn't laugh at the Medusas anymore. At least, not much.

Karen was on the verge of going stir crazy staring up at the blue-white ceiling of her tiny hut in the late morning of training day four when the storm finally let up. Vanessa called over the radios for the Medusas to assemble outside in five minutes.

Hallelujah. Something to do. Karen suited up and crawled out of her shelter. It was noticeably warmer than yesterday. She estimated the temperature was all the way up to zero or so. And more to the point, the sun was shining. The storm had broken.

Jack stood beside his shelter, chatting with the Norwegians. He looked downright chipper this morning. Drat. That never boded well for the Medusas. He announced briskly, "There's been a change in plans. Oberstløytnant Larson will fill you in on it."

Karen's eyes narrowed as the Norwegian stepped forward. "Based on our initial report to our superiors on your performance, our headquarters would like to continue observing your training exercises. To that end, the FSK—the Norwegian Defense Special Command—will be participating in your ongoing training henceforth."

What the hell did that mean? Had they liked what they'd seen enough to want to see more? Or did it mean they had yet to see anything that convinced them the Medusas were competent enough to work with?

Karen groaned under her breath. Yippee. More making nice with male chauvinist pigs. After Larson's unfortunate slip of

the tongue, she'd pretty much been able to avoid any contact
with him. But whether or not she could keep that up over the
next several weeks was anybody's guess.

Jack picked up the narrative. "Most of our Norwegian col-
leagues will be leaving shortly. They will be flown across to
the mainland where they will establish a covert operations
post. Your job, ladies, will be to locate their position and disable
their outpost." He added slyly, "Without getting your butts
kicked this time."

Karen ignored the jab. After all, the Norwegians had walked
right into the ambush. Had the Medusas used weapons, they'd
have killed all the Norwegians where they stood. To Jack, she
said, "Define disabling their outpost."

Jack grinned at her. "Don't blow it up. At least, not with
anyone inside."

The Medusas nodded casually while the Norwegians looked
faintly alarmed.

"Oh, and Oberstløytnant Larson will be staying with you
ladies to act as an observer. He is not to be regarded as a
member of your team for planning purposes."

Karen spoke up. "What guarantee do we have that he won't
act as a spy or saboteur on behalf of his men?"

"You have my word on it," Larson said a bit sharply.

Karen looked him square in the eye, intentionally took a
moment to weigh his words, and finally drawled, "I'll hold
you to that."

His eyes narrowed, but he made no reply.

Out of the corner of her eye, Karen thought she saw Jack's
mouth twitch in amusement. Jerk. In fact, all men were jerks.

Oslo, Norway, March 2, 7:00 a.m.

Detective Jens Schumacher looked around the crime scene
dispassionately. Gad, what a lot of blood! It sprayed the ceiling,

ran down the walls and soaked the carpets at the entire far end of the room. Krag had really done a number on his boss.

According to the preliminary report the initial on-scene murder detective—a good-looking kid named Ivo Dahl—was making to him right now, Krag had also slashed fourteen of his coworkers. All of them had needed medical attention and three of them required hospitalization for their injuries.

Jens shrugged off his olive-green, army-surplus parka and passed a hand over his rapidly balding head. He really ought to look into doing something about his hair, but who had time? Even if he did get plugs or a weave, it wasn't like he had time for women. Between work and Astrid, his nineteen-year-old daughter who'd just moved back in with him, his life was in enough turmoil.

Jens interrupted Dahl's dry narrative of what blood spatter had come with which victim to ask, "What are his coworkers saying?"

"They're appalled."

"Of course, they're appalled," Jens snapped. "What do they think of Krag? Did he have it in him? Did they see this coming? Was he angry over anything?"

Dahl lowered his voice. "They all were angry. The new CEO pushed them into a deal with the European Union and set an impossible timetable for creating a telecom network of some kind. They've all been working long hours and been under a lot of pressure."

"Was Krag the sort to crack under pressure? Any history of violence?"

"No to both, according to his coworkers. He's been here…" Dahl looked down at his notes, "…nine years, and has been through high-intensity deadlines before."

"Did he have a beef with the CEO?"

"No more than anyone else around here. They're all fairly guarded in their comments about the victim. I gather he was not particularly well liked."

Jens glanced over where the dead executive had been sprawled on the floor. The guy's head and face had looked like a hamburger. "I should say he wasn't liked at all. Anybody jump up to defend the Dane when the attack happened?"

Dahl shook his head. "Witnesses say it happened very quickly. No warning."

Jens frowned. That was the odd thing. Disgruntled employees always gave fair warning to their bosses before they did the deed. They sought redress for their grievances before they resorted to murder. They didn't just get up in the middle of a meeting and slash their boss to death. What had set Krag off like that?

"Is there a transcript of the meeting?" Jens asked.

"No, sir."

People on certain drugs were known to do random and violent acts. "Was Krag a drug user?" Jens asked.

"Folks I've talked to say he might have taken something to keep him wired through the long work hours."

Jens glanced over at Krag's body, which lay on its side, stiffening, arched backward in a violent death spasm.

"What killed Krag?"

"Medical examiner wants to autopsy before he makes a ruling."

"Yeah, yeah. What did he say to you off the record when he took a look at the guy?"

"Said the guy had a seizure of some kind. Maybe something blew in his brain. An aneurysm or a stroke made him nuts and then killed him."

Jesus. A blown blood vessel could make some average, law-abiding citizen flip out and do all of this? To Dahl, he said, "Find out who Krag's close friends were. The kind who'd know whether or not he might have done coke on the sly."

The kid nodded.

Another cop poked his head into the bloody conference room. "Schumacher, there's a television crew out here. You wanna talk to them?"

"Hell, no! I didn't get my beauty sleep last night. Get them out of the building."

Jens stepped into the kitchen from the garage, shedding his parka as he went. It was really cold outside today. Normally, he'd stop by a lunch place and grab a sandwich to eat on the way back to the office, but the morning's murder scene—yet another random explosion of violence—had been only a few blocks from his house, and a hot meal sounded good. Even if it was microwaved leftovers.

He looked up, startled to see Astrid seated at the kitchen table. She gazed up at him vaguely, not quite focusing on him. "Hi, Daddy," she drawled.

"Hi, honey. Are you all right?"

"Yeah, sure."

He frowned. He wasn't a cop for nothing. She looked stoned to him.

"Aren't you supposed to be at class?"

"Didn't feel like going."

He moved over to the refrigerator and pulled out last night's casserole. "Why not?"

"Too cold out."

He plopped a glob of the congealed noodles and salmon into a bowl and tossed it in the microwave. When Astrid had moved back in with him, she'd said it was because her mother had

turned into a "total drag." Buttons beeped as he programmed
the oven. Yup, parents had a way of turning into drags when
their kids were stoned and skipping college classes. He
probably stood a better chance of getting the truth out of her
while she was still high than he did once she came back down.
He turned around to face her.

"What'd you take, Astrid?"

"Huh?" She squinted up at him.

A dreadful thought struck him. What if she'd gotten into
some of the stuff that was making all those people go crazy?
Not Astrid. Not his little girl. Images of the gory murder scenes
of the past several days flashed through his head. He asked
more urgently, "What are you on?"

"The chair?"

Very funny. He restrained his growing panic. He, like most of
the homicide division, was convinced the recent rash of murders
was tied to drugs. They'd been able to link four of the five mur-
derers to drug use. They didn't know exactly what drugs yet, or
if something was wrong with the drugs they'd ingested. But now
was *not* a good time to be fooling with street drugs in Oslo.

He leaned down and took Astrid by both shoulders. "What
are you on?" he demanded.

She began to whine about how he was hurting her. The microwave dinged to indicate his food was hot. But he ignored it
all, forcing her to look at him. "You're not in trouble. But I *have*
to know. What did you take?"

"Some coke," she mumbled. "And some other stuff."

"What other stuff?"

She zoned out on him, her head lolling to one side. He gave
her a shake and repeated forcefully, "Tell me! Your life may
depend on it!"

"I dunno. Pills. Willie said they were a real kick in the pants."

Willie. Her on-again, off-again boyfriend. Soon to be dead boyfriend, god damn it! Jens turned his daughter loose. "I'm going to call a chemist friend of mine, sweetie. She knows a lot about drugs. She'll know what to do for you. Just rest your head on the table for a minute. Okay?"

Astrid didn't answer. She'd passed out somewhere on the way down to the table.

The Arctic Circle, March 2, 1:00 p.m.

Breaking down camp had been a matter of jumping on the roofs of their shelters and collapsing them into shapeless piles of snow. After a several-hour maintenance delay, two helicopters had finally arrived. Jack climbed aboard the first one with the Norwegians. All except Larson, of course. He piled on the second helicopter with the Medusas.

To Karen's chagrin, the other women arranged for Larson to be smashed up against her in the chopper's crowded belly. Once the helicopter took off, they had to shout to be heard. Except if a guy put his mouth practically against your ear. Turned out you could hear him just fine then.

"Have I done something to anger you?" he asked.

Hell, yes, he'd angered her! None of the Norwegians had shown the slightest acceptance of the Medusas as their equals the entire time they'd been up here training. For the past four days, Larson had treated Karen and her teammates like overgrown Girl Scouts earning merit badges.

She took a deep breath. Jack had talked to the Medusas before they came to Norway about working with soldiers from another country's armed forces. He'd warned them the Medusas' existence would be a tough sell and that it was going to take mountains of patience to get through to their foreign counterparts. She sighed. That probably didn't include picking fights with the foreign country's observer.

She turned to shout into his ear. "Do me a favor."

"What's that?"

"Don't think of us as women. Treat us like you would any American soldier over here for Arctic exercises."

"But you're not regular soldiers," he protested.

"You're right," she shouted back. "We're not. We're Special Forces operators who are smarter, tougher and deadlier than any regular American soldier you've ever met."

He frowned and obviously considered making some sort of snappy comeback, but ultimately refrained. *Wise man.* She'd hate to have to push him out of the helicopter. He might turn out to be useful for something, yet.

Their helicopter landed them on a barren stretch of beach. Abundant icebergs bobbed in the sea at their backs and gravel crunched under their feet. The coast rose up away from them, rocky and bare, and the smooth slope of a glacier ran down to the sea off to their left. Yet another garden spot of the north, apparently. The helicopter's crew wrestled a large canvas bag out of the back of the cargo compartment and tossed it to the ground. Then, the aircraft commander opened his door and held out an olive-green cloth folder encased in clear vinyl. Karen had worked in a helicopter maintenance unit in the marines, and was the most comfortable around choppers, so she ran back under the rotors to retrieve the mission briefing package.

The bird lifted off, and silence settled around them.

"I say," Karen commented drolly, "it must be all the way up to ten or fifteen degrees out here."

Larson took off a glove and held up his hand for a few seconds. "Minus ten Celsius," he announced.

Karen did the math in her head. Fourteen degrees Fahrenheit. "Good grief, it's nearly summer."

While the other women smiled, he replied, "It is unseasonably warm for this part of Norway."

"All I have to say is anyone who'd live in this climate is nuts."

He laughed and gestured around them with his hand. "You notice the absence of human habitation around you. We Norwegians agree with you. Only a few Sami hunters and herders live up here."

"Sami?" Karen asked.

"The indigenous people. They used to be called Laplanders, but that's considered a pejorative these days. They prefer their own name for themselves, which is Sami."

"Are they the folks who herd reindeer?" she asked.

He nodded. "They also hunt seals, walrus, bears and rabbits, much as your own Alaskan Inuit people might, and they fish the seas as well. But they are primarily known for being a nomadic people who follow the great reindeer herds."

The Medusas quickly unpacked the bag of additional gear Jack had arranged for them to have, noting thankfully, the six pairs of those cool folding snowshoes. They weighed only a few pounds, but the difference they made, even just standing around like this on the edge of a glacier field, was incredible.

Vanessa opened the vinyl folder. It contained laminated maps, both regular ones that depicted sparse roads and villages, none of them nearby, and several much more useful topographical maps in various scales. In their line of work, it was all about knowing the lay of the land.

And then, of course, there was a mission briefing packet. Vanessa read aloud the written version of the instructions they'd gotten earlier. Somewhere in this general area was a Norwegian Army outpost, which they were to find and take out. And then Vanessa rolled her eyes.

"Get this." She read on. "Norwegian patrols are active in the area and should be considered hostile. They are under orders to find and neutralize any intruders who approach their secret facility."

Karen groaned. Staying alive in this extreme climate was going to be hard enough. And how they were going to find some dinky hut in the middle of this mountainous terrain with its thousands of valleys and rocky rifts, she had no idea. But now there were going to be hostiles chasing them, too?

Vanessa read through the rules of engagement—standard stuff. Simulate lethal force. Load rubber bullets only. Don't harm anyone for real. Don't destroy civilian assets. But pretty much anything else went.

Karen's background prior to serving in the Medusas included a fair bit of land reconnaissance training since that was a primary mission of the marines. It was no surprise when Vanessa looked at her as she asked, "Any suggestions on how we proceed, ladies?"

Karen answered right away. "First thing, get to the highest ground we can and have a look around. Then, try to figure out what an outpost up here would be doing, and deduce the most logical place for it to be."

The other women nodded while Larson crossed his arms and looked interested.

Vanessa asked, "What's strategically important up here? Naval activity in the Arctic Ocean? Communications?"

Karen replied soberly, "Oil."

The others looked at her in surprise.

"It's always about money. Norway makes a fortune on its oil industry. A third of its gross national product or something like that."

Larson looked startled that she knew something like that. People always assumed that because she was a marine she was stupid. *Wrongo, buckwheat.* She continued, "Except the bulk of their production is in the North Sea, way down south in Norway. Unless they've made a new find up here in the Arctic they're not telling anyone about."

Ol' Anders looked even more startled, and Karen did her best not to read anything into his expression. They dared not use him as a meter of their correctness. He was Special Forces after all. Which meant he was a trained liar. She wouldn't put it past Jack to have pre-arranged for their Norwegian escort to mislead them.

Vanessa spread out the topographical map and they all crouched around it. "Right here," she stabbed a finger at the map, "is the highest peak in the immediate area, and it happens to be fairly near the coast. What you say we go have a look at it?"

The other women nodded. But Larson protested, "That's nearly five miles away! And you have a great deal of gear to carry."

Karen gritted her teeth. "We're each hauling about forty pounds. We routinely train in seventy pounds. And we had to hike eighty miles in one session to pass our initial training."

His eyebrows shot straight up, but all he said was, "It's your mission. Walk as far as you like."

Karen's eyes narrowed. That sounded suspiciously like a challenge.

They hiked into the mountains for several hours, and probably covered half the distance to the mountain. The snow-shoes were a godsend. Plus, it helped that all the Medusas seemed motivated by Larson's skepticism over their ability to go that far carrying gear.

The sun had passed low on the horizon from one side of the

sky to the other, and was about to begin its short dip behind the western mountains when Isabella, who was on point, raised a fist in the visual signal for them to stop.

Karen frowned. Isabella had done that sharply, like she'd spotted a threat. Her frown deepened as Isabella signaled that she'd spotted two targets ahead. So soon? Had the Medusas already run across a Norwegian 'patrol'? It seemed too easy.

Vanessa signaled the women to get down on their bellies and proceed forward with caution. Karen inched forward to where Isabella sprawled in the snow, peering over the ridge through her binoculars. Karen pulled out her own field glasses and had a look.

At first, she didn't see anything. But then, that wasn't necessarily a surprise. Isabella was one of the top photo intelligence analysts around and had an incredible eye for detail. And then a black speck moved against a field of white, and Karen zoomed in on the target. Male. Dressed in a bulky fur coat. But beyond that, she couldn't make out anything.

Vanessa breathed across the throat mikes and earphones they all wore, "Let's move in and identify them."

The Medusas moved fast whenever they were tucked down in a swale and out of sight of the targets. But they flowed like molasses over the ridgelines when they would be in view of the hostiles. In about fifteen minutes, Isabella held up her fist again. And this time she signaled that the targets were over the next ridge at a distance of roughly two hundred feet.

The Medusas shed their camping gear and donned only their combat equipment for this last approach. Vanessa signaled them to fan out and surround the target. Karen and Misty were assigned to get around to the far side of the two men, who were together now. And then it was time to move out.

Karen low-crawled on her belly through the snow, tunneling her way forward underneath the crisp line of frozen snow that rimmed the ridge in front of them. As soon as she emerged, she spotted the targets. Two men, wearing odd, extremely high-tech looking sunglasses, narrow slashes that wrapped around their heads. Practically no skin was visible on either man. They wore rough fur coats with hoods and masks of some kind covering most of their faces. At a glance, they might be mistaken for bears.

The two men were gesturing with their hands as if they were having a conversation.

Karen eased left, swinging wide around the men. She stayed low, moving only when neither man was looking in her direction. It always amazed her how soldiers could be right out in plain sight and not be spotted. It was all about the eye seeing movement, not still shapes.

One more spurt forward and she'd be in position. She looked out of the corner of her eye without moving her head and spotted Misty making a quick crawl forward. She was almost in position, too. Given that the two of them had had to travel significantly farther than the others, she expected the rest of the team was in place already.

And then another subtle movement caught Karen's attention. It came from behind her. Moving only her eyeballs, she scanned the snow, looking for the source of that visual flutter. Son of a—

Larson was no more than thirty feet behind her. He'd followed her out here! And put them all at risk by doing it! He could've been spotted tailing her like this! And besides, it really grated on her nerves that he'd followed her for this long before she'd seen him. The guy was good, dammit.

Karen clicked her throat radio once to indicate she was ready to go. Five more individual clicks answered hers. A pause, and then three fast clicks to signal the go.

Karen rose to her feet and charged the targets all in one

movement. Her MP-5 submachine gun leveled at the targets, she raced forward.

The two men started violently as six white, armed apparitions rose up all round them. They threw their hands up in the air, jabbering in what sounded like Finnish, but Karen wasn't sure. It definitely wasn't Norwegian. From the men's tone of voice, they'd scared the snot out of these poor schmucks.

Misty, a Russian speaker, tried that tongue on the men. They shook their heads in the negative. And then one of the men tried English. "Please to not kill us!"

Vanessa raised the muzzle of her weapon up and away from the men, but the other Medusas kept theirs trained on the men. "Who are you?" Vanessa asked.

"Hunters. Who are you?"

"We are hunters as well. What are you way out here hunting?"

"Rabbit," the man blurted. "You?"

Vanessa took a long look at the guy, then answered, "Men."

She pushed her hood back, revealing her face, and the two men stared. They pulled down the knit masks that covered their faces, bunched them around their necks, and stared some more.

"You hunt for men?" the spokesman repeated incredulously. "You wish to find husbands out *here?*" He said something in the other language, and both men burst out laughing. Uproariously.

Karen could see the humor of it from their point of view. Perhaps Vanessa should have been a bit more specific about which men they sought and why. However, her gaffe seemed to have broken the ice with these guys.

Karen happened to glance over at Larson. He was grinning fit to beat the band. And for some reason, that irritated the living heck out of her. Her eyes narrowed. And an idea occurred to her. She turned to the two men and pushed back her own hood to reveal her gender as well. "Are you, by any chance, Sami warriors?"

The English speaker nodded. He seemed pleased to have been called a warrior.

"Perhaps you could help us, then. All six of us are women, and we're *all* looking for men. You wouldn't happen to know where to find more just like you, would you?"

The other Medusas followed her cue and pushed back their hoods as well. The Sami men looked around in disbelief. "Six women?"

Karen nodded.

That provoked a spate of what must be an indigenous Sami dialect between the two men. Then one of them turned to Karen and asked, "Are you the warrior goddesses come to us from the hall of Sessrumnir to fulfill the prophecy?"

Karen did not have the foggiest idea what they were talking about, but the guy asked the question with such earnest intensity, she decided to roll with it. "We are. Perhaps you can take us to your people?"

The two men nodded in what for all the world looked like awe. "We have an encampment not far from here."

Bingo. "How many of you are there?" Karen asked.

The second man answered in heavily accented English, "Ten hunters. Women and babies. About fifty."

"Come with us," the first one said. "We take you to them. And then we send out message to Sami nation that time of prophecy come."

The Medusas nodded and fell in beside the hunters, who set off inland toward the south.

Larson stomped up beside Karen to mutter, "What in the bloody hell are you doing?"

"Increasing our reconnaissance force from five to fifty-five. We can't cover all this terrain alone. But these guys will know it like the backs of their hands."

"But they think you're *goddesses*. And you're letting them," he replied in outrage.

Karen looked at him blandly. "Who's to say we're not goddesses to these people? I think we come across as pretty godlike. Don't you?"

"But…" he spluttered, "It's a lie."

"No, Oberstløytnant. It's a job."

Chapter 4

Oslo, Norway, March 2, 1:30 p.m.

"**D**etective Schumacher, there's been a triple murder in the red light district. Report just came in to Homicide."

Irritated, Jens looked up from his desk, where he was reading through the initial affidavits in the Krag case. "If you're going to work with me, Ivo, call me Jens. Hearing my last name all the time makes me feel old."

"Yes, sir, Jens." A pause. "Sir."

Jeez. As if being called sir was any better! The kid sounded scared of him. He rolled his eyes and returned to looking at the witness statement. "And why is this triple homicide of particular interest to us?"

"Because the perpetrator, after randomly going psycho, is still alive."

Jens looked up quickly. "Really? Can we talk to him?"

"Her. She's in the Rikshospitalet University Hospital."

"Let's pay her a visit her, shall we?"

Ivo nodded and held up a set of keys. "Thought you might say that. I'll drive."

Jens closed the Krag file and picked up his ratty coat. He had a thing about wearing decent clothes to crime scenes and ruining them. A waste of perfectly good money.

When they got to the hospital, Jens was disappointed to find out the woman was in a coma and not expected to live. Apparently her bodily systems were experiencing what the doctor called cascade failure. A nice way of putting it.

He tried hard not to picture Astrid lying in the same bed so still and lifeless. He would *not* let this happen to his little girl! What the hell was going on out there in the streets of Oslo that was making people go crazy like this?

"What was she on, doc?" Jens asked.

The doctor shrugged. "We're running blood toxicology now, but I couldn't say for sure. She doesn't show the usual symptom set for anything. Apparently got wired real tight, attacked several people, then briefly went extremely lethargic, and passed out."

"Let me know what you turn up." Jens passed the physician his business card and did his damnedest to ignore the panic twisting in his gut. *Not Astrid.*

The doctor nodded. "I'll call you as soon as we have something."

Somewhere in the North Sea, March 2, 6:00 p.m.

A satellite phone rang nearby, but there were other people to answer it. The man lying in the swinging hammock was too seasick to care who might be calling the ship right now anyway. At least the rope bed was damping out the worst of the boat's rocking. But not enough. He hadn't kept down a bite of solid food since the small cargo vessel left Glasgow yesterday.

He'd argued strenuously against placing the lab in such a godforsaken corner of the world where rough seas and bitter cold would make transportation and supply operations a royal pain in the rear. But he'd been overruled by his superiors. They'd insisted on utmost security for this most secret and important of operations and had chosen the most unlikely, most remote place on the planet for him to run this show.

He only hoped they were enjoying sitting on their fat asses on a Pacific Island, sunning themselves on a beach while he froze his ass off up here. He'd never express such a sacrilegious thought aloud, of course. He'd be struck down dead before the words barely left his mouth

"Phone's for you, Isa," one of the crewmen said too goddamned cheerfully. They all seemed to be having a great laugh over his misery.

"Tell them I'm dying. I can't talk now."

"The call's from Indonesia."

Isa swore under his breath. *His boss.* He stuck out his hand for the phone. Why couldn't the sailor have said so in the first place? He planted the phone against his ear as the ship—and his stomach—gave a great, heaving roll.

"Hello, sir. This is Uthman."

As always, the top brass in the network didn't beat around the bush. Afraid of traces on their calls. This call would last under a minute. "How's the Oslo experiment going?"

Isa brightened a little. It was always good to have positive news to relay. "Beyond our wildest expectations, sir. The city is falling into chaos, and we only released a single kilo of the chemical."

"How much is stockpiled at the production site?"

"Roughly three hundred kilos so far. But, I've got my men working round the clock making more. In another several weeks, we should have close to five hundred kilos ready to go."

"Make it six hundred kilos and have it ready in two weeks."

Isa sucked in a quick breath between his teeth. "We're green-lighted to go with the global release, then?"

"That is affirmative. Our spiritual leader has received a vision from God. It is time to punish the decadence of the West. We will release your chemical into the drug supply across the western world—North and South America, Europe, and Australia. Our heroin producers in Afghanistan and Pakistan are prepared to cut your additive into their outbound supplies as soon as it can be delivered."

"Understood."

Another voice cut into the conversation. It announced emotionlessly, "Thirty seconds elapsed call time."

"Two weeks, Isa."

And then the line went dead.

Northern Norway, March 2, 7:00 p.m.

Karen studied the encampment in fascination. On the surface, it appeared crude, but upon closer inspection, it was incredibly efficient. The families lived in a tight cluster of sod huts. A large communal building stood on one side of the circle, and a lean-to shelter attached to it provided a windbreak for a huddled herd of reindeer.

Hard to imagine that it was the twenty-first century and people anywhere on the planet were still living like this. Surely it must be a source of tension between the Sami people and other Norwegians. She'd bet Sami kids were deserting villages like this in droves. It was a shame, really. This culture had survived for thousands of years pretty much like this, and it was probably only a few decades from disappearing entirely.

"The *siida-isit,* he comes soon," one of their guides announced. "For now, we go to gathering place."

"What's a *siida-isit?*" Karen murmured to Anders.

"*Siida* is the Sami word for their tribal unit. It's mostly clan based. This group of hunters and their families is one *siida.* Their chief is called the *siida-isit.* He is village leader, shaman, counsellor, and justice giver all in one."

Karen nodded. In other words, the big dog.

The Medusas and their hosts ducked inside the main building. It was about the size and shape of a quonset hut and would probably seat thirty or forty people. Although, given how small these people were, maybe it would hold more like fifty. Among the women and children who'd crowded around to stare at them when they arrived, she'd felt like Ms. Jolly Green Giant.

Several men lifted aside the reindeer-skin door and stepped into the hut. A woman followed, scuttling around them to throw more reindeer chunks on the fire. The small, smoky fire filled the space with a strong smell of manure. The woman offered them skins of what turned out to be water so cold it made Karen's teeth ache. Which was probably just as well. The aftertaste of bear grease and reindeer skin was foul. She'd hate to experience it warm.

Isabella, the team's resident language sponge, started pointing at objects around the room and asking the Sami word for them. Before long, all the Medusas had joined in and were repeating the words aloud, to much laughter and many corrections by the locals. The Samis seemed pleased at their effort to learn the Sami tongue. Bowls of stew were passed around, and the Medusas dug into their own packs and contributed beef jerky and chocolate bars to the impromptu feast. Nothing like a little Hershey's diplomacy to loosen things up.

Through it all, Larson sat quietly in the corner. The men kept turning to him and trying to engage him in conversation as if he was the team's leader, until finally he said something in what sounded like quick, fluent Sami. Show off.

Whatever he said, it made the native men stare, open-mouthed.

"What did you just say to them?" Karen asked.

"I told them I was a servant of the goddess and you'd beat me if they didn't quit treating me like you."

It was Karen's turn for her jaw to sag. "You didn't."

He looked her dead in the eye. "I did."

Her own gaze narrowed. So that's how he wanted to play this game, eh? Fine. "Then get me something to drink, oh servant of mine."

His eyes glinted in the firelight, flashing silver irritation. But, he rose from his cross-legged stance to his feet in one fluid movement and ducked outside the tent.

Karen glanced at her teammates, who were all staring at her. "Everything okay, Python?" Vanessa murmured.

"Yup. Couldn't be better," Karen replied cheerfully. She was all over ordering Mr. Chauvinist around like her servant.

The skin swung aside, and Karen looked up expectantly. But instead of Larson, a wizened little man stumped into the room, wrapped in a bulky fur blanket. He looked about a hundred and ten years old. He gazed around the group of women. His black, bird-bright gaze lighted on Karen, and he startled her by bowing deeply. He rasped something in the Sami tongue. Ten-to-one he'd just welcomed her to town. With some difficulty, he straightened once more, looking at her expectantly.

O-kay. What was she supposed to do now? Vanessa flashed her a subtle hand signal to say something.

Karen said, "Please, have a seat by the warm fire your kind tribeswoman has provided for us." While somebody translated for her, she gestured toward the fire and then indicated with her hand that he should sit.

It must've been the right thing to say, for the old man smiled and rather creakily folded himself down to the floor underneath his fur robe. The same woman who'd tended the fire tucked the blanket in around him and pressed a steaming mug of something into his hand. He sipped it slowly and seemed to relax.

Larson slipped back into the tent, but Karen hardly noticed him, so fascinated was she by this character before her. Short, old and unassuming though he might be, his presence was commanding. Here was a leader among his people. Of that, she had no doubt. Larson sat down behind her and to her right.

Finally, after the old man had drained his mug, he looked Karen in the eye and said in heavily accented English, "Is it time?"

"For what?" Karen asked.

The elder answered in Sami.

Karen looked over at her impromptu servant. "Translate, will you?"

"Isn't that using me to help your mission?" he asked dryly. "I wouldn't want to break the rules."

She rolled her eyes. "Enough people here speak English or Russian or something else one of us speaks that we'd eventually communicate with these people. I dunno 'bout you, but I'm tired and hungry. Let's get this over with this week. Just translate." Then, in the interest of diplomacy, she flashed him her most winning smile. "Please."

It was a blatantly girly tactic, but she wasn't above using her gender as a weapon. All was fair in love and war—this being war, of course.

Larson shrugged. "And I quote the village elder, 'Ah. You test me. We have received the prophecy and faithfully repeated it for all the Sami to hear. Your *yoik* has spread like a great blizzard driven on the strongest north wind across the land.'"

"What the heck is a *yoik?*" she muttered to Larson.

"A chanted song. Used to record history, legends and religious prophecies."

Louder and to the old man, she said, "May I hear this *yoik?*"

He nodded and began chanting in a warbling, rusty, old man's voice. In the native language, darn it.

Larson murmured as the guy sang, "The old ways are lost by all but a few. The old beliefs are gone. It is time to restore them. We come to make it so. Restore your people. Restore your lands. Restore the faith. We come presently, and we are the sign. I shall cleanse your lands of the scourge upon it now, and then you shall be free. So said the warrior goddess to Naliki who walked in dreaming wakefulness."

The old man fell silent.

"Who's Naliki?" Karen asked the *siida-isit*.

The old man answered, speaking rapidly at Larson. He must have realized the Norwegian soldier was translating for the women.

"Naliki is the *noaide* to whom the goddess—that's you—gave the vision. And the *yoik* he just sang was written by this Naliki person. Apparently, the Sami people have been waiting for a sign from the gods for a while that it's time to rise up and take back their native lands and lifestyle." Larson added lightly, "And here you are."

Karen turned to stare over her shoulder at him. "You're kidding."

"Nope."

"What's this gentleman's name?"

Larson said something in rapid Sami.

The old man replied in halting English, "I am Padmir, *siida-isit* of the Siida Cholma."

Larson interjected, "*Siida-isits* are highly respected among their people. It is a great honor that he speaks to you as outsiders."

Padmir retorted, his black eyes snapping. "It is a great honor *for you* that I speak to you, Norse man. It is a great honor for me that the goddesses sit at my fire and speak to me."

Karen laughed at the chagrined look on Larson's face. She liked this old guy, Padmir. He'd certainly put the big, bad Norwegian commando in his place. "Translate for me, please, Oberstløytnant Larson."

He nodded with a certain amount of annoyance.

Looking at the old man, she said, "*Siida-isit* Padmir, my companions and I come on a quest. We seek six strangers to these lands, much the same as us. They have come recently and set up a camp of sorts. Do you, by any chance, know where to find them?"

Larson scowled, but seemed to translate the message verbatim.

Padmir said something to the other men, who until now had been seated quietly behind him. The hunters' faces lit up, and there was a spate of animated talk, accompanied by a great deal of hand waving.

Larson muttered, "They've already been looking for the place where you will cleanse the land of outsiders, and they say they've found it. Apparently, it's less than a day's walk from here to the north and east."

She was a little confused as to how the Samis knew to be

looking for intruders a full day before the Medusas came, but she wasn't going to look this gift horse in the mouth.

Larson muttered, "This is cheating. You were supposed to find my guys on your own."

Karen muttered back, "The rules of engagement said to use all the available local resources at our disposal. I'd say these guys are local resources, wouldn't you?"

Larson didn't reply, but his narrowed gaze was answer enough.

"Sit there and be quiet, like a good servant," Karen bit out. "It's part of Delta training to make friends with the locals and then enlist their help. And if you ask me, we girls are doing pretty well at both with these folks."

A woman came in, carrying another big, steaming pot, undoubtedly more food of some kind. Larson jumped up to help her with it and hung it on a hook by the fire for her. Whether he did it out of chivalry, or to rub Karen's nose in his ability to make friends, too, she couldn't tell. Either way, the native woman smiled shyly at him.

It turned out to be reindeer stew. It tasted surprisingly good. Nonetheless, Karen ate sparingly. These people didn't look like they did much more than subsist, and seven soldiers with hearty appetites would no doubt strain the tribe's limited resources.

Padmir finished his soup and set aside his carved wooden bowl. Larson translated as the chief announced, "Tonight, I send forth the word for a gathering of all the Sami people in the heart of our native lands The Great Restoration is upon us."

"Great Restoration?" Karen repeated.

Larson shrugged. "Don't ask me. I'm only the hired help."

She rolled her eyes at him.

Vanessa piped up. "Would it be possible for these guys to draw us a map to the encampment of the outsiders?"

Larson relayed the question to the Sami men. "They'll do you one better and will guide you goddesses to it. It will be an event to sing *yoiks* to their grandchildren about."

Vanessa replied dryly, "Really, a map will be fine."

Larson shrugged. "You won't talk them out of it. If they don't lead you, they'll follow you."

Vanessa sighed. "All right. We'll head out first thing in the morning. That'll put us in range of your guys by nightfall. And I'd really rather hit them in the dark if I can."

Oslo, Norway, March 2, 9:00 p.m.

Jens dug his cell phone out of his breast pocket and took a look at the caller ID. *Finally.* The Oslo Police's forensic chemist. And a really nice lady. He flipped open the phone.

"Hi, Marta. Thanks for returning my call. What can you tell me about my daughter? Is she displaying any of the classic signs of violent psychosis that the other victims have just prior to their deaths?"

"No." Jens couldn't help letting out a sigh of relief.

"That doesn't mean she's out of danger, though. We're just now interviewing surviving family members and friends of the attackers. This drug seems to build up in the system over a period of time, and the symptoms become more pronounced and more…severe…gradually."

"How much time?" Jens asked tensely, his gut right back in the twist it had been in ever since he'd discovered Astrid stoned at the kitchen table on God knows what.

"Days or maybe weeks. Hard to tell. Most of the victims, as far as we can tell were regular recreational drug users or outright addicts. We're fairly certain a bad batch of drugs was put out on the streets, and that something in the drugs is interacting with other chemicals present to cause the psychotic episodes, convulsions and death."

Jens cursed under his breath. "What do I do for my daughter?"

"Keep her off any drugs at all, and at the first signs of erratic behavior, get her to a hospital and in restraints, for her own safety and yours." The pathological chemist added grimly, "And you could pray. Whatever this stuff is, it's powerful and nasty."

That was one way of describing it. People were dying all over Oslo. In the past week, they'd had more murders than the city averaged in a normal year.

"Thanks, Marta."

"I'll let you know if I find out any more."

Jens disconnected the call. He knew of something else he could do besides wait and pray—neither of which he could do worth a damn. He could find out who Astrid had gotten her drugs from. Starting with that louse, Willie.

Northern Norway, March 2, 10:00 p.m.

The Sami people shifted around their sleeping arrangements and freed up two turf huts for the Medusas and Larson. When Karen and Larson were shown to one hut and the rest of the Medusas to another, Karen wasn't the slightest bit amused.

He translated dryly; it turned out that as the preeminent goddess among the group, Karen was expected to have her own quarters. And of course, she'd want her servant with her to wait on her. The lesser warrior goddesses were given the other hut.

Unfortunately, said lesser goddesses were so busy containing gales of laughter that they weren't the slightest bit of help at all in talking the Samis out of this sleeping arrangement. Fuming, Karen was forced to retire to her own hut. With her manservant.

The sod structure was surprisingly warm. Even with only a

small fire in the center beneath the smoke hole in the roof, the interior was shirtsleeve warm. Either that, or Karen was acclimating faster to the cold than she'd realized. A Sami woman carried in a load of dried reindeer dung and a fresh skin of water, and then, backed out of the hut. Karen and Larson were alone.

She pulled out her sleeping bag and plunked down on top of it, glaring at her roommate. "Okay, Einstein. Talk to me about Norse mythology. Who, exactly, am I supposed to be?"

He leaned back against his pack, stretching his feet out to the fire. "The Samis think you're no less than Freya herself."

"And Freya is?"

He grinned. "The Norse goddess of love and fertility. Oh, and she's also the goddess of war and patron of all female warriors."

"Female warriors?" Karen echoed.

He shrugged. "The Vikings have a long history of women fighters. When the men were away conquering and pillaging foreign lands, somebody back home had to protect the village from being taken and plundered."

"Tell me more about this Freya."

"She was exceedingly beautiful and clever, as any self-respecting goddess should be. She possessed several notable magic items, including Brising's necklace, which made her so beautiful that she was irresistible to men. She also had a cloak made of falcon skins that she used to fly with on occasion. She shared Odin's love of battle, and the two of them split the spirits of all warriors who fell in battle. Half went to Odin's hall, Valhalla. And the other half—including all the fallen women warriors—went to her hall, Sessrumnir."

"Ahh. That's the place the first Sami guy asked me if I'd come from."

Crud. Maybe it hadn't been such a great idea to go along

with this business of the locals thinking she was Freya. But darned if she was about to admit that to Larson! "Anything more I ought to know about Freya?"

"She got her golden necklace by sleeping with four mythical dwarven smiths. In return, they crafted Brising's necklace from the stars and the fruitfulness of the earth. It enhanced her beauty so much that mortal men could hardly bear to look at her, and all men who saw her fell hopelessly in love with her."

Karen made a face. "Who'd want men fawning all over them all the time anyway?"

Larson grinned. "I know plenty of women who think it would be wonderful to have men worship at their feet."

Karen shook her head. "They'd get in the way. You'd end up tripping over guys everywhere you went."

He laughed. "The American warrior is practical as well as smart and strong and beautiful. Maybe you do have a bit of Freya in you after all."

More than a little uncomfortable with this whole goddess comparison thing, she abruptly changed subjects. "Tell me about yourself."

Larson looked startled. "Not much to tell."

"Where are you from?"

"I come from a little island called Heng. It's off the coast of southwestern Norway, not far from Stavenger."

"I gather then you grew up around water and boating."

He laughed. "It's hard not to in Norway. And yes, I did. My father is a ship captain."

"What sorts of ships?"

"He started in the Norwegian Navy but spent the last twenty years of his career piloting a container ship. One of the super-cargo carriers."

"A military family then. Was he tough?"

Larson's eyes darkened from light blue to dull gray. "You could say that."

Well, then. *That* hit a nerve. "Okay. So you grew up around boats and the navy. Do FSK officers have to go to college?"

He nodded. "I studied ship design and Norse history at the University of Oslo."

"Then what?"

"Then I joined the army."

Yup, definitely tension between father and son. "Going army had to really twist your father's knickers, what with him being navy and all."

Larson answered too blandly, "I suppose it did."

"Any hobbies?"

He frowned. "Who has time for hobbies?"

Karen grinned. "I know what you mean. Ever since I took this job, I've been going nonstop. If it's not a mission, it's more training. It's like drinking from a fire hose."

He laughed. "Your Special Forces aren't so different from ours, except for—"

He broke off, and his next words hung unspoken in the air. Except for the part where the U.S. allowed women inside the fence.

He said hastily, "I do like to cross-country ski. I race in biathlons."

"You're one of the Olympic medalists who were chasing us, then?"

"Yeah." An awkward silence fell. Into it, he said, "Biathlons originated in the Norwegian Army in the 1760s. We take it as a point of pride to be the best in the world at it."

It was startling to realize that she and the Medusas had been keeping pace with an Olympian for the past few days. But then her gaze narrowed. "You've been taking it easy on us women, haven't you? You threw the fight with me because you didn't want to hurt me," she accused.

He retorted, "No, I didn't. You surprised me and took me off guard. And then you put a superior wrestling move on me."

She subsided, surprisingly disappointed. It might have been nice to think he was bigger and stronger than her. But no. She was the Freya look-alike. A manly-girl who could whup up on an Olympic athlete for God's sake. Humiliation roiled in her gut.

"But I'll win next time," he added confidently.

Right. Because after all, he was a man. And she was only a woman. A woman who couldn't make up her mind about whether she liked this guy or hated his guts. Nothing like a little good old-fashioned dose of "you can't live with 'em and you can't live without 'em" to mess up a girl's head.

Karen hmmphed and crawled into her sleeping bag. She turned her back to Larson in disgust and tried to think small, feminine, fragile thoughts.

It didn't work.

She fell asleep pondering creative ways to break Larson in half.

Northern Norway, March 3, 6:00 a.m.

It might as well be the middle of the night for all the light there was out here, but that was okay. The night belonged to them. The Medusas and their Norwegian sidekick were suited up and ready to go when the Sami trackers gestured that they, too, were ready to head out.

Karen walked past a number of Sami girls and women milking the reindeer and picking up the night's deposits of fresh fuel by the reindeer. All in all, she'd rather be toting forty pounds of electronics, explosives and weapons and heading out to kick some Norwegian Army butt.

They walked until after sunrise, breaking at midday for a bite to eat and a short rest. And then they walked most of the afternoon without pause. These Sami men might be small, but they were tough as nails. Even Anders was showing signs of having to work a bit to keep up with them.

The sun set, and they walked about one more hour, which made it about four-thirty in the afternoon. And all of a sudden, the Sami men stopped and crouched. They murmured something to Anders.

"The hut of the outsiders you are here to cleanse from the land is over the next ridge. You can see the heat rising off it now."

Karen looked where the hunters were pointing. Now that they mentioned it, she could see a faint shimmer of warm air rising in a column. There was no visible smoke, just that nearly invisible disturbance in the air. Good eyesight these Samis had. Must come from hunting for a living.

Vanessa spoke quietly. "Karen, tell these guys to head home."

Karen turned to the two men. "Thank you for your guidance. Now it is time for you to leave."

It didn't take a translation of their agitated outburst in reply to figure out these guys didn't want to leave. They wanted to hunt beside the goddess. She swore under her breath as Larson threw her a big, fat, I-told-you-so look.

She huffed. "Tell them this is our quest. We shall return to the village to fulfill the prophecy when we are finished here. But this is not a fight for men. It is ours."

He raised his eyebrows but made the translation.

An 'ahh' of comprehension came from the two hunters. They nodded their understanding and turned immediately to go. Leaving six women alone to fight a gun battle, they couldn't wrap their brains around. But a quest by the gods—that they could understand.

The two Sami men disappeared over the ridge behind the

Medusas. "Okay, fellow goddesses. Let's get on with this quest," Vanessa commented dryly.

The others laughed quietly.

Their surveillance showed no activity outside the building. The Norwegians must not expect the Medusas to find them for several more days. And why should they? Had the Samis not led them right to it, locating this log cabin would've been like finding a needle in a haystack. The structure looked like an old hunting lodge. It wasn't huge, but given the expense of hauling in all those logs, it looked downright luxurious for the region. The women guessed it slept maybe a dozen men.

There had only been five Norwegians and Jack on the helicopter, but that didn't mean they hadn't picked up more manpower before flying here. The women decided to plan for twelve men. Two to one odds wasn't bad, especially when they had the element of surprise on their side.

The next step was some close-up surveillance to figure out what, exactly, these army types were doing way out here. The final step would be the fun part—the surprise assault where the Medusas got even for their loss in the unarmed-combat encounter. This time around, they'd have rubber bullets and rubber-bladed knives. The Norwegians wouldn't stand a chance.

The Medusas eased forward, each taking a window in the structure to peer through. Keeping a sharp eye out for booby traps, Karen inched forward, one elbow at a time. Surprisingly, she ran across no traps. Maybe the other women hit them on their approaches. But, given that no snaps, pops, bangs or other explosions of noise gave away their approach, her teammates must've been successful at disarming any traps they ran across.

Karen tried hard not to think about Larson, creeping along right behind her, but it was hard not to. He dogged her every step, like a pesky shadow that wouldn't let go of her ankle.

Finally, she eased up to the wall of the cabin, sitting on the ground beneath the window. A stack of twenty or so storage drums of some kind stood beside her. Probably spare fuel and provisions, given how far out in the middle of nowhere this place was. She extended her flexible mini-periscope and tucked its end up over one corner of the window sill over her head.

She was looking at a common room of some kind. It was a large space with a big, stone fireplace off to one side. Except instead of furniture in the room it looked more like a…lab. There were long tables, and machinery that looked way, way too high-tech to be sitting out here in the wilderness. The only light in the room came from a doorway on the other side of the house, so she couldn't make out a lot of detail as to what kind of equipment it was. But it definitely looked scientific.

"Report," Vanessa breathed.

Kat reported a bedroom with no activity. Misty and Vanessa reported a kitchen with four men eating in it. Jack was not among them.

Isabella, who was around the corner from Karen's position, reported a bedroom stacked full of large metal drums and a dozen additional drums sitting outside beside her. They appeared unmarked but were shipping containers of some kind. Anders glided off in the darkness to have a look at the drums, and Karen was glad to be rid of him. Then it was Karen's turn.

"The living room appears to have been converted into a lab of some kind. It's full of electronics and scientific-looking equipment. If it's toys the Norwegian Special Forces are using, I've never seen anything like—"

A loud, ominous rumbling noise interrupted her. She whirled around with her back to building. If that was a trap going off, it was a hell of an explosion. It sounded like a freight train coming down the hill.

The whole mountain behind her seemed to be sliding toward her. *Crap.* Avalanche. She estimated the amount of flat land between the cabin and the mountain. Was there enough space for the snow to come to a halt before it slammed into her?

Larson sprinted around the side of the building, shouting, "Get to the lee of the building!"

That answered that. She dived around the end of the cabin, and joined her five teammates and Larson as the first boulder-sized chucks of ice and snow came hurtling past. The building at her back shook as the remnants of the avalanche slammed into it.

Shouting came from inside the building. Another slamming noise. This time of the front door flying open. Two men leaped out, back-to-back, each facing to the side.

It was a toss-up who was more surprised, the Medusas or the men staring back at them. Everyone raised their weapons simultaneously.

The reports of rifles exploded, deafeningly loud at such close range. The Medusas dived for cover around the ends of the building. Something hot burned across Karen's left thigh just as she ducked around the corner. She'd been hit by rubber bullets before, and they didn't feel like that at all.

Larson landed beside her, tearing his rifle off his back.

"What the hell kind of ammunition are your men using?" Karen bit out. "I just got hit and it hurts like hell!"

"Lemme see."

She rolled onto her side, left leg up, as she pulled out her own rifle and yanked on a pair of night-vision goggles.

"You're bleeding," he bit out. "Looks superficial, but you've been shot."

Just then, Vanessa's voice crackled over the radio, "What ammo are your men using, Larson? Kat and Isabella are both bleeding."

He ripped the periscope out of Karen's belt and poked the end around the corner of the cabin. Larson stabbed at his throat mike. "These are *not* my men. And those are *real* bullets they're firing."

Karen glanced down at her own weapon, loaded only with harmless, rubber dum-dum rounds. *Oh, shit.*

Cindy Dees

Chapter 5

Vanessa started barking orders. "Around the back side of the building. Now. Get down in the snow."

Snow wasn't worth spit at stopping bullets, but it would provide visual cover so the bad guys wouldn't know where to aim their fire. Karen jumped to her feet and turned to sprint through the snow—and was confronted by a *wall* of the stuff. The avalanche. She climbed into the tumbled mess, diving for cover as more shots rang out.

A quick glance over her shoulder for Larson. *He wasn't behind her, dammit!* Where'd he go? She flattened herself behind a boulder-sized chunk of snow to look for him.

"Pull back, Python. We're about thirty feet behind you."

"No can do, Viper. I've lost Larson."

"Anyone got a visual on him?" Vanessa bit out.

Silence was the only answer to her question.

Vanessa asked, "Anders, where are you?"

More silence. Which meant he was close enough to the hostiles that he dared not speak aloud.

"I'm going back down," Karen announced. "And yes, I'll be careful and keep my head in the game," she added before her boss could remind her.

She poked her periscope around the end of the building and groaned under her breath. Four hostiles were fanning out in the snow, moving away from the cabin. The good news was they were headed generally away from the avalanche field and the Medusas' location. The bad news was that they all were toting various weapons at the ready. Digging fast, she made a hollow long enough to swallow her torso and legs—just in case it came to a shootout. Then she peered around the end of the building again.

She scanned the snow for Larson or some sign that he'd buried himself out there. Nada. *C'mon, golden boy. Where are you?*

And then, without warning, she saw him. Rising up out of the snow right behind one of the tangos. He had a knife in his right hand and slashed it across the guy's neck. The tango went limp in silence, and Larson eased him to the ground. But, God, the blood. The snow turned crimson all around the two men. No way the other hostiles would miss that. And sure enough, they didn't. A shout, and all three men whirled to face Larson, who'd at least had the good sense to scoop up the downed man's shotgun and head for cover. He was just sprinting around the far end of the house when the men opened fire. Karen ducked as bullets flew every which way.

"Anders. You okay? Report." she whispered frantically as the tangos commenced floundering back toward the cabin through the snow.

"I'm behind the barrels."

"You heard Viper. Pull back to the avalanche field."

"This is a drug lab. I need to collect a sample for evidence."

With scant patience, she retorted, "We're not armed. We have to get out of here. We can come back later with real bullets. Hell, call in an air strike by your air force."

"After I get a sample."

Exasperated, Karen plastered herself flat in her little hollow as one of the tangos came into sight about fifty feet away from her position. Most amateur shooters couldn't lethally hit a human-sized target at that range. But she didn't know if these guys were amateurs or not. And she didn't want to bet her life on it. She had to assume the worst, that these guys were proficient with those guns.

Dammit, the tangos were heading back toward the cabin. And Larson. Fast.

"Incoming," Vanessa murmured. "Three men. Range fifty meters. On foot, fast-walk pace. Floundering in the snow. Lots of vertical movement. Aim low."

Katrina's voice chimed in. "These rubber bullets may not be lethal, but put one in an eye or hit the throat or bridge of the nose, and it'll render the target combat-ineffective for a while."

Karen snorted. She was a good shot, but targeting the bridge of some guy's nose was out of her league.

Viper again. "What range can you reliably target eyes at, Cobra?"

Kat answered, "On a moving target, about twenty-five meters."

Damn, she was good.

"Start moving, Cobra," Vanessa ordered. "Get twenty meters or so from Anders' position. We'll cover you. Adder, Sidewinder, take Cobra's right flank, Range from her ten to fifteen meters. Fire for the eyes or throat. I'll take her left flank."

Karen felt useless over here on the far side of the building. Maybe she should try to move around the back of the cabin and join Larson. But then she took a second look at the geometry as the tangos continued to stalk the pile of barrels where they'd last seen Larson. They wouldn't expect her on their right flank like this. She'd get shots at a range of eight meters or so. But then, of course, they'd want to fire back—at nearly point-blank range. She'd have to shoot and run like hell. And hope the crossfire from her teammates confused the tangos enough so they didn't know where the shots were coming from.

"I have only two shots in this weapon," Larson murmured.

"Then make them count," Vanessa muttered back.

The remaining tangos approached the cabin. Karen watched in an agony of suspense as Viper whispered their range to Larson, who was blind on the far side of the barrels. Twenty meters. Fifteen. Ten.

Then all hell broke loose. A single shot rang out, and one of the men screamed. He dropped his weapon and plastered both hands over his left eye. The other two men opened fire, blasting wildly toward the barrels where Larson hid. Single shots began to ring out among the continuous hostile fire. The Medusas had opened up. But Larson was still pinned down. He was the only one with real ammunition, and he couldn't fire!

Karen raised her rifle to her cheek and put her eye to the sight. She exhaled slowly and was just about to take out the tango nearest her when the front door burst open and two more men came charging out. In a millisecond she took in the silhouettes in their hands. *Crap.*

"Two new tangos incoming!" she transmitted urgently. "Armed with AK-47s. Expect automatic fire!"

And then the deafening burst of two fully automatic submachine guns fired into the fray. The users were being idiots, holding down the triggers and laying down a curtain of lead. At that rate, they'd be out of ammo in thirty seconds. Assuming any of the Medusas were still alive in thirty seconds. Her team-mates were crazy close to bring their own weapons into effective range.

She took aim at the eye socket of the nearest new entrant into the fight. She didn't have a clean shot at it, but worst case, she'd plink the side of his nose and distract him. She lined up her sights and took the shot. The guy lurched and stopped firing. He turned slightly toward her and she took aim on his other eye. Squeezed through the trigger smoothly. He yelled at that one and doubled over.

The second tango had his AK down by his hip, and was raking it side-to-side across where the barrels ought to be. Please God, let the containers be filled with fluid or something solid enough to stop all that lead from ripping right through them! And *please* let it not be flammable!

She pushed to her feet to charge the remaining shooters and go hand-to-hand.

"Hold your position, Python!" Vanessa ordered sharply. "Medusas, fire at will."

Karen froze in the act of bolting around the corner. Instead, she knelt by the corner and fired left-handed around the wall. The tangos were moving around too much now for her to get a clean shot at an eye, but she just aimed for the head and called it good. Why Vanessa had ordered her to stay put, she had no idea. But she trusted the woman with her life. And in a fire-fight there was no time to be questioning orders. There'd be time enough after they survived this fiasco to sort out the whys and wherefores.

And then Karen had her answer. The withering barrage of what the tangos no doubt thought were real bullets drove them back into the cabin. They came running around the corner and dived into the building, slamming the door shut behind them.

And Karen had the best angle to fire inside the door if the tangos cracked it open. She aimed her rifle at the door just in case. And sure enough, a few seconds later, it opened a few inches and a gun barrel poked out. She fired a shot at the dark spot just over the barrel of the shotgun where the shooter's face should be. A sharp cry and the door slammed shut again.

"Cobra. Relieve Python. Meet us behind the cabin, Python."

In a few seconds, the small sniper tapped on Karen's shoulder. Karen stood up while Cobra went low, crouching between Karen's feet. When the sniper nodded that she'd acquired the target, Karen gingerly stepped over her comrade and backed out of firing position. She scrambled around the back of the cabin, diving beneath the nearest window and crouching in the snow beside her teammates.

"Any idea where Anders went?" Vanessa breathed.

Karen nodded. "Behind the barrels. He took out one tango and got the guy's shotgun."

"He's still not answering. The tangos must be looking out the window he's sitting under. Python, go signal him to pull back. You two cover our retreat with Cobra. We'll pull back in a standard fighting retreat formation. Anders can tag along with you in the rotation. We'll head over the ridge, due south of the cabin and rendezvous there. Alternate rendezvous will be one kilometer due east of that."

Karen nodded and took off crawling. She ducked under the second window and paused to peer around the corner. Larson was, indeed, crouched beside the eastern facing window, looking down the barrel of his stolen shotgun between a gap in the metal drums. Carefully, she tapped his foot. It was never a good thing to surprise a Special Forces operator in full combat mode. He nodded fractionally to acknowledge her presence.

She eased up beside him, plastering herself close to him to

avoid being seen if anyone happened to glance out the window. She breathed into his ear, "Fighting retreat, stay with me. Pull back due south over the ridge. Alternate meeting point one click east of that."

"When?"

"Now."

"I need a sample of what's in these barrels."

"We're mostly unarmed against hostiles with deadly intent. Viper has given the order to retreat *now.*"

"Get me a sample while I move up to the corner of the cabin. I'll keep an eye out to make sure we don't get company."

Karen glared at him. They *so* didn't have time to sit here and argue over how to proceed. He knew better than to contradict the team leader's orders!

He glanced over at her. Murmured, "I'm not trying to make trouble. But it's vital that I get a sample. Help me out on this, and I'll retreat wherever and whenever you want." When she continued to glare at him doubtfully, he added, "I promise."

Reluctantly she nodded. Arguing never did any good in combat. She pushed up to a crouch by the wall of the cabin while he eased around in front of the pile of barrels, out of sight. She pulled out her field knife, a wicked-sharp blade eight inches long, and stabbed the nearest barrel. The blade cut through the steel not quite like butter, but close. She yanked it out and stabbed again, perpendicular to the first cut and forming an X. She twisted the blade this time, opening up a small hole in the side of the barrel.

One corner of the barrel dropped a few inches, causing the whole pile to lurch slightly. Using her blade as a spatula, she pulled out a sample of what turned out to be white powder. She reached into the pocket of her parka where she'd stowed emergency medical supplies and pulled out a gauze pad. Using her teeth, she ripped the paper package open. She rubbed the pad across the blade. The sterile fabric shouldn't contaminate whatever that powder was.

A tremendous blast sounded nearby. Crap. Larson had just fired. The tangos must be thinking about coming out to play again. A second blast exploded, and the pile beside her gave a big lurch. Recoil from the shotgun must've hit it. An ominous, metallic, grinding sound echoed above her. She looked up.

And was just in time to see the pile wobble. Tilt. And begin a slow-motion collapse directly toward her.

A white shape hurtled toward her, slamming into her and knocking her clear as the entire pile of barrels, at least twenty of them, came tumbling down.

The impact of Larson flying into her knocked her a good ten feet backward, landing her on her back in the snow. A barrel rolled on top of her leg, harmlessly pushing it deep into the snow. She tried to roll the barrel clear and was startled by its massive weight. She could barely move it. The thing must weigh close to two hundred pounds. Instead, she wiggled her foot and leg deeper into the snow and pulled the limb free with no trouble. The cloud of powdery snow raised by the crash began to settle, and she looked frantically for Larson. There was no sign of him. He must be buried. *Under the barrels.* Make that under tons of steel and unidentified white powder! Not good.

"Man down," she transmitted in an urgent whisper. "All free hands to the pile of barrels. It collapsed and Anders is buried."

Viper transmitted immediately, "Cobra, hold your position, and keep the tangos busy at the front door if you can. Everyone else, to Python."

Karen looked at where she'd landed and estimated what direction Larson must have come from to tackle her like that.

She started digging frantically in the snow around a partially buried barrel. She encountered something hard. She dug even faster. A boot.

Crap. He was buried under the entire pile of barrels. He'd suffocate if they didn't get all that weight off his chest fast. Adrenaline roared through her. With great difficulty, she exhaled slowly and studied the pile. They'd have to work not only fast but also smart to get him out of there. They had a minute, maybe two, to free him. The pattern in which the steel drums lay began to unfold before her. If they started with that top barrel, then rolled aside those two, they could lift that fourth barrel, and then have access to a couple of more barrels that, good Lord willing, were the ones lying on top of Larson.

Vanessa sprinted around the corner. Karen pointed and her boss nodded. They each grabbed an end of the barrel and gave a heave. It moved aside. They dropped it by the cabin window. Aleesha and Isabella stacked it in front of the window, partially blocking where the others were working from view. Good idea. Karen and Vanessa rolled aside the second barrel.

Misty joined Vanessa at the far end of the next barrel, which had to be lifted up in the air and then moved aside. Karen exhaled hard and lifted with her thighs, her back straight. What she wouldn't give for a wide, leather, weight-lifting belt to support her back right about now! Although with the adrenaline screaming through her, she could probably lift a car and not feel it. The seconds ticked away in the back of her mind.

None of the barrels sloshed as though they contained liquid. More of that white powder in all of them perhaps? The weights seemed generally uniform—which was to say they were all freaking heavy.

They lifted off two more barrels. With weights like this,

Larson might not be breathing. He could very well be crushed under this pile. Fear for him goaded her.

And then Karen spied a gloved hand in the snow. She started to lean down to check on him, and the entire pile of barrels shifted. Damn! She dived in and planted her back against the one that threatened to roll down and collapse the whole stack on top of him again. The weight at her back shifted, and she planted her feet in the snow on either side of his hand. She literally had to grunt to breathe through the effort of holding who knew how many hundreds of pounds of barrels from crashing down on top of Larson.

"Hurry," she grunted.

The other Medusas pushed and pulled at the barrels like maniacs. She had to give them credit. They were giving it their level-best effort. Her legs trembled, near the point of collapse. *Dig deep. Breathe. Stand firm.* His *life* depended on it. Beads of sweat popped out on Karen's forehead and her thighs began to give out. Too much adrenaline screamed through her for much pain to register, but her body was nearly at its limit.

"Just a couple more barrels," Vanessa panted.

Karen nodded her understanding. She blew out short fast breaths. Must keep oxygen flowing to her muscles. It felt as if an entire mountain was sitting on her back. Larson's legs appeared. Two more barrels to go, one on his torso and one lying across his head and shoulders. One barrel lifted away. One more to go. She could do this.

As the last barrel came away from him, she saw that his face was intact. His chest seemed normal under his parka, too, not crushed. But he was unconscious and not moving.

"I can't hold this much longer." Her knees were screaming in protest, the joints themselves threatening to give way.

Aleesha crouched by his head, cradling his neck and head

in a nifty arm hold and then, with the help of the others, dragged him clear of the pile.

Vanessa and Misty grabbed Karen's parka and put tension on it. "On the count of three," Vanessa bit out.

Karen nodded.

"One…two…three!"

Karen leaped to the side while Vanessa and Misty yanked her for all they were worth. She rocketed into the clear as the entire pile of barrels came crashing down on the spot where she'd just stood. One of the top barrels bounced off the moving pile, and went airborne. It hit her squarely in the middle of the back, knocking her flat on her face in the snow. The already weakened sheet metal, riddled with bullets, gave way, and the entire contents of the barrel emptied all over her back.

Good news, the barrel wasn't heavy any more. Bad news, she was practically buried in a pile of white powder. She leaped up, shaking it off and wiping it away from her eyes.

Katrina's weapon fired several times in quick succession.

"Can you run?" Vanessa bit out.

Karen drew an experimental deep breath. "I'm good," she panted.

"Medusas retreat. Cobra, give us thirty seconds, and then pull back. Two rotation fighting retreat. Python and Mamba, you've got Anders. Sidewinder and I will cover you. Cobra and Adder are the other rotation."

Karen nodded. Thank God she'd landed in deep snow and not on a hard surface. That barrel could have crushed her ribcage otherwise. She stumbled to her right toward Aleesha, who had hastily wrapped an inflatable neck brace around Larson's neck and pulled the auto-inflate tab. Too bad there wasn't time to go looking for his shotgun and its real ammo. But at least neither he nor she was a pancake.

"Adder, get eyeballs on the back windows," Vanessa ordered.

"I could use some help before I pull back," Kat transmitted.

Misty grabbed her MP-5 and its useless rubber bullets off the ground. "I'm on it."

Karen rushed over to where Aleesha was performing a quick check on Larson. The doctor reported tersely, "He's been knocked out. No broken bones, no apparent crushing. How's your breathing?"

"Normal. My ribs are intact. I inhaled a little of the white stuff, though."

"Any symptoms?" the doctor bit out as she finished running her hands down Larson's legs.

"Not yet."

Aleesha said tersely, in full trauma-surgeon mode, "We'll need to send some of that powder out for analysis. Lemme know if you feel out of the ordinary in any way."

"Yes, Mother."

Aleesha grinned up at her briefly. "Your boy's ready to move. You want the head or feet?"

"Help me lift him into a fireman's carry. It'll be faster if I haul him out. You take my pack and rifle."

Aleesha nodded. Unlike Larson, she knew not to argue in a situation like this. Each of the Medusas knew their own capabilities. If one of them said she could do something, the others knew she wasn't exaggerating.

Aleesha helped her lift his limp form and drape his arms over Karen's shoulders from behind.

Karen shifted his weight, settling it more firmly against her back, and then turned. She took off, jogging clumsily through the snow. Oh, God, this sucked. He would have to be a big, muscular guy. He weighed around 220 pounds if she had to guess. The slope was uneven, and the snow varied from hard-packed old snow that held her weight to light powder, stirred up by the avalanche. There was no predicting from step to step whether the snow would hold their combined weight on the surface or whether they'd sink hip-deep. She floundered forward doggedly.

Aleesha moved ahead of her to forge a bit of a trail and that helped some. But it was still grueling to haul a man Larson's size up the ragged slope. Karen hurt just about everywhere a person could hurt. Her thighs, already exhausted by holding off that pile of barrels, were further tasked. They cramped, but she had no time to stop and stretch them out. Her entire chest cavity hurt from where the barrel had crashed into her, and her lungs were going to explode any second. She couldn't even spare the energy to swallow. Instead, she spat whenever her mouth filled with saliva. Her breathing turned into a wheezing series of gasps, and each exhalation was a grunt of pain.

"Forward rotation, halt," Vanessa ordered.

Karen staggered to a stop, panting like a broken-down race-horse. It was almost more painful to rest than it was just to keep pushing through the agony. Katrina and Misty raced up.

"Ready to go, Python?" Misty asked.

Karen nodded at the two women who would now take up escort duty. How long it took them to climb that long slope, Karen didn't know. But it was the toughest few minutes of her life. The others offered to spell her, but they all knew she had more upper-body strength than anybody else on the team. And besides, they couldn't afford the time to stop and transfer him to someone else. The tangos could come out any second. And with their ammunition, they could easily kill the Medusas before they reached the top of the ridge.

About three-quarters of the way up the hill they reached the starting point of the avalanche, and the snow smoothed out. The team paused long enough in the lee of a huge block of snow mostly out of sight of the cabin to put on their snowshoes.

Aleesha and Isabella pulled in close beside her and supported her under her arms for the last part of the climb. It was a technique they'd learned in their initial training when Jack routinely ran them to the point of collapse. They'd take turns propping each other up so everyone made it through the run.

At last, they topped the ridge. Karen laid Larson down in the snow and collapsed beside him, sucking in great lungfuls of fiery cold air.

Aleesha knelt beside him, checking his vitals again. "Blood pressure and pulse are strong. He should come around before too long, I'd think."

"Good," Karen panted. "He can walk under his own power then."

Isabella called out from where she lay at the ridgeline, observing the cabin. "Cobra and Sidewinder are in their final retreat. Looks like our tangos decided to hole up and not come play anymore."

"Thank God," Karen replied. "If they had any idea how outgunned we were, they'd have killed us all."

Isabella grinned back over her shoulder. "That's why we didn't stand up and announce it to them."

Karen would've stuck out her tongue at her teammate if it weren't so damned cold out here. She didn't relish carrying Larson any further. But as soon as the others joined them, they'd all need to bug out. She glanced over at their gear.

Then she asked Aleesha and Isabella, "Did either of you happen to throw in a spare tent pole when you packed your gear today?" During their first couple of days of field training, the

Norwegians had shown them a dozen handy things a person could do with a length of rigid aluminum tubing.

"As a matter of fact, I did," Aleesha answered.

Isabella nodded as well.

"So did I. If one of the others threw in a pole, that makes four, and we ought to be able to rig up a skid to drag the golden boy on. I gotta say, I have no desire to carry him any farther than I have to. He's big, darn him."

Isabella started rummaging in the packs and pulled out tent poles and rope. "Ah ha! Viper has a spare pole, too. One skid coming up."

While Karen rested and Aleesha took Larson's vitals again, Isabella lashed the tent poles into a travois—a crude, roughly triangular drag. Now all they had to do was lift Anders onto the contraption, and they'd be good to go.

Too soon for Karen's aching body, the other Medusas joined them. "Let's get out of here," Vanessa said briskly.

The women loaded Larson, still out like a light, onto the drag, and Vanessa and Misty took the first shift pulling him. Karen, Isabella and Aleesha picked up Vanessa's, Misty's and Anders' field packs in addition to their own, and Kat went ahead to scout out the easiest route. They rested every five minutes and rotated positions to keep everyone fresh. Or more accurately, to democratically spread the pain around. They had a long night of hiking ahead of them.

About an hour into their trek, Aleesha was on point and stopped the team cold by announcing, "Incoming. Two targets at twelve o'clock."

Now what?

Chapter 6

Oslo, Norway, March 4, 2:00 a.m.

Jens woke up, disoriented, in the dark. What had yanked him to consciousness so abruptly? Then he heard it again. Someone was pounding at the front door. *Jesus, what time was it?* He rolled over and squinted at the digital alarm clock: 2:07. He groaned as he rolled out of bed, stumbled to the closet, and pulled on jeans and a T-shirt. He picked up his shoulder holster and unsnapped the leather strap holding down his service revolver. Rubbing sleep out of his eyes, he padded barefoot into the hall.

"Stop banging, already!" he bellowed. "I'm coming."

Astrid nearly ran him over as she came barreling out of her room. "Daddy, if it's Willie, don't hurt him. I told him you might be asking him some questions—"

"Jesus, Astrid! What were you thinking? Do you want me

to have to arrest both of you for impeding a police investigation?"

"Daddy!" she wailed. "You can't arrest Willie!"

Like hell he couldn't! He drew breath to argue the point, but whoever was at the door pounded again. It was two o'clock and he was dead tired, dammit. He'd been putting in ungodly hours with all the murders in Oslo, and now this.

She hurried down the hall ahead of him toward the front door.

"Astrid!" he ordered sharply. "Don't open that!"

He stepped around her up to the peep hole. A person couldn't be too careful with all the nutcases on the streets right now. *Aww, hell.* He threw the dead bolt and swung the front door open in disgust. "What do you want, Ivo? It's the middle of the flipping night."

"May I come in?"

Jens stepped back. The young detective followed him in and stopped cold when he spied Astrid. "Is this your daughter?"

Jens rolled his eyes. Right now, she was mostly a whiny pain in the butt. "What's up?"

"The initial toxicology reports are in."

That woke him up. Like a bucket of cold water in the face.

Wow. That was fast. It could take two to three weeks to get tox reports back. And this set had been run in two to three days. His eyes narrowed. The folks at the lab were going to regret demonstrating to him how fast they really could run their tests.

Jens stared expectantly at Ivo. "And?"

"You were right. There's a match in all three of the initial murders. I swung by the office on the way over here and picked up the files."

"Bring them into the kitchen. I need coffee if I'm to function at this hour. And what's up with that godawful shirt?" Ivo was wearing a psychedelic monstrosity that for all the world looked like a polyester leisure shirt. Add a puka shell necklace and the horror would be complete. Jens turned to head for the kitchen.

Ivo answered, "I was at a club, Val Hall, when I got the call. You should go sometime."

Jens's head whipped around. Astrid gushed, "Isn't that for members only? I hear it's gorgeous and the music is incredible. What's the dance floor like? Is it as wild as they say?"

Ivo grinned. "Next time I go I'd be happy to take you."

"You're a member?" she squeaked.

Jens rolled his eyes. He'd hated disco the first time it came around, before either of these two were born. Still hated it.

Astrid followed them into the kitchen. Jens said, not unkindly, "Skedaddle, kiddo. There are grisly crime-scene photos in these files, and they're police business anyway."

She made a face at him. "I've probably seen worse on television."

"Go!" He added darkly, "We'll talk later."

Astrid threw a sulky look at him and then turned her gaze on Ivo. He didn't want to think about what kind of look that was she threw at his partner.

Jens sat down heavily at the kitchen table. "What's the match?"

Ivo spread three files out on the table. "Each of the perpetrators tested positive for two drugs. Cocaine and pseudoephedrine."

A powerful combination. People who mixed those two substances could be jacked up for a couple days at a stretch. He'd seen prisoners high on that cocktail stand in a cell and spin for three days straight, before passing out from dehydration and low blood sugar. People were known to die when their aortas, or even their hearts, ruptured from the strain of the intense stimulation.

So. All three perpetrators were high on powerful stimulants. Thing was, he'd never heard of that mix of drugs making people go psychotic. He asked his extremely book-wise partner, "Have you ever heard of coke and Sudafed causing violent psychotic episodes?"

Ivo shook his head. "It wires folks tight as hell and can make them a little nuts, but not this violent." He waved his hand over the files of grisly photos. "Each of these killers was criminally insane at the time of the murders. And there's one more thing, sir."

"And that is?"

"The initial tests found something else in all three perpetrators."

"Don't make me beg. What was it?"

"The forensics folks have never seen it before. They're going to run more detailed spectroscopic analysis. It's a complex molecule, resides in fat cells, and bears a passing resemblance to LSD. But beyond that, they don't know much. Oh, and none of the perps had much of it in their systems. It was just a trace amount. Our chemists think it might be a marker molecule they can use to track down a particular batch of drugs."

Jens nodded. "That's good news. How long until they know exactly what the chemical is?"

"Couple of days if they rush it."

"They've rushed everything else. They'll rush this. But Ivo. Don't wake me up at 2:00 a.m. again to tell me what it is. Understood?"

"Yes, sir."

Northern Norway, March 4, 4:00 a.m.

Thankfully, Aleesha's incoming targets turned out to be their Sami guides. They'd hung around the area just in case, God bless them. They ended up helping to haul Larson and the extra packs. Even better, they were thrilled to death to do it.

It was around five o'clock when the combination of frigid

temperatures and sweat finally got the better of Karen. "Viper," she said quietly, "If I don't get my clothes off and dry out soon, I'm going to be in serious trouble."

Vanessa nodded and turned to the other Medusas. "Any idea how we ask our guides if there's somewhere nearby we could go to warm up and dry off a bit?" With Larson out cold, they'd lost their translator. And neither of their guides spoke a language a Medusa did.

Isabella spoke up. "Let me give it a try."

Karen was impressed as Isabella said something in what sounded like passable Sami. Dang, that woman was a natural at languages! The Sami men said something back.

"I think they said there's a shelter close by and something about building a fire."

"Perfect," Vanessa answered.

Isabella said something back to the Sami men, and they veered left toward a steep cliff face. The men weren't kidding when they said shelter was close; it took them maybe ten minutes to reach an uneven crevasse in the stone wall. The men led the way inside the cave. The opening was too narrow to horse the skid and Larson through, so Karen half-carried, half-dragged him inside. He was going to owe her big when this was over. She'd almost gotten him over to the blackened circle on the cave floor that indicated where a fire would soon be when the golden boy himself mumbled something against her neck. Intense awareness of his mouth on her skin shot through her. He pulled weakly against her.

"Stop that, Anders," she groused. "It's hard enough dragging your heavy butt around as it is." Not to mention the butterflies in her stomach were distracting.

He mumbled something unintelligible and, thank goodness, subsided.

She deposited him gently on the floor. The Samis already

had a small fire going from a supply of reindeer chips stacked in one corner. Good idea, having a little spot like this out in the middle of the hunting grounds for just such an emergency.

"Aleesha," Karen said worriedly, "he's not awake yet."

The team doctor crouched beside Anders. "Not good. I'm concerned that swelling's developing around his brain." She rummaged around in her med kit. "I'm gonna hit him with an anti-inflammatory."

Karen watched Aleesha give Larson a hefty injection. "How long should that take to work?"

"If it's going to help him, he should come around within an hour or two."

"And if it doesn't help?" Karen asked quietly.

"Then your boy's in serious trouble. He'll need a first-rate trauma center ASAP."

Karen snorted. "And where's the nearest one of those?"

Aleesha gave her a worried look. "Not nearly close enough."

Karen looked down at Larson. "He's strong. He'll be okay."

Aleesha put a commiserating hand on her shoulder. "From your lips to God's ear," she murmured.

Isabella had a quiet word with the Sami men, and both of them threw Karen an alarmed look and bolted from the cave.

Karen turned on her teammate, demanding, "What did you just tell those guys?"

Isabella grinned. "I think I told them you were going to take your clothes off and if they didn't want to be enslaved forever by the sight of you, they might want to leave."

Karen rolled her eyes while the other Medusas laughed. She had to put an end to this whole goddess thing as soon as they got back to camp. Nonetheless, she did strip off her clothes. Aleesha joined her, as did Isabella. All three of them had worked up sweats at some point in the evening's fun.

While they were huddling around the fire, drying out, Karen asked Isabella, "How is it you speak so much Sami in one day?"

She shrugged. "It's in the same language family as Finnish. And while I don't actually speak much Finnish, I did a term paper on it in a linguistics class in college. Once you have the hang of the grammar structure, it's pretty easy to plug in vocabulary. And, once you've got several hundred words, you'd be surprised how much you can express if you phrase things creatively."

Karen shook her head in awe. "Thank goodness you're on this team." Of course, that was part of what made the Medusas effective. They pooled their skills and functioned as a single entity.

In a matter of fifteen or twenty minutes, all three women were dry and dressed again. Karen knelt beside Larson and felt the back of his neck. It was warm. It wasn't a foolproof method of determining body temperature, but it was good for a rough estimate. If his neck was warm, then his core temperature wasn't dangerously low. She gazed down at his unconscious face. Like this, he wasn't nearly as intimidating. He actually looked like a nice guy.

"He mumbled and moved a bit when I was carrying him in here," she told Aleesha, who'd knelt beside her.

The doctor nodded. "That's a good sign. Don't worry. I won't let him do anything stupid like go and die."

Karen said wryly, "He's no fool. He's nice and cozy wrapped in those Sami furs while we do all the work."

Aleesha smiled. "He'd do the same for you."

"Yeah, I know. And that's why I'm doing it for him."

"Good thing you were here. You're stronger than any of the rest of us." Aleesha shrugged. "Without you, I don't know if we'd have gotten him out of there in one piece."

Karen's cheeks heated up. "It's no big deal. You would have done what you had to and pulled him out." Someday she had to learn how to take a compliment. But not today.

"Ready to go, ladies?" It was Vanessa. "I'm antsy being out here unarmed like this."

Karen nodded. Yup, that had been a hell of a lesson for them all. Even in training, they needed to go ahead and suck up the extra weight of carrying actual ammo.

Larson mumbled some more when Karen carried him outside. But when they laid him down on the skid and tucked the Sami's furs in around him again, he settled quickly. *C'mon. Wake up already.*

The remainder of the night passed in a blur. It was cold and dark, and heavy going. But eventually, they made it back to camp. Sleepy Sami women stirred the fires, and kettles of stew were put on to heat.

Aleesha and Karen lifted Larson onto a sleeping bag, and they stripped off most of his outer clothes. Karen couldn't help but notice what a gorgeous body the guy had. As in *gorgeous*. Even Aleesha remarked, "Whoa. Nice specimen."

Karen laughed. "Don't let Michael hear you say that."

Aleesha grinned back. "Girlie, when me stops lookin', me be dead and pushin' up daisies." She dropped the accent. "Besides, Michael knows how I feel about him. He's not worried."

"How's his training going, anyway?"

"Jack said he's having to work hard at the physical stuff but is sailing through the mental stuff."

Karen snorted. "Everybody struggles to meet the physical standards."

Aleesha smiled fondly. "I built a workout program for him before he went to Delta training to help him get in their kind of shape. He ignored it, of course."

Given the blush staining Aleesha's cheeks, Karen could guess what sort of workouts Michael had preferred. Must be nice to have that kind of relationship with a guy as great as

Michael Somerset. Aloud, Karen commented, "Anders is one of the Olympic medalists from the Norwegian team."

Aleesha nodded. "That explains it. Even for a Spec Ops guy, he's ripped."

"An unconscious Spec Ops guy. Why isn't he awake yet?"

Aleesha laid a hand on his forehead in the age-old gesture of a healer. "He's starting to move around and showing neurological activity. Give the anti-inflammatory a little more time."

Karen sighed. "I'll stay up and watch him. I couldn't sleep anyway. You go get some rest."

Aleesha replied. "I'll take a quick nap and then come sit with him so you can get some sleep."

"Take a decent nap. I'll be okay for a while."

Aleesha snorted. "You've had a tougher day than any of the rest of us. I'll let you stay up for an hour or so, but then you're going to bed. End of discussion. As for him, don't worry. He's tough. He'll wake up any time now as grouchy as a bear and with nothing more than a headache."

Karen nodded. She was starting to feel pretty rough around the edges. Hauling around a two-hundred-pound-plus man did catch up with a girl after a while. As Aleesha ducked out into the night, a blast of cold wind swirled in. The wind was kicking up again and the temperature was plummeting even more. This climate was simply not fit for human habitation. The Sami people were either the toughest people she'd ever met or just too plain stubborn to know better than to live here.

Karen pushed ashes up around the edges of the fire and added several reindeer chips to it, and then she pulled her sleeping bag around her shoulders.

As the fire gradually beat back the cold, she studied Larson's features in the dim firelight. He sure was good-looking. Even out cold, his face was noble. It'd be real easy to fall for him.

Not only was he cute, but he was tall and muscular enough that he didn't make her feel like a giant freak when she was around him. There was something innately appealing about his Norwegian heritage. It was a solidness. A sense of being hard-working. Fundamentally decent.

He reminded her of the people she'd grown up with, mostly farmers and likewise salt-of-the-earth souls. Maybe she and he weren't so very different after all. Even if he was a glamorous Olympic athlete and she was a pig farmer's kid from Iowa.

Yeah, right. In her dreams.

If only she had the supernatural abilities the Samis gave her credit for. Then she could heal him. Maybe she could get him to fall in love with her, too.

The North Sea, off the coast of Norway, March 4, 6:00 a.m.

Isa screamed into the phone, "What the hell do you mean, you were *attacked?*"

"You heard me, boss. At least a dozen guys jumped us. Shot the shit out of us. Slit Ian's throat."

"Anyone else dead?"

"No, sir."

"Then you didn't get shot up that bad. How's the lab?"

"Okay. They didn't get inside. We fought them off."

"And the stash?"

"Well, that's the thing. The bastards shot up most of the barrels outside pretty good. The stuff that was stored inside the cabin is okay, though."

Isa swore violently. "How much did we lose?" he snarled.

"'Bout half of it."

Isa swore luridly under his breath. "We're supposed to have six hundred kilos of this stuff ready to go in two weeks. Work around the clock. And send out patrols. Make sure no one else gets anywhere close to the lab. If anyone tries, blow his head off."

"There aren't enough of us to run the lab and trek up and down the mountainsides looking for intruders, too."

Isa snapped, "Make it happen. The prophet has willed it so." He thought fast. His ass was grass if he didn't deliver on his promised six hundred kilos. God might be magnificently forgiving, but the prophet was not. "I'll send some more men. They'll join you in a couple of days. But in the meantime, keep that lab running at full steam. I'm not throwing off the whole god-damned global timetable because of this attack. Understood?"

"Yes, sir."

Northern Norway, March 4, 4:30 a.m.

All of sudden, something grabbed Karen's wrist and jolted her from her reverie of gazing into the fire. She gathered herself to fight when a voice murmured, "Relax. It's only me."

Larson. He was awake. Thank God. "How do you feel?" she mumbled as the adrenaline surge stood down, but didn't entirely drain away.

"My head hurts."

"Mamba said it would. Are you as grouchy as a bear, as she also predicted?"

He laughed, then winced and smiled painfully. "So far so good on that count."

While he sat up gingerly, she tossed more dung on the fire and took a pull of water out of the water skin. His gray-and-white camo pants rode low on his hips and were sexy as hell if she did say so. He wore no shirt. He had just enough chest hair to be too sexy for his own good, but not so much that a girl would have to worry about fur on his back. And the guy had shoulders that did not *quit*.

The red glow of the embers took on a yellow, flickering cast as the new fuel caught fire. The light danced across his skin like an eager lover. "What happened?" he asked.

She blinked, jarred out of her musings about his attributes. "I beg your pardon?"

"How'd I end up here? How'd the fight end? Last thing I remember was three guys charging me, shooting like crazy, and the pile of barrels collapsing on you."

She nodded and picked up the narrative. "You did the big-hero thing and shoved me out of the way. But in the process, you got knocked out by a barrel and buried under the pile. We convinced the bad guys they were about to die and they went back in the cabin. While Cobra held them at bay, the rest of us dug you out. Then we dragged you over the ridge and out of range of the cabin. From there, we built a sledge for you and hauled you out."

"All the way back here?" He sounded impressed.

She shrugged. "Our two Sami guides caught up with us, and they helped pull you and haul the extra gear."

He absorbed that one in silence. The look on his face morphed from surprised to definitely impressed to—if she wasn't mistaken—respect.

"I thought you said you Medusas didn't haul heavy things for long distances."

"I said we didn't like to. I didn't say we couldn't do it."

"You must be sore. Any time I have to hump a hundred kilos for any length of time, I feel it the next day."

Karen grinned. "I haven't tried to move yet."

He smiled in commiseration. "Roll over, I'll give you a rubdown. Doing something will help take my mind off this headache."

A rubdown? As in put his hands on her and touch her all

over? As in learn where she was ticklish or sensitive or tender? "Uhh, that's not necessary," she replied, alarmed.

"It's the least I can do. You saved my life."

Well, wasn't he just being Mr. Friendly all of a sudden? Of course, if someone had just saved her life, she'd probably be pretty well-disposed toward them, too. Maybe the Medusas had finally made their point with at least one of the Norwegians. "I didn't save your life. I just carried you out."

He skewered her with a laser-sharp look. "I'm an operator, too. Don't bullshit me. You bloody well did save my hide."

She grinned. "I can certainly see you learned your English from Special Forces guys."

He snorted, unfazed by her attempt to distract him. "Those barrels were heavy. I tried to move a couple. And I remember enough of that fight to know we were in big trouble. Completely outgunned."

"I'll concede you that point. Our rubber dum-dums were no match for that gang's AKs. And speaking of drug dealers, any chance you've got an operational radio with you?"

"No. Jack was afraid you ladies would steal it and use it."

Karen grinned. "We would have." Then she added, "Too bad. We were hoping you could call in an air strike and make a fireball out of that cabin."

"Indeed. Whatever those men at the cabin were doing, it wasn't legal. My men have radios. If we can find them, we can use theirs."

Karen frowned. "Any idea where your guys are?"

"No."

Was he being straight with her? Was it possible he didn't want to give away his men's location because he didn't want the Medusas to show up his team? "Seriously. All training aside, do you have any idea at all where your men are?"

His eyes glittered with irritation. Didn't like having his honesty questioned? In her book, that was a good thing. He replied evenly, "Seriously. I have no idea where they are."

She nodded her acceptance of his answer. "Any informed guesses?"

"If I were in charge, I'd find a nice, dry cave to set up shop in. Or, if their scenario requires them to be more out in the open, I'd build igloos and camouflage the heck out of them. Trust me, they'll be damned hard to find either way."

"Do you know if the scenario includes them making radio transmissions?"

"I did see comm gear in their packs."

Karen thought hard. "If we could get near even rudimentary civilization, we could probably get enough bits and pieces to rig up some sort of signal detector."

He shrugged. "If we get that close to civilization, we can borrow a cell phone and call my headquarters."

Karen laughed. "Well, there is that. I was still thinking in terms of pretending to be in hostile territory, I guess."

He nailed her with a piercing look. "I don't think being in hostile territory would slow down you Medusas much. The way you're making friends with these Samis, you'd have the locals in any hostile territory—how do you say it—eating out of your hands in a matter of days, no matter how hostile they might be toward your government."

He'd noticed, huh? Cool.

Larson continued. "The Samis have been treated pretty badly over the past couple of centuries. First, scientists came to study them like lab rats, and then a program of 'Norwegian-ization' was forced upon them that all but wiped out their culture. They tend to be extremely suspicious of outsiders. Yet, you ladies waltzed in here and had them volunteering to help you in a matter of hours. Extraordinary."

Delta operators were renowned as masters of "going native." But no matter how good their male counterparts were at it, the Medusas felt they had a special advantage in that department. Women were simply less intimidating than men.

Aloud, she said, "How soon after we make the call can your military blast that drug lab off the map?"

Larson frowned. "The Norwegian military doesn't randomly blow up civilian structures. They'll want verification that it's a drug lab before they pop it."

If an airstrike were, in fact, called in, it would do a little more than 'pop' the cabin. The building would be blown to kingdom come, and the largest piece left would be the size of a toothpick. In her experience, Spec Ops troops universally seemed to agree that if a thing needed killing, it was worth killing *really* dead.

Karen shrugged. "If you need verification, Mamba took samples of the powder from the barrels. As soon as we get somewhere with mail or courier service, we can fire it off to a lab and identify it."

"Excellent." Larson took a moment to stretch the kinks out of his back while Karen took a moment to gulp at the sight of him flexing his muscles. Dang, that man made her weak in the knees.

She cleared her throat. "So, we have two options. As soon as possible, we either head for civilization to mail the powder and get to a phone, or we go looking for your team and get access to their radios."

"The weather will likely determine which one is more feasible. Up here you don't fight Mother Nature, for you will surely lose."

She nodded in agreement. "The good news is it's the Medusas' style to flow around obstacles, not try to brute-force through them." Karen continued thinking through scenarios.

Talking aloud helped her organize her thoughts. "If the Samis have weapons and ammunition, we could always pay another visit to the cabin."

"And do what?" he asked in alarm.

"Make independent verification that it's a drug lab. Then we torch it ourselves."

Larson blinked at that one. "You don't hesitate to take the initiative, do you?"

She blinked back in return. "Are you referring to the Medusas as a team or me personally?"

"Are they different?"

That gave her pause. Professionally, neither she nor the Medusas hesitated to seize the moment and go on the offensive. But personally? She was more the cautious type. At least when it came to matters of the heart. In fact, now that she thought about it, she was downright gun-shy about such things. Probably came from a lifetime of intimidated men making fun of her. It was damned hard to form a meaningful relationship with some guy who was scared you were going to hurt him.

"Roll over."

Karen started. Dammit. She'd been hoping he'd forget about the back-rub thing.

She opened her mouth to decline again, but he cut her off. "Consider it an operational necessity. I need the distraction. And you need to be in top form. The next couple of days may be more strenuous than we originally planned. I promise I won't get—how do you Americans say it?—fresh with you."

Karen nodded reluctantly. "That's one way of putting it."

"So, don't be a chicken. Lie down on your stomach."

Okay, that did it. No hunky Norwegian operator was calling her a coward. She flopped down on her belly, bunching up the top part of her sleeping bag under her head for a pillow. Unfortunately, she'd taken off her bra when she stripped down earlier—while Larson was still out cold. Now she was stuck wearing only a far-too-revealing T-shirt and silk leggings. She hugged the sleeping bag a little closer.

Big, warm hands settled on her shoulders. After the first shock of his touch, she managed to relax fractionally. But she was still stiff as a board. He didn't comment on her tense, knotted muscles however. He just commenced kneading her shoulders and upper back. When her irrational fear that he might attempt something stupid didn't pan out, she forced herself to relax enough to close her eyes.

"How do you like it?" he murmured.

Her eyes flew back open. The wooden pole frame of the wall with its sinew lashings and sod arched upward in front of her. "Excuse me?"

"Hard or soft?"

"Huh?" she mumbled, shocked at his bluntness.

"Do you like it deep or light?"

Ooo-kay. *That* called several completely inappropriate mental images to mind. Please, God, let him be talking about a back rub. "I dunno."

"I'd recommend a deep-tissue massage to loosen up the lactic acid and then follow-up with a light massage to increase circulation and start carrying away the toxins from your muscles."

Whew. He'd had her worried there, for a minute. "You're the mega-athlete, massage guy. You do what you think is best to keep me operational."

"Karen, I have my hands on your back. Trust me. You're a mega-athlete, as well."

He would bring that up. It was a big, fat mood killer to any boy-girl thoughts she might be having about him.

He worked on her back for a while in silence. She had to

admit, he never did anything the whole time that was the slightest bit out of line. His hands never strayed anywhere that would make her even remotely nervous. Except, she was acutely…something. Maybe not uncomfortable. But certainly *aware*. The guy's hands were all over her, for heaven's sake.

After he'd kneaded her back into a boneless mass of jelly, he worked on her legs and then her arms—and it felt so good it surely couldn't be legal. Her brain actually shifted into acceptance of the massage, and by degrees, finally shifted into outright enjoyment of it. In fact, she almost found herself getting annoyed that Anders was being so well-behaved. Couldn't he maybe be just a little more…exploratory?

Whoa. Rewind. No explorations. The guy was working loose her muscles. Nothing more. No way did he find her attractive. This guy was just like Colonel Scatalone. The same colonel who called her: She-man, a manly-girl, Queen Kong.

It was decent of Larson to be polite. But she didn't really think for a minute that he was truly attracted to her. Norway was full of willowy, sweet, gorgeous Nordic beauties. The guy was an Olympic athlete. In this ski-crazy country, he was no doubt a celebrity. He could have any woman he wanted.

She realized his hands had stopped moving and rested, warm and easy on the small of her back. "What is it?" he asked.

"What is what?" she replied cautiously.

"Your back just went rock-hard. What tightened you up like that? What are you thinking about?"

Yeah, right. Like she was going to tell him. "Uh, I've decided I've had enough of this whole pretending-I'm-a-goddess thing."

He retorted dryly, "Don't you like sharing a hut with your manservant?"

Well, there was that. A definite bennie to the whole misunderstanding. "No, no, that's not it. I'm just uncomfortable with this whole adulation business. First thing in the morning, I'm telling these folks that I'm a plain old soldier. Nothing special."

"Bull."

"I beg your pardon?"

"You are *not* a plain old soldier. Not even close."

And suddenly the hut felt way too small and way too hot and way too private. A burning need to force the conversation into less dangerous waters overwhelmed her. "That's kind of you to say, Anders. I'm glad the Medusas are making a good impression on you."

His hands lifted away from her. She looked over her shoulder, pinning him with a look that dared him to say it aloud. To admit he hadn't really meant the innuendo in his words. He sat back on his heels and frowned at her. Opened his mouth to say something. Frowned again. Shut his mouth.

Yeah, that was what she thought. When push came to shove, he couldn't pretend he was actually attracted to her. He might flirt a little and make nice with her, but he couldn't honestly say he liked her.

In a way, she respected Jack Scatalone's attitude more. At least he'd look her in the eye and tell her what he thought of her.

Unfortunately, even that grim thought didn't put a dent in her attraction to Anders Larson.

Dammit.

Chapter 7

Larson eased his hands away from her now-boneless body. "Do you lift weights to get such excellent definition in your back muscles?" he asked lightly.

Please, God, let the conversation turn to anything other than her muscles. She sighed and answered in resignation, "I used to power-lift, but since I joined the Medusa Project I haven't had time for that. We stay so active, though, I don't think I've lost much strength."

"Tell me about the Medusas."

She shrugged under his hands. "Some folks in the U.S. government decided to silence women once and for all on the subject of being allowed to join the Special Forces. A project was funded to select a team of six women and run them through full-blown Special Forces training. We were supposed to fail."

"But you didn't?"

"But we didn't."

"Then what?"

"Then a few people with serious clout went to bat for us and got us permanently funded. And here we are."

He snorted. "It's not as easy as that. You keep forgetting I've been through the same sort of training you have. It's incredible to think a group of women survived what I did."

"Yeah, we get that reaction a lot from our American male counterparts."

"How did you do it?"

"Same way you did. We gutted it out and worked as a team. For what it's worth, we try to compensate for our lack of muscle by applying extra brain power to scenarios. Plus, our handlers try to profile missions to take into account our lack of strength. We have no illusions about being as strong as a male team."

"Had you ladies used weapons in your ambush of my team, you'd have had us all, you know."

"Yup, we know. We chose to go hand-to-hand to test ourselves—and to prove something to you. We still have a ways to go before we can beat a male Spec-Ops team unarmed, though."

"It was a near thing that my men managed to win. That little one—Katrina—she all but had Ollie. Her hand got wet and slipped a grip, or she'd have taken him down. And two of the other women nearly won as well."

Wow. She'd had no idea. She'd been so tied up dealing with him she'd had no time to check on her comrades during the ambush.

"One advantage you've already got over many of the other Special Forces teams in the world is the breadth of your training. I talked with Colonel Scatalone at some length about what you women know how to do, and your résumés are impressive."

"Enough for the FSK to consider training a female team of its own?"

"A few days ago, I'd have laughed at the notion. But after seeing the way you women handled yourselves in that firefight at the drug lab, I might consider it."

Karen commented dryly, "You ought to see us when we have real bullets."

Anders grinned. "Have you ladies checked with these Samis to see if they have any ammo?"

"Viper was going to ask when we got to this camp. I haven't talked to her yet to see what the answer was."

"When we get access to a radio, I can call my support center and have ammo flown out to us. You carry standard MP-5s, right?"

"Yes. Our sidearms are also 9 mm." She added, "And you can never go wrong with a few pounds of C-4 and some grenades."

An awkward silence fell between them. Karen wondered idly if discussions of weapons and ammo usually killed the chatty mood between normal men and women. But then, neither she nor Anders was at all normal. She'd lay odds most girls didn't think about tucking grenades in their hip pocket.

To break the moment, Karen said, "On the hike back here, the Medusas had time to talk things over. We think we need to move this encampment and get the Samis back to a major village where they'll be safer."

"You think those drug dealers will come after us?"

"Maybe. We left a trail a mile wide for them to follow."

"What's the local weather doing?" Anders asked tersely.

Karen shrugged. "It's blowing hard. Beyond that, I don't know. You'd have to stick your head out and have a look."

He pushed fluidly to his feet and did just that. A gust of icy cold burst into the small space and the fire guttered. He pulled the crude door shut again and came back down to sit by the fire. "It's getting cold."

Karen laughed shortly. "It has *been* cold."

He shrugged in concession. "Perhaps I should say it's getting colder. Wind's picking up. Weather the next few days could be nasty. The last forecast I saw was for some heavy weather to pack in and stay for several days."

"Lovely."

He grinned. "What did you expect at eighty degrees north latitude at this time of year?"

Certainly not a bronzed god like him. She shrugged. "Doesn't make it any less cold just because I expected it to be that way."

"True." The look he gave her was anything but cold, however.

As much in self-defense from further looks like that as in real sincerity, Karen said, "We probably ought to try to get some sleep. Next couple of days could be long if we end up slogging around trying to move this encampment and tracking our drug-maker friends in a blizzard. How do you feel? Maybe I shouldn't let you sleep until Mamba has a look at you. You were unconscious a long time. I'd hate to have you go to sleep and lapse into a coma on me."

"Is Major Gautier a good doctor?"

Karen snorted. "She's a topnotch trauma surgeon. Harvard Medical School."

Anders nodded, suitably impressed. "I'm sure I have a concussion, but I'm not feeling symptoms of anything more severe."

"Nothing beyond a headache?"

"No."

"No dizziness, personality changes, feeling foggy? No memory gap except just before the accident?"

"Nope."

She gave him a suspicious look.

He retorted, "Are you this untrusting of everyone you know, or just me? You really need to stop questioning everything I say. I promise, I will always tell you the truth."

Karen started. Her? Untrusting? She started to give him a snappy comeback that she didn't question everything he said…until it occurred to her that he was absolutely right. She frowned. She wasn't usually suspicious of people. Why him?

And then it hit her. Of course. She disliked and didn't trust Jack Scatalone. And Anders reminded her a great deal of Jack. Great. Now she could add ruining her for any future relationships with guys to Scatalone's list of sins against her. She cursed under her breath.

"Sorry. I didn't catch that," Anders said mildly.

He darn well had heard her. He was sitting about a foot from her…and she was doing it again. If he said he hadn't heard her mumbled imprecation, then he hadn't heard it. Sheesh.

She looked him square in the eye. "I'm sorry. You haven't given me any reason whatsoever not to take you at your word. You just happen to remind me of someone I don't trust very much."

"Ahh. I'm sorry."

She laughed without real humor. "Don't be sorry. It's not your fault. It's my problem. I'll try not to transfer my ambivalence for him to you."

"This word *ambivalence.* It means…"

"Simultaneous attraction to and repulsion from someone or something."

"Attraction? Perhaps you should concentrate on that aspect when you are with me and leave behind the repulsion."

Karen's stomach flip-flopped. She blurted, "Nothing about you repulses me. You're okay on that score."

Her cheeks exploded with heat. Why in the hell had she just said that aloud? As she glanced around the hut for a rock to crawl under, she noticed something out of the corner of her eye. Damned if his expression wasn't unfolding into the sexiest, most incendiary smile she'd ever laid eyes on. Well, then.

Maybe it hadn't been such a bad idea after all to make that little true confession.

He lay down and pulled his sleeping bag up around his shoulders, and she did the same. And that sexy smile was still on his face as she risked a peek at him across the fire.

"Sweet dreams, Karen."

Crud. She still had to work with this guy, and she was about a millimeter from going around that fire and crawling into his sleeping bag with him. Okay, so maybe it had been a really, really bad idea to confess her feelings.

Northern Norway, March 4, 6:00 a.m.

"How are we coming, men?" Jack Scatalone huddled deeper in his parka and pulled the hood farther forward. The Norwegian team in front of him was crouched around a deceptively simple-looking radio setup.

"Just about ready. Batteries are almost up to operating temperature," one of the Norwegians replied.

Larson's men were good. They were almost like working with his own Delta 3 team stateside. He watched as one of the men took off his gloves to complete the last step—inserting oversized field batteries into the body of the main transmitter. Jack started counting in his head. *One potato. Two potato. Three potato…* The guy had about ten seconds to expose his fingers to the raw air before frostbite would start to set in.

At six, the guy nodded and pulled his glove back on with a grimace. It was gratifying that even these Norwegians thought it was stupidly cold this morning. He'd take a jungle any day over this arctic misery.

"We're ready, Colonel."

Jack nodded. "Flip the switch."

The Norwegian communications expert did just that, sending a broad-beam jamming signal out in all directions. All radio frequencies within thirty miles of this innocuous-looking little black box were now officially shut down.

"How long do you think it'll take your girls to realize we're jamming everything and come find us?"

Jack retorted, "A word of advice. Don't call them girls to their faces. I get away with it because I trained them and I know exactly what they're capable of. But they'd break you into little pieces if you gave them that kind of motivation to do so."

The other men made the requisite sounds of skepticism that any woman could hurt them, but he saw doubt flicker in their eyes. Hmm. That hand-to-hand encounter with the Medusas must've been a closer thing than these guys had let on. The Norwegians had given him the impression that they'd handled the Medusas easily. Maybe not. Next time he saw his team, he'd have to get their side of the story.

One of the Norwegians commented, "Well, maybe that big blond one could hurt one of us."

Another one retorted, "Nah, she just surprised Anders. She'd never take him in a fair fight."

Jack's eyes narrowed. He'd trained Karen Turner himself, and he was damned proud of her ability in unarmed combat. "If you're referring to Python, she routinely fights to a draw with me. She can hold her own with most male special operators. I wouldn't suggest crossing her in a dark alley."

One of the Norwegians muttered, "Scary woman."

Jack's jaw rippled. He was here to make nice with the allied nation soldiers. But he'd dearly love to see Karen get a hold of this joker. Making a concerted effort to remain calm, he said, "In answer to your earlier question, I'd guess the Medusas will find us in under a week."

"So quickly?" one of the Norwegians blurted.

Jack nodded casually, "These aren't Girl Scouts we're talking about. They're essentially Delta operators."

"Still. A week? They've got hundreds of square kilometers to cover."

Irritation flared in Jack's gut. How the Medusas put up with chauvinistic attitudes like this, he couldn't fathom. The women usually grinned and shrugged it off. But it made him want to pound the shit out of someone. He crossed his arms casually. "Care to place a little wager on it?"

"Like what?"

"A bottle of Louis Treize to the winner?"

The Norwegian grinned, sharklike, and nodded. A bottle of the aged cognac ran a cool two thousand dollars U.S. "Say five days?"

Jack nodded tersely. "Done."

Northern Norway, March 4, 9:00 a.m.

Karen woke on a burst of cold air that made her hunker down deeper into her sleeping bag. The fire had burned down to little more than a pile of ashes and someone had just come in, letting in even more frigid air.

"Rise and shine, Python," Vanessa announced.

Karen groaned under her breath, but painted on a game smile. "'Morning, Mom." She sat up, still in her sleeping bag, as did Anders. He looked about as thrilled to be awake as she felt. Until he went outside, she wasn't about to get naked and get dressed.

Aleesha asked cheerfully, "How'd you two lovebirds sleep last night?"

Karen's cheeks burned. *Lovebirds?* She threw her teammate a withering glare. Almost in spite of herself, she glanced sidelong in Anders' direction to see how he'd reacted to the comment. Karen's eyes opened wide in surprise. He was as red as a cherry. He was embarrassed? Was he that humiliated at being associated with her romantically? Had she completely misinterpreted his comments last night? What an *idiot* she was! The heat spreading across her face and down her neck took on an unpleasant burning quality.

Isabella tossed some more fuel on the fire while Kat laid a long, ungainly parcel wrapped in reindeer hide beside Karen.

Vanessa plunked down by the fire and got right to business. "There are currently two working rifles in town and a couple of hundred rounds of ammunition for each. There are two more non-functional rifles. Python, I'm hoping you and Cobra can restore them to operational status."

Karen took the decrepit weapon Katrina unwrapped from the skin and passed to her. She inspected it quickly. Rust inside the barrel, which was in need of re-rifling. Corrosion in the firing chamber. It needed a new firing pin. The stock's balance was terrible, but the sights were in pretty good condition. Jack had made them repair and fire worse before. "With the right tools, I can get this working in a few hours."

Vanessa grimaced. "You may have to improvise your tools."

Karen shrugged. Jack had made them do that, too. "I'll check with the Samis and see what they've got. Speaking of which, have you talked to the head dude about moving the encampment back to the nearest major village?"

Vanessa frowned. "The *siida-isit* wasn't receptive to the idea. They're having good luck hunting this area and he wants to stay a while longer."

"Bummer. I really do think they'd be safer in a larger population center."

Vanessa sighed. "I agree. I think you need to ask the *siida-isit* to take his people back to the main village."

"He already said no to you. My asking won't do any—" But as soon as the words were out of Karen's mouth, she saw where Viper was going. Because the natives were half convinced Karen was some sort of Viking goddess reincarnated, they might listen to her. *Crud.* "Look, Viper. I think we really need to explain to these people that I'm just a regular soldier like the rest of you."

"Fine. *After* you convince the chief to move his people."

Karen exhaled heavily. She understood Viper's logic, but that didn't mean she had to like it. Anders smirked over at her. She scowled back at him.

"Get out of here so I can dress, servant guy," she snapped.

He grinned at her unrepentantly and pulled on a sweater, boots and parka. "I'll be back in ten," he murmured on the way out.

Misty commented as the door shut behind him, "That is one fine example of Y chromosomes at work."

The other women agreed. And—crap—all looked over at her. Karen shrugged. "Okay, so he's a hunk."

"Anything else?" Aleesha asked.

"No! And even if there was something between us, it would be none of your business," Karen groused.

Aleesha laughed warmly. "Ahh, you gots it bad, girlie. Bit wit' de love bug. Heart a goin' pitter-patter."

"I do *not* love Anders Larson."

The other women laughed. She might think of these women as sisters, but sometimes they got on her nerves like sisters, too. Karen unzipped her sleeping bag and threw it open. Damn, it was cold. She ducked behind the reindeer skin in the corner to use the chamber pot and then hustled into her clothes, doing her best to ignore the banter about her and Anders from her teammates.

It was an eternity before Anders finally knocked on the door and rescued her from the other Medusas. She was actually grateful to head outside and trudge across the camp in frigid conditions to speak with the *siida-isit* if it meant escaping their humor at her expense.

Karen stepped into the chief's hut while Anders held the door for her. Several men sat around a fire eating what looked like power bars. As soon as she sat down, one was offered to her. Yup. A peanut-butter protein bar. Nothing like a little incursion of the twenty-first century into this native culture. Lest she forget entirely where she was, however, she was also offered reindeer jerky and a bowl of something white and lumpy that smelled suspiciously like seal blubber. *Eeyew.* She declined the blubber politely and stuck with the jerky and the power bar.

While she chewed, Karen pondered the best approach to take with the tribal elders seated across from her. Finally, she said, "I understand you're reluctant to rejoin the main village."

Anders translated quietly for her.

The chief nodded. "The hunting here is good. We must feed not only ourselves but much of the village with what we take."

"Can you not hunt near the village?"

The old man's eyes widened slightly. He'd caught the fact that a little harder tone had crept into her voice. "Aye, Golden One, we can. But there is rarely game so close to humans."

Time to play the supernatural card. She took a mental deep breath. Man, this went against the grain for her. She said reluctantly, "What if I tell you there will be plenty of animals to hunt near the village if you return to it?"

All the Samis' gazes went wide at that one. She'd just put their faith in their own mythology to the test. She called upon her training in effective lying and looked the chief square in the eye. Held his gaze steadily. Easily. Confidently.

The *siida-isit* looked away first. *Bingo.* He'd bought it. Anders turned his head so the others around the fire couldn't see his face and briefly raised his eyebrows at her. He, too, had read the chief the same way.

"Honored *siida-isit*," she said gravely. "My request is a matter of life and death. If you stay here, I foresee a tragedy befalling your people. But if you do as I ask and return to the village, I promise, the spirits of your warrior gods will be with you and you will know great success in the hunt. There will be food aplenty for all in your village." Even if she had to buy a couple tons of supplies and ship them in at her own expense, dammit.

The *siida-isit* considered her in silence. He, too, was accomplished at putting a person on the hot seat to see if they'd squirm. She schooled her muscles to relax. To be still. C'mon, buy the explanation. She'd shot her wad. If that line didn't work, she was pretty well hosed. She'd hate to have to force these people to move, but she would if she had to. She was absolutely certain, down deep in her gut, that it was not safe to stay this close to that cabin full of armed drug makers.

Anders said something soberly to the chief in the Sami tongue and received a surprisingly lengthy answer back.

Karen muttered, "What did you say?"

"I said the Golden One has spoken and asked why they hesitate."

"Good grief, you make me sound like a high priestess or something."

"That would be the idea," he replied dryly.

She huffed. "I don't like this."

He drilled her with a hard look. "Your idea. Not mine."

"Yeah, yeah, I know," she groused under her breath. "What did the chief say back to you?"

"I'm not sure. Something about getting word last night that their young men are getting worse. Your intervention is needed urgently."

Karen frowned. "What's that all about?"

"No clue."

While they were having their murmured exchange, the Samis were having a whispered one of their own. The chief met her gaze for a moment but then bowed his head. "It shall be as the Golden One decrees. We return to the village. Tomorrow."

"Today," Karen retorted.

The men looked startled.

"How long will it take them to break down the village?" she asked.

Anders asked the question and relayed the answer. "Four hours or so. Will that be acceptable to the Golden One?"

Karen nodded. "Impressive. That'll be great. I'll go tell my…" what to call her teammates? "…companions to prepare for the journey. If there is anything we can do to help you, let us know. And thank you for your cooperation."

The *siida-isit* nodded regally.

God, she felt like a heel for tricking him like this. But it was for his people's own good. The Samis would be in real danger if they stayed out here undefended. She rose to her feet, uncomfortable sitting there wallowing in her lies any longer.

Northern Norway, March 4, 4:00 p.m.

Karen felt a hundred times better with actual bullets in her weapon, even if it was a Second-World-War surplus rifle. It had taken her most of the four hours while the Samis packed to fix it. They didn't have enough ammo to do much test firing once she and Kat repaired the last two rifles, but the weapons were safe, properly sighted and fired reasonably true.

A thin line of red fury lined the western horizon where the sun was just skating sideways behind the mountains. Darkness would come quickly now. She looked down the line of sleds pulled by reindeer. The Sami people looked like bears in their bulky fur coats. But at least they looked warm. Which was more than she could say about herself. She was cold yet again. After this training was over, she was going to go sit on the hottest beach in the hottest sun she could find for a good long time.

"Python, take the north flank. We're getting close to the cabin."

In point of fact they were actually a couple miles from the drug lab. But, based on what the Samis were telling them of the route the group needed to take through the mountains to reach the village, the caravan was approaching the trail's closest point to the lab.

"Look sharp," Vanessa murmured to her off microphone. "I've got a bad feeling."

Karen nodded at her boss to acknowledge the comment. The Medusas were big believers in listening to their intuitions. Their gut feelings had helped them anticipate trouble on more than one occasion.

Karen touched her mike button. "Mamba, are you getting any of your voodoo warnings?" Aleesha was famous for her intuitions of when trouble was coming.

"Me belly's a rumblin' all right."

Katrina, uncharacteristically, spoke up, too. "The back of my neck's itching. I don't like this. We're sitting ducks out here."

Karen looked at the mountain peaks towering over them like dark sentinels. It would be so damned easy for a sniper to sit up there on one of those peaks and pick people off out of this caravan. Ideally, the Medusas would clear each of those peaks before the caravan passed it, but it just wasn't possible. The snow was too deep, the mountains too steep, and the reindeer moving too quickly for the Medusas to get ahead far enough to clear the route that thoroughly.

Fortunately, the Samis took breaks now and then, and that gave the Medusas a chance to get a little ways ahead and have a look around. Now was one of those times.

"Medusas, fan out. Four hundred yards ahead of the Samis, one-hundred-yard intervals."

Karen waited her turn in the usual rotation and clicked her acknowledgment of the order. Her lightweight snowshoes were a godsend as she took off jogging to the left. The slope began to climb more steeply under her feet. She no doubt owed her stamina now to Jack and all the countless miles he'd made them run through the Rocky Mountains as part of their initial training. But that didn't mean she had to like him for it.

The landscape around her was all stark shapes and contrasts—upthrusting rock, planes of snow and deep shadows. Black on black. It reminded her of urban operations—plenty of objects to hide behind, but no cover to speak of between them.

She was on edge tonight. Itchy. Spoiling for a fight. That wasn't like her. Maybe it was all these enforced dealings with Jack Scatalone doing it to her. One of these days, she was going to get him off by himself, and the two of them were going to have it out. She hiked hard up the mountain, burning off the steam that even thinking about Jack Scatalone built in her gut. Oh yes. The two of them all alone. No weapons. Hand-to-hand until only one of them was left standing. She might not win, but she'd by golly take a good chunk out of his hide before she went down.

She stumbled and her attention snapped back to the terrain around her. She'd drifted to the middle of the glacier that climbed this mountain, where the going was the easiest—and where she was out in plain sight, visible to anyone who happened to take a casual look around. Sheesh! She knew better than to stroll along completely without cover like this!

She veered to the side, toward the edge of the glacier. Her breathing accelerated as she climbed the much more slow and difficult path up the snow field's stony margin. This was where the moving ice deposited boulders the size of small cars and casually tore huge chunks of granite off the mountainside in its millennia-long journey. She wove in and out around the detritus, glad for the strenuous going to distract her from thoughts of wringing Jack's neck.

She came out into a clearing not far from the top of the ridge. All clear. She probably could turn back now and rejoin the caravan. She glanced over her shoulder. The Samis were showing no signs of moving out yet. It was only a hundred yards or so to the summit. And there was just something about the top of the mountain in front of her that made her want to climb to the top of it. A challenge. A dare, even. Come and get me. And she was feeling invincible tonight.

What the heck. She plowed onward. The snow up here was smooth, a thick, wind-scoured crust that easily held her weight. As she took the last few steps to the top, the temptation was huge to throw up her arms and dance around. Hey, she didn't climb a mountain every day. Why not?

She flung her arms wide and turned her face up to the sky. She spun around until she was dizzy and breathless. God, the view was breathtaking from up here. She could see for miles in every direction. The moonlit landscape was a stunning black-and-white photograph, too perfect, too pristine to be real. It felt like the whole world stretched away at her feet. She was, indeed, Freya—warrior goddess and immortal, mistress of all she surveyed below. No wonder people climbed Mount Everest. This feeling was beyond exhilarating. It was intoxicating! Note to self: take up mountain climbing in her spare time.

Or maybe she was just giddy with hypoxia from the altitude.

Viper's dry voice tickled her ear. "Having fun up there? You've got the Samis down here about ready to start sacrificing animals and small children to you."

"Come again?" Karen asked, startled.

"You look like a goddess standing up there on top of your mountain. The Samis are freaking out. The *siida-isit* is beating a drum and singing one of those prayer-chants of theirs, and the whole lot of them at staring up at you like they expect you to start hurling lightning bolts down on them at any second."

"Oh, for crying out loud," Karen muttered. She plopped down into a sitting position that took her out of sight of the tribespeople.

Vanessa's voice came back, filled with laughter. "That got 'em good. You ought to hear them oohing and ahhing. They think you just disappeared into the mountain."

Karen scowled. "I'm going to tell them to sacrifice you to me first. How does being boiled in oil sound?"

Vanessa laughed openly now and didn't bother to reply.

Roundly irritated, Karen stood up again and turned her back on the foolishness below. After taking a moment to breathe deeply and slowly, she said more calmly, "The view's unbelievable. You guys should come up and take a look."

Misty answered this time. "Can't. The Samis are getting ready to move. It's either that, or stop and build a temple to you. I think Viper's got them almost talked out of that, though. Can you make your way down the east face and meet us in the next valley over, Athena?"

"It's Freya," Karen retorted sourly. "Athena's Greek. The Viking goddess of war is Freya."

Now all the Medusas were laughing. *Wenches.* "Y'all better

watch out. I'll tell the Samis you're my handmaidens, and I'll make them worship you, too."

As the ribbing flew back and forth, she looked to the east. Snow stretched away from her at an easily hikable angle. Too bad she didn't have a snowboard with her. This mountain just begged to be surfed. "By the way, all you comedians, I can make it down the back side of this hill, no problem."

Isabella replied this time. "Great. The Samis say we should reach the floor of the next valley in a half hour. Can you be there that soon, or will we need to stop the caravan and wait for you?"

Karen eyed the slope. The valley on to the east was much lower and farther away than the one she'd just climbed out of. But it was downhill travel. "I can make it in twenty." The way she was feeling right now, she could do it in ten!

"Roger," Vanessa replied, back up on frequency. "We'll probably lose radio signal until we're all on the same side of the mountain. If you get into trouble, give us a few minutes to top the pass and then holler."

"You got it, boss."

"You sound like you're having entirely too good a time up there, Python."

"Me? You're the one egging on the Samis to make sacrifices to me! All kidding aside, it's gorgeous up here."

"I believe you. The view's not bad from down here. Anders seems particularly enthralled with the view at the top of the mountain."

"He'd better not be up on this frequency," Karen blurted in alarm.

More laughter. "He's not." Vanessa added, "Have fun and we'll see you on the other side."

Karen glared as the caravan, a string of tiny black ants

below, moved out. She turned and surveyed the slope she
needed to traverse. She started hiking downward, and her teammates went out of sight as the mountain began to grow behind
her. She'd been half jogging downward, each foot sliding up
to six feet more than the length of her stride, for less than a
minute when a movement below made her halt suddenly. She
slid to a snowy stop. Something had moved down there. Something big.

Great. It wasn't her turn to be carrying one of the four rifles
and she was about to have to detour around a polar bear! Not
that the creaky old rifles the Medusas had right now would do
anything to a bear other than make it mad.

She stopped. Pulled out her field glasses. Dropped to her
knees, low and still in the snow, to take a better look. Holy crap!
That was no bear. It was a man!

Was Jack or one of Anders' Norwegian buddies following
the caravan? Maybe setting up an ambush for it? Or was it
someone more sinister, like one of the drug dealers? Her eyes
narrowed. Only one way to find out. God, she hoped it was
Jack. She'd love nothing more than to sneak up behind him and
scare the living crap out of him.

The guy was well below her and moving downward quickly,
but not as if he were fleeing her. He hadn't looked back over
his shoulder once since she'd been watching him. He definitely acted like he didn't know she was up here.

She needed to catch up with him before the Sami caravan
topped the ridge and came into this guy's sight. In seven, maybe
eight, more minutes the caravan would come into view, and she
had to be in position to neutralize this guy before then. She'd
never make it down the mountain in time. Unless…

She might not have a snowboard, but she did have a thick
tarp in her pack. If she folded it into a square and held the front

edge up like a toboggan, it would get her down the mountain really fast.

Since she was only armed with a knife, she'd have to get right up to the hostile below to take him out, which was risky. But the way she was feeling right now, that was just fine with her.

It took her only a few seconds to fashion a makeshift toboggan. She took a running start and plopped down on the impromptu sled, sitting Indian-fashion. She held up the front edge to keep it from plowing into the snow, and pushed with her other hand as she started to accelerate.

Her sled hit the smooth, icy sheet of the main snowpack, gathering speed. And more speed. In a matter of seconds, she was flying down the mountain, the wind flailing at her face until tears streamed out of her eyes.

She had to be pushing fifty miles per hour. And that was okay in the wide-open, snowy space at the top of the mountain. But as the glacier narrowed, squeezing its way into the valley below, steering became necessary. She experimented and was mightily relieved to discover that if she leaned left she went left, and if she leaned right she went right. She could probably use her feet to slow herself down, but if one or both of her heels dug in too much, she could send herself into a tumbling fall-cum-crash down the steep slope, and that wouldn't be good at all.

She didn't check her watch, but she must've made it most of the way down the two-thousand-foot vertical drop in no more than three minutes. The sled finally came to rest on a relatively flat section of snow a couple of hundred feet above the valley floor.

She sat there for several seconds, catching her breath. The hostile should be off to her left. No telling how far he'd moved while she'd been flying down the mountain. She'd been too busy watching where she was going to try to spot him.

She stood up, dropped her field knife out of its wrist sheath and into her right hand and glided forward. Time was of the essence. She had only a few more minutes until the caravan topped the ridge and came into weapons range. Moving from boulder to boulder for cover, she leapfrogged down and to the left. *Please be Jack. Please be Jack.* Each time she took up a new position, she stopped to listen. And each time, she heard only the whooshing sound of the wind sweeping ice crystals before it.

But then she stopped again and heard another noise. A faint, rhythmic crunching.

Bingo. Target acquisition.

Chapter 8

Oslo, Norway, March 4, 4:45 p.m.

Jens pinched the bridge of his nose. He was getting old. Didn't deal as well as he used to with a lousy night's sleep. He looked around the briefing room. Everyone was working extra hours and lots of his fellow cops just coming off shift looked bleary-eyed. Rough night?

The outgoing shift commander stood up. "We're getting preliminary reports from the Tromsö and Nordkapp areas of similar crime sprees erupting. Whatever's going on in Oslo has spread."

Great. Jens wondered idly if maybe it had started up north and migrated south to Oslo and not the other way around. He'd have to think about that later.

The briefer continued, "The mayor is monitoring the situation. If it continues to deteriorate, he may consider declaring a curfew or even a state of emergency. The folks in the labs tell us the Oslo crimes definitely appear related to drugs. If you have informants or contacts you can work to find out what's going on in the drug scene, work them ASAP."

Jens frowned. *Willie.* Time to pay the little prick a visit.

The briefing ended, and Jens headed back to his desk to call Astrid's pal. He reached for the phone, but it rang under his hand, making him jump.

"Detective Schumacher," he growled.

"Detective. This is Doctor Malchik over at Rikshospitalet University Hospital. The young prostitute who committed the murders has expired."

It took him a second to translate in his head. Oh. She'd died. Christ. The guy made her sound like a magazine subscription. "Did she ever regain consciousness? Say anything?"

"No, no," the guy said impatiently. "That sort of thing only happens on television programs. She experienced an intractable grand mal seizure that apparently involved her heart muscles. They did not respond to treatment, and we were not able to sustain vital functions."

"In plain language, please."

"She had a massive convulsion, her heart stopped beating, and she died."

And the bastard couldn't have said that from the beginning? Why? Doctors. Always had to impress everyone with how much they knew.

"Thanks." Jens disconnected the call with his thumb and as soon as he got a dial tone punched in a new set of numbers.

"Tromsö Police. How may I direct your call?"

"Homicide."

"One moment."

A tired-sounding male voice came on the line. "Yurgen here."

"Good morning. Detective Schumacher down in Oslo Homicide."

"'Morning. Just got off the phone with some of your guys. I can't tell you anything new about the murders. We're seeing the same M.O.s up here that you are."

"Any idea where your drugs are coming from?"

"We think our dealer must be living nearby, maybe coming into town from an outlying area and trading drugs whenever he happens to be here. The pills that we think are causing the problem seem to be showing up in spurts. Every two to three weeks a handful of them have been hitting the streets."

"Are you searching the local area for your dealer?"

"Can't. We've got a big military reservation nearby, and there's some exercise running. The army won't let us anywhere near it."

Jens swore under his breath. "Tell *them* to find your dealer, then, if he's hiding out on their turf."

The Tromsö cop's voice lowered conspiratorially. "The way I hear it, the FSK is running Special Forces exercises out there. I'd hate to be the drug dealer if they catch up with him."

Jens grinned. "I hear ya. Keep me informed of any new developments, and I'll do the same for you."

"You've got it."

Jens hung up again, and again dialed a new number as soon as he got a dial tone. Now for Willie. The kid would cough up the name of his supplier, or so help him, Jens was going to break him in half.

Jens opened his car window. The rush of cold air felt good. The car's heater was blasting him out. "Astrid!" he called to the girl walking down the sidewalk. The beige neo-classical buildings of Oslo University rose behind her.

His daughter whirled, her backpack sliding off one shoulder. "Dad! What are you doing here?"

"Get in. We'll give you a ride home."

"I don't need a ride. I'm enjoying the sunshine."

"Don't argue. Get in. All hell's broken loose and you're not safe on the streets."

"It's broad daylight! I'm perfectly fine. Besides. I'm over eighteen. I'm an adult."

Jens rolled his eyes. Did other teenagers actually get results by flinging that "I'm an adult" line at their parents, or was he the only parent in the world who didn't care if she was eighteen or thirty-eight? She was still his little girl. Always would be. "You may be an adult, but I'm bigger than you and I'm carrying a gun. Now, get in."

He scowled as she ducked down to see if Ivo was driving. Yes, Loverboy was here. Jens gritted his teeth as that seemed to sway his stubborn offspring. She opened the back door of the unmarked car and slid across the back seat until she could look at Ivo in the rearview mirror.

"Hi," she said shyly to his partner.

"Hi." Ivo gave her a stunning smile.

"Can you believe he's picking me up from school now, like I'm six?" she groused, all smiles and flirty looks.

Ivo replied seriously, "He's right to be cautious. This crime wave is terrible. I don't think a pretty girl like you should be out by yourself, either."

This earned his partner a perky pout followed by a brilliant smile. Jens clenched his jaw as she simpered, "But it's so boring to be all cooped up inside at home with nothing to do but study."

Hell, even he'd caught on that she was angling to get Ivo to ask her out. Jens interjected, "You need to study if you want to get decent grades." That earned him rolled eyes from the back seat.

They got home and waved goodbye to Ivo. Astrid didn't take her eyes off him as he drove off. Jens opened the kitchen door and shed his parka while Astrid put down her book bag.

"Have a seat, honey." He gestured at one of the kitchen chairs.

Astrid sat down cautiously. "Are you gonna lecture me again about drugs? I swear I haven't done any since you lectured me yesterday."

He sighed. "No lecture. Can I make you a cup of hot chocolate?"

"Hot chocolate? What's wrong?"

Damn. She knew him too well. He sat down across from her and forced his hands not to fidget. This was hard to do with total strangers. It was damn near impossible with his own daughter. "Honey, I went to see Willie this morning. Just to talk. To ask him where he got those pills and what was in them."

"Dad—"

He held up a hand, and uncharacteristically, Astrid fell silent. She must sense that something bad had happened. "I have some bad news for you."

She nodded reluctantly, clearly bracing herself. Except she had no idea what was coming next. He took a deep, steadying breath. God, he hated to do this.

As gently as he knew how to, he said, "We think his roommate had a psychotic episode. The tall, skinny one."

"Nicklaus," Astrid supplied.

"Right. Willie and the other boy who lived with them—"

"Randal."

"Yeah, Randal. He and Willie were both dead when I got there. We found Nicklaus at his girlfriend's apartment. Both of them were dead, too."

Astrid went as still and white as a block of ice, her eyes enormous and dark. He reached across the table and took her icy fingers in his. No amount of chafing brought any warmth back into them.

"I'm so sorry, sweetie."

In a heartbreakingly small voice, she asked, "Am I going to go crazy and die, too, Daddy?"

Northern Norway, March 4, 5:00 p.m.

Karen peered through her flexible periscope around the corner of a shoulder-high boulder. To her great disappointment, the target turned out not to be Jack. She'd so been hoping she could rough him up. Neither was this guy one of the Norwegian special operators she'd met.

Which meant he was more likely than not a hostile. And for some bizarre reason, that sent a surge of intense satisfaction through her. Maybe she'd get to pound the heck out of someone after all. It didn't really matter who she unleashed her pent-up anger on at this point. This guy was as good as any.

The hostile peered around his own boulder toward the valley floor below. What was he up to?

Patience, Karen. The rules of engagement the Medusas had agreed upon for their reconnaissance sorties today was that they wouldn't harm or kill any stranger who showed no intent to harm members of the caravan. They would merely capture and question anyone they came across. However, if they ran into anyone who did demonstrate hostile intent, the rules of engagement were to kill on sight.

Karen had trained to kill like this for the past year. Now, faced with a man she might very well have to execute in cold blood, the idea ought to be daunting. But it wasn't. Not at all. She *relished* the idea, even.

If it came down to him or her, it wasn't a hard choice. If it came down to him or her teammates, or even him or the Sami people, it wasn't a hard choice either. No matter how much she was jonesing to kill something right now, she *would…not…*kill for pleasure. With great difficulty, she forced herself to set aside her unnatural glee and settled into the cold, emotionless focus the moment required.

There. The first reindeer team and sled had just topped the mountain pass. Her target lurched. Stared intently through his binoculars at the caravan. The second sled—with Misty jogging alongside it, rifle clearly visible—came into view.

Her target spun fast and dropped to the ground behind his rock. Crap. He was facing right at her. She didn't even have time to pull back the periscope. Now she'd have to stay perfectly still and hope he didn't spot the distinctively man-made circle of the lens next to the ragged outline of her boulder.

Her heart surged into high gear, practically pounding its way out of her chest. What was up with that? She was in better physical condition than this. And her adrenaline wasn't that out of control.

She froze every other muscle in her body, standing perfectly still, and watched her quarry. Breathe in. Count to four. Breathe out. She counted in a slightly slower tempo than her heartbeat, willing it to relax. Slow down. Be calm. Gradually, her pulse responded, slowing to a more sensible rhythm.

Hostile or not hostile? Capture or kill? She waited with the infinite patience of a predator, already tasting its prey, her unblinking stare riveted on her target. Slowly, she got a firmer grip on her knife. Any second now he'd show his cards. And when he did, she would make her decision and spring into action in an instant. She allowed her muscles to coil into relaxed readiness, prepared to spring into battle. Breathing or not, this guy was going down in the next few seconds.

Because she didn't know if he was alone or not, she'd have

to take him out in total silence. Not a problem, just a slightly more violent method of attack required.

The hostile fumbled in his backpack and pulled out a long, thin, black tube. Time shifted into slow motion as she identified the object. That looked like the barrel of a sawed off shotgun.

If he pointed that thing at the caravan, he was dead where he stood.

This guy didn't carry himself like a killer. He was nervous about how he handled the weapon. She bided her time, waiting for the final, damning act that declared him hostile. She wasn't about to off someone on anything less than ironclad evidence of criminal intent.

He fumbled with the weapon's safety, shrugged on its shoulder strap, and psyched himself up to shoot, exhaling hard several times. *Amateur.* In the first place, the Medusas never carried a weapon in anything but the ready-to-fire position. Second, if she had to pick up a weapon and ready it to fire, she could do it in a single smooth, blindingly fast movement that sacrificed nothing by way of accuracy.

Finally, he rose to a half-crouch and turned around to lay his rifle barrel on the rock before him. His finger reached for the trigger. Bad decision, buddy.

She pounced.

It was over in about one second. Knife held chest-high in front of her, she took three running strides forward. With her free hand she grabbed his parka hood, and with the other hand, her knife hand, she slashed powerfully across the guy's throat. Her strike had the same cold efficiency and deadly effect Anders' had had the day before.

The hostile dropped to the ground. Blood soaked into the snow, dissipating like syrup into a snow cone. And she felt nothing but cold satisfaction.

Then he was still.

She pushed back his glove and felt for a pulse in his wrist. Nada. Dead.

She lifted the shotgun out of his hands and backed away from him, her gaze still wary upon him. Never trust a tango to be dead until the meat wagon has hauled him away. She'd learned that one from Jack. He'd played possum on her once. Had about broken her ankle as she'd turned away from him and he'd grabbed her foot.

Propping the weapon against her hip with her finger on the trigger, she used her left hand to key her microphone.

"I have one hostile down. I'm at the bottom of the pass, thirty yards to your left as you come down the mountain."

The effect on the slope above her was tremendous and immediate. Reindeer sleds scattered in all directions. The Samis dived into the snow and behind boulders, disappearing from view in a matter of seconds. Dang, they were good at blending into the scenery! Must be all that hunting they did. Had she not seen them go, she'd never have guessed nearly fifty men, women, and children ranged across that mountainside.

Vanessa transmitted tersely, "More hostiles?"

Karen replied, "None sighted."

"Medusas, spread out. Fan formation. Anders will stay in the area with the Samis to guard them. Python, say status of hostile."

"Dead."

Vanessa didn't question her decision to kill the guy. It went without saying that Karen wouldn't have taken him out if he hadn't shown violent intent. All her boss said was, "Threat is high, ladies."

Karen knelt and searched her kill. His face was already a ghastly shade of blue-gray. No identification. No radio, just a cell phone. She flipped it open, and a message on its face said it wasn't receiving any signals. The cell phone the Samis had with them in case of an emergency wasn't operational, either. Must be the mountains interfering with the signals. She pocketed the phone. She'd try it on the next mountain peak.

The guy had enough gear to stay out here for a couple days. Must be cave-camping because he had no tent. But, he had a good sleeping bag, food and water, maps, assorted survival supplies, and a handful of ammo. Idiot! What person came out here with a weapon and only a couple of dozen shells to fire from it? The Medusas commonly carried several thousand rounds of ammo for their weapons.

She threw the shotgun sling over her shoulder and moved out, carefully clearing the rock-strewn hillside nearby. God, it felt good to have a loaded weapon—a *real* one—in her hands again. An almost sexual thrill shuddered through her. She frowned. What was wrong with her tonight?

The Medusas combed the valley for over an hour looking for more hostiles before Vanessa finally called the all clear. Karen's guy had been alone.

But the Samis refused to come out of hiding until Karen personally hiked back up the mountainside to where they were hiding and told them herself that it was safe. Then they came out. *Ahh, the downside of being a god. Everyone wants a piece of you.*

Anders emerged as well. He was carrying one of the Sami rifles, and danger fairly oozed from him. He strode up to her, all business. "Who'd you kill?"

"Single male. No identification except a few pages torn out of a book. They look like Arabic verses. Koran, maybe. Dark hair, dark eyes, dark body hair. He pulled out this baby—" she held out the shotgun "—and aimed it at the caravan as soon as he saw one of the Medusas."

He nodded tersely. No questions asked. Apparently, he

trusted her judgment. And for that, she was grateful. At the moment, as weird as she was feeling, she wasn't sure she trusted her own judgment.

Anders said, "We need to retrieve the body. My headquarters will want to ID it."

Karen nodded and led the way back to the corpse. She took the dead man's feet and Anders took his shoulders, and the two of them carried the body down to the valley floor. The Samis weren't thrilled to have to repack their sleds to make room for this new, grisly cargo, but they did it when Karen asked them to. The dead man's more useful supplies were distributed among the Medusas, and the rest packed with the body.

The caravan set out once more.

Nobody complained when they traveled much longer than had been originally planned. Everybody wanted to put some distance between the caravan and the site of the killing. The really deep freeze of the night had settled in before the *siida-isit* finally called a halt.

Anders translated. "He says the reindeer are exhausted and can go no further. We will stop here for the night."

"Here" was a small, sheltered valley with sheer vertical cliffs rising some three hundred feet at their backs and to one side. A good, defensible position. A watch rotation was set up, two Medusas and three Samis at a time—with an operational weapon for each.

Vanessa came over to where Anders was helping a couple of Sami women pitch a skin cover over a curving wood frame. Karen was helping several girls unpack other gear—cooking utensils, sleeping furs and food.

Karen, who was untying a heavy sack of grain, looked up as her boss crouched beside her. Lord knew, the reindeer had earned a good meal tonight.

"You okay?" Vanessa asked quietly.

"Yeah. Why?"

"Well, you killed a guy tonight. Just wanted to make sure you were cool with it."

Karen rocked back on her heels, considering her boss. "I don't like killing. But it had to be done. He aimed that shotgun at the caravan. Him or us. Not a hard choice."

The two of them were silent for a moment. Then Vanessa asked reflectively, "If someone had told you two years ago you'd be in these mountains slitting guys' throats and not batting an eyelash over it, would you have believed them?"

Karen snorted. "Not in a million years." She looked around at the tired Samis stumbling through the motions of setting up camp. Kat and Misty were across the clearing helping some women pour water from heavy skins into a cooking pot. Aleesha was looking into some kid's ears and throat with her little doctor flashlight, and Isabella was talking to a couple of men and pointing at various objects around the camp. Still soaking up the Sami tongue.

She looked back at her boss. "It's a good life, isn't it?"

Vanessa nodded. "Yeah. It is." A pause. "I'm glad you're part of this team."

Karen grinned, a little embarrassed. "Hey, you're the one who picked me. All I did was say yes. Thanks for having me."

Vanessa grinned back. "How could I pass up selecting a Viking goddess?"

Karen gave her boss's shoulder a shove and knocked her off her heels and onto her behind. She started when Anders spoke to Vanessa from directly behind her. "Watch out. When Freya gets angry enough she chops people's heads off with her battle ax."

Karen rose to her feet and whirled around. How much of her exchange with Vanessa had he overheard? That looked like something very close to admiration shining in his eyes.

"Your hut's ready," he announced to her.

"Does it have an altar in it? Maybe a sacrificial lamb or two?"

He laughed. "No, I managed to stop them from turning it into an all-out shrine. They did insist on sprinkling your bed with sweet-smelling herbs, though."

"You're kidding."

"Nope."

Karen groaned.

Vanessa spoke up. "Take the first sleep rotation, Python. You've had a rough couple of days."

Karen didn't argue. She was beat. Definitely off her game emotionally. She headed for her hut. And paused in the doorway to look over her shoulder. Anders was, literally, on her heels. "What are you doing?"

"Guarding my mistress, of course."

"Oh, puh-lease."

"If not me, the Samis will do it. After your little display on the mountaintop, and then the way you found and killed that guy, there's no doubt in their minds you're the real thing. A full-blown reincarnation of Freya herself."

She closed her eyes in acute annoyance. She took a long, calming breath. "I'll deal with that in the morning. But right now, I'm going to sleep."

"And I'm coming with you."

She was in no mood to argue with anyone, let alone Anders. She shrugged and ducked into the hut. It was much smaller than the sod hut of the last encampment, but it was airtight and held the heat of the tiny fire reasonably well. Sure enough, her sleeping bag was already spread out on a pile of furs, and dried—sharp and pokey—bits of leaves were sprinkled all over it.

She brushed the herbs off as best she could, stripped down

to her long underwear, and crawled into her sleeping bag. Silence fell over the hut. It did smell good in here.

"What herbs did they use?"

"Laurel, lavender and rosemary leaves."

"It's nice."

Anders replied dryly, "I'll tell them you like it."

Her eyes flew open. "You'll do no such thing! Don't you encourage them or I'll have you boiled in oil along with Vanessa."

His light eyes glinted back at her in amusement. God, he was sexy when he smiled like that. "Get some sleep. You've earned it. You did well up on that mountain today. I continue to be impressed with how you handle yourself."

He wouldn't have been so impressed had he known how close she'd come to losing control and battle raging for no apparent reason. Nonetheless, warmth spread through her at the compliment. "Thanks. I'll pass that along to my superiors. They really want the Medusas to make a good impression on the first foreign counterparts that we have trained with."

Anders crawled into his sleeping bag, his face partially hidden by the glowing fire. "Although I am impressed by your entire team, I wasn't talking about them. I was talking about you. Personally."

And as she gaped, he rolled over, presented her his back and went to sleep.

Chapter 9

Lakvik, Norway, March 5, 4:00 p.m.

Apparently, word of some kind had managed to precede the caravan that the Sami hunters and the Medusas were coming to town. The Sami village, named Lakvik, consisted of several rows of tiny wood-frame houses, a two-room school and a Viking-style longhouse that apparently acted as a central gathering building. A large cluster of sod huts formed a suburb of sorts. And beyond that, a veritable tent city had been erected. Some of the tents were bright-colored nylon, but most of them were made of reindeer skins stretched over wooden frames.

People bustled around everywhere, laughing and talking, carrying food and furs and firewood. *Cool. Real wood.* It would be nice to smell a fire that didn't reek of manure. It was clear at a glance that a large celebration of some kind was already well into preparation. Samis milled around by the hundreds. No way did all these people fit in the permanent structures Karen saw in town.

"Where did everyone come from?" she asked Anders.

He spoke to the nearest pair of Sami men, who were carrying what looked like an entire frozen reindeer carcass toward the giant wood fire now roaring in the middle of town. Anders turned back to her. "Samis have been coming in from all over northern Norway for a couple of days now. Ever since your arrival was reported."

Karen stared. "All these people are here to see us?"

"No. They're here to see *you*."

"This has got to stop. *Now*. Who do I tell that I'm not a goddess to get all this insanity to go away?"

She was thankful that Anders didn't indulge in an "I told you so."

"Probably the head shaman type here. I'll ask around and see if I can find out who he is."

Yet again, she and Anders were installed in their own hut while the rest of the Medusas shared another one. She didn't know whether to be pleased to be alone with him or as jumpy as a long-tailed cat beside a rocking chair. She settled on being a little of both.

As they finished unpacking their meager possessions, he suggested, "Why don't you take a nap? It could be a long evening if all these people want to meet you."

Unaccountably furious at the prospect of all these strangers wrangling for her attention, she glared at Anders and flopped down onto her sleeping bag.

"Are you all right?"

"Yes, I'm all right!" she flared up. She blinked, surprised at the vehemence of her outburst.

Unperturbed, he said, "You've seemed a little edgy since the firefight."

"Yeah, well, we're all a little edgy." And now that she stopped to think about it, she was actually being more than a little bitchy. She released a long, slow breath, and one by one unclenched the major muscle groups in her body. "I'm sorry," she sighed. "I don't know what's up with me. I'm usually not anywhere near this nasty."

He smiled kindly. "We all deal with stress in different ways. I've seen guys get wound a lot tighter than you on missions."

Thing was, she never got wound tight. This mission was a complete anomaly. Maybe it was just the stress of having to live up to being a goddess that was doing it to her. Or, if she was being brutally honest with herself, maybe it was the close proximity to a gorgeous hunk she had a ferocious crush on. Either way, she really did need to chill out. Maybe she'd feel better after a nap. She closed her eyes and let sleep claim her.

Lakvik, Norway, March 5, 8:00 p.m.

When Karen woke up, she didn't feel better. In fact, she felt noticeably worse. She was grumpy and out of sorts. Absolutely everything irritated her. At least Anders left immediately after she woke up, so she didn't subject him to much random sniping.

The rest of the Medusas ducked into her hut almost immediately.

"Hey there, sleepyhead," Vanessa said cheerfully.

Karen grumbled something unintelligible under her breath. As her boss's eyebrows raised fractionally, Karen pulled herself back in sharply. She took a deep breath and asked as civilly as she could muster, "How's the party going?"

Aleesha laughed. "Now that you're awake, oh Exalted One, it can start."

Karen gritted her teeth and smiled. "Any luck getting a call out to Anders' ops center?"

Isabella, their communication specialist, answered that one. "None. Nothing's coming in or going out."

"Has anyone hiked to the nearest mountain peak to give one a try?"

Isabella shook her head. "Not yet. But that's what I'm about to do."

Karen grinned. "Hurry back or you'll miss the highlight of the party where I have Viper tarred and feathered for her impertinence."

The whole team laughed at that one.

Karen felt marginally better, but still fought an underlying…something. If she didn't know better, she'd call it simmering anger. But she wasn't mad at anybody. She must be PMSing. Although that wasn't something she usually suffered from, nor was it time for that.

And then the feast swallowed her, all light and noise and color and teeming people. With great fanfare, the Samis led her to a wide bonfire and seated her in a place of honor atop a stunning pile of furs. She identified bear, wolf, beaver and mink pelts, all thick and gorgeous. Anders was installed beside her to act as translator for the dozens of Samis who lined up to meet her. The receiving line went on forever. She was beginning to have downright uncharitable thoughts about her hosts by the time the celebration took a decidedly more raucous turn.

It didn't take her long to spot the source of the increased joviality. The Sami people were passing around skins of some unidentified liquid libation. Booze, no doubt. A shout went up for her to have some. Normally, the Medusas wouldn't dream of drinking on the job. But the Samis weren't going to be denied on this one. Karen glanced over at Vanessa standing on the far side of the fire. She got a slight nod from her boss.

Reluctantly, Karen took a skin and hoisted it high using the back of her elbow to tilt it up. When the spout was well above her face she pulled her thumb away from the spigot and let a stream of liquid squirt into her mouth. Oh, geez. She'd expected it to be alcoholic, but this rotgut was lethal! She was on fire from her lips to the bottom of her stomach!

She duly choked and spluttered—to the vast amusement of the assembled masses. God almighty, that stuff was strong! She'd tossed back 151-proof rum with Delta Force operators before, but this stuff made that taste like cough syrup.

Someone offered her the skin again. Laughing, she waved it away. She was already way off her game. She didn't need to add drunkenness on top of her lousy frame of mind.

After about an hour of hard drinking, the Samis started singing, although that was a generous word for it. They were performing more *loiks,* the half chants, half songs they used for storytelling, for passing down their oral history as a people, and for conveying spiritual visions. Anders translated a few of the *loiks,* but they all started to run together in her head. They were predictably epic and involved lots of nature imagery and convoluted language. If she were waxing literary tonight, which she bloody well wasn't, the *loiks* were actually incredibly sophisticated.

Anders left the fire at some point and came back a few minutes later with a liquid-filled skin. He handed it to her. "Water," he murmured.

She nodded her thanks and took a long drink. A roar went up as the Samis incorrectly assumed she'd actually just put away a good liter of their moonshine. She made a production out of wiping her mouth and smacking her lips, and the roar got even louder. *Whatever.* As soon as this feast was over, she was bursting their bubble once and for all. She couldn't blow her nose without these people oohing and ahhing like she'd just converted lead to gold. Enough was enough.

She glanced up and happened to catch Misty's gaze across the fire. Karen's eyes widened in surprise as her teammate flashed her a subtle hand signal. There was a problem? A serious one? What the heck kind of serious problem could they have at a glorified weenie roast?

She leaned over to Anders. "Gotta go. Sidewinder just signaled. Something's wrong."

His pleasant, relaxed expression didn't change, but he muttered tightly, "What's up?"

"Don't know," she said absently, keeping an eye on Misty for any further signals. "Let's go find out. Tell the Samis I'm taking you out behind a hut to have my way with you. We'll be back in a while."

And then her gaze whipped around to him. Good Lord, that had been a careless thing to say! It was *totally* unlike her to blurt something like that out. Anders was staring at her in shock. And then he threw back his head and howled with laughter. Should she be unbelievably insulted, or had she just shocked the life out of him?

He said something in Sami and a huge shout went up from the crowd. Dammit. He'd gone and translated exactly what she'd said. The cad.

"I can't believe you repeated that to them!" she ground out.

"Why not? If I'm lucky, maybe you *will* take me out back later to fool around."

Now it was her turn to stare. Heat climbed her face that had nothing to do with the fire before her. And that indefinable, uncomfortable disturbance deep in her gut churned up a little higher. "Let's go," she said shortly.

She stood up, and by way of revenge, grabbed the collar of Anders' coat to drag him away with her. More hooting and shouted comments erupted. She was relieved beyond words not to understand a bit of what they were saying.

They stepped beyond the bright circle of the fire and she turned him loose. They made their way back toward their hut in silence. When Karen ducked inside, all the other Medusas were already there. Isabella was still red-cheeked from her recent climb back down the mountain.

"Did you get through?" Karen asked her.

"Nope."

"Wow. Not on any frequency?"

"I tried every radio or phone they have in this town. They even had a cell phone with a satellite uplink. And nothing's working. Nada."

Karen's college degree was in mechanical engineering. But more to the point, she'd worked most of her marine career in a helicopter-maintenance squadron. As such, she knew a whole lot about radios. "So, is it just me, or do you think we're getting jammed?"

Isabella nodded at her. "That's exactly what I'm thinking."

Vanessa leaned back, her gaze narrow. "Jack and his Norwegian buddies are jamming us? What range would their jamming equipment likely have?"

Karen shrugged. "Let's assume they're ground-based. From a plane or satellite you can jam frequencies for hundreds of miles in any direction. Their range will depend on how high up they are. Jamming signals tend to be line of sight. So, they'll be sitting on top of a mountain with a black box. Depending on the terrain, they can throw a signal somewhere between five and fifty miles, if I had to guess."

Misty spoke up. "So, if we head for the highest mountain in the area, we should find them?"

Karen replied, "Maybe. They may sit on a smaller peak and accept that the tallest mountain will block their jamming signal in that particular direction."

Vanessa leaned forward. "Correct me if I'm wrong, but isn't a jamming signal a radio signal, too?"

Karen nodded.

Vanessa continued, "Then, is there any way we can track their signal?"

Hmm. Interesting idea. Karen mulled over what she knew about homing devices. If she could create something that measured signal strengths, she might be able to find the jamming frequency and then figure out in which direction the signal was strongest. "I might be able to build a crude signal tracker. Question is, where would I get the electronic gear to do it?"

Vanessa answered, "Let's ask the Samis what they've got. After all, they had a satellite uplink phone in town."

Karen nodded. "Want me to go ask them now?"

"Nah, don't spoil their party. After all, you are the guest of honor. Tomorrow morning's soon enough."

Karen grinned. "And it won't hurt Jack to sit on top of a frozen mountain for another night anyway."

Vanessa just shook her head and smiled. Karen probably ought to quit sniping at the guy in front of her boss, since Vanessa was head over heels for the guy, but she just couldn't. He was an itch under her skin that wouldn't leave her alone— an irritation that heated the bubbling cauldron in her gut a little more every time she thought about him.

Anders spoke up. "I hate to interrupt, but just before we left the fire, the Samis were saying that the *noaide* Naliki was asking after Karen. He may want to speak to her soon."

"Isn't that the shaman who had the vision about me and started this whole mess?" she snapped.

"The very same," Anders answered mildly.

Okay, now she felt bad for her snippy tone with him. More rationally this time, she asked, "And what does this Naliki guy want with me?"

Anders shrugged. "Probably wants to consult on whatever omens and foretellings of the future you care to share with him."

Karen rolled her eyes. "Is this the head shaman guy you were looking for earlier? The one that I can tell in no uncertain terms that I'm not Freya?"

"I think so. Everyone seems a little afraid of this guy."

Vanessa interjected quietly, "Karen, I know this whole situation has bothered you. But be nice to this guy, okay? We need Sami help if we're to find Jack and get access to a working phone. And we need to blow up that drug lab before anyone else gets hurt."

Karen sighed. "Fine. I'll break it to Naliki gently that I'm not a goddess. But I *am* telling him."

"Fair enough," her boss replied.

Anders stood up and held down a hand to help her to her feet. Karen shivered, hyper-aware of the warm contact between their palms. His gaze met hers, and for an instant, the connection between their hands was mirrored in their eyes.

Staggered, Karen allowed him to pull her easily to her feet. She followed him from the tent, at a loss as to what to say after *that* little exchange. He led her to a sod hut on the far edge of the village. It was unique in that its exterior walls were decorated with all kinds of tidbits—reindeer hooves, bear claws, eagle feathers and various bones, bleached white and glimmer-

162   *The Medusa Prophecy*

ing in the moonlight. It looked like a throwback to a more
primitive, mystic place and time.

As she ducked into the hut, that sensation intensified. The
inside walls were covered with more of the same decorations,
and absolutely everything else in the dwelling was handmade
in the old tradition. An incredibly old person wrapped in a fur
blanket sat on the floor across a small wood fire.

In raspy, flawless English the woman—a woman!—said,
"Ahh, there you are, child. Come in. I've been waiting to speak
with you for most of my life."

Chapter 10

Karen stared at the elderly woman. "I beg your pardon?"

"Come. Sit. We will speak together."

Karen sat. This old woman had an authority about her a person didn't say no to.

"Your young man can go. We don't need him to translate for us."

Karen glanced over at Anders. He stood in the doorway, the firelight playing off his features and making him look more godlike than she ever could. He nodded his respects at the shaman and turned to go.

"Handsome lad you've picked for yourself," the old woman commented.

Karen winced. Anders hadn't left yet! His back was turned to her, but his hand froze on the door latch. He'd heard the shaman, all right. Silently, he let himself out into the night. The door closed behind him.

Karen turned to her hostess in no small dismay. "I haven't picked him," she bit out, "and I'd appreciate it if you didn't say things like that around him!"

The old woman laughed, a gay, girlish sound that surprised Karen. "See how you blush! You *have* picked him. You just haven't admitted it to yourself."

Karen scowled. Fine, dammit. So she'd picked the guy. Big deal.

"Look into the fire, child. Your soul is unquiet."

Rather than argue, for this woman had all the hallmarks of someone who could be implacably stubborn and incredibly infuriating, Karen played along for the moment. She fixed her gaze on the dancing flames. The fire was warm and soothing. It smelled good, too. Like a green summer afternoon. Staring into it did push back the anger roiling inside her. "Where did you learn to speak English?"

"My grandfather worked with a British spy who parachuted into Norway during World War Two to help the resistance. They taught me."

Something in the woman's voice made Karen ask, "Did you help them?"

A smile creased the old woman's face into a thousand wrinkles. The shaman leaned forward and whispered conspiratorially, "I did. And no one ever suspected a thing. I was just a girl, and I walked right past the Nazis every day carrying important messages down my shirt."

Wow. Who'd have ever guessed this unlikely little old woman was a war hero? "My name is Karen Turner. I'm a soldier in the United States military."

"I am called Naliki. I am a *noaide*. Do you know what that is?"

"As I understand it, you're a shaman. A healer, counselor and mystic."

Naliki shrugged. "Close enough for an outsider. I am a bridge between the spirit world and this world. A telephone wire through which communication passes."

Karen wasn't particularly into such spiritual mumbo jumbo, but she remembered Vanessa's instruction. Make nice with this lady. "My teammates and I are here in Norway for Arctic survival training. But we've run into a bit of a problem. We thought we were staging a mock attack on a Norwegian military unit, but instead, we attacked an actual drug lab. We desperately need to get in touch with our Norwegian command center so they can come take care of the lab. But, our trainers are jamming all the electronic frequencies in this area, and we can't contact anyone. We're hoping your people can help us."

A slow nod from Naliki. "So you have done what you said you would."

"I beg your pardon?"

"In my vision of you, you said you would find and destroy the source of the drugs that are tormenting our young people."

"I did?" Karen was startled enough by the accuracy of this so-called vision to forget to doubt it for a moment. "What else did I say?"

Naliki laughed. "You said in return you would set my people free."

"Free from what?"

"From outside pressure to change our ways. We want to preserve our language. Run our own schools. Teach traditional values and folklore to our children so our ways are not lost. We need land—preserves—set aside for us so the reindeer herds continue to have places to graze without oil pipelines or electric lines or hazardous waste dumps contaminating them."

Karen frowned. "And I said I'd do all this for your people?"

"All in good time. My visions do not lie. First, the drug lab.

More and more of our young men are having fits—we must stop that first."

"Fits?" Karen repeated. "Could you be more specific?"

"They fall to the ground in a seizure. If anyone tries to touch them, they strike out violently, with no care for who they harm. And then they fall unconscious. One boy never woke up from the deep sleep."

"Are you saying he *died?*"

The shaman nodded soberly.

Yikes. "And drugs are causing these potentially fatal fits? What sort of drugs?"

Naliki nodded. "Neither I nor any of the other healers know what it is. It is unlike anything we have seen before. And unfortunately, we are familiar with all the drugs of the outside world. I can tell you the drugs come from the lab our hunters showed you."

Holy cow. The Medusas needed to report this to the authorities right away! "We really need to let our superiors know about this. But the team we're chasing is jamming all the radio and telephone signals in this area. To fix that, we need to get out of the range of the signal jamming so we can make a phone call, or we need to find the Norwegian military team who's jamming us and get them to stop."

Naliki's eyes drifted closed and her head jerked a couple of times as though she was dozing off. Karen frowned. Should she reach over and shake the woman's shoulder?

"How far must you travel for your modern gadgets to work?"

Oops. The elderly shaman was still awake. Karen shrugged. "Maybe as little as a few miles, maybe up to fifty miles."

Naliki shook her head. "A storm is coming. A grandfather of a blizzard. You will not have time to travel so far."

"How do you know there's a storm?"

Naliki smiled wisely. "It hangs heavy in the air."

Karen couldn't argue with that. Back on the farm when she was a kid, everyone could feel a big thunderstorm building long before they could see it.

"Surely you know the signs," Naliki said in a faraway tone that wasn't quite a whisper. "The way the leaves flutter in panic on the trees, showing their pale undersides? The stillness that presses against your ears? The animals clustering tight, shouldering each other and rolling their eyes until the whites show?"

Karen stared, transfixed. She knew *exactly* what Naliki was talking about. But how did the shaman know she would recall those particular images?

"There's something I have to tell you, *Noaide* Naliki."

When Karen didn't continue, the shaman nodded encouragingly.

Karen took a deep breath and had at it. "Your people have gotten the wrong idea about me. They got the impression I'm some sort of reincarnated figure from Norse mythology." Lord, it felt good to get this off her chest. She searched for the right words to use in her confession.

"I'm afraid I led them to believe it when we first met. A Sami hunter asked if I was the person a prophecy foretold would come to lead them to freedom. I said I was because it was easier than explaining that I wasn't. It was a mistake. It was disrespectful of your beliefs and I shouldn't have done it. But now this thing has spun completely out of control."

The words came more quickly now, tumbling out of her. "Now they think everything I do is a portent of some kind. They're wining and dining me and giving me my own hut and treating me like royalty. I feel terrible about it. I don't want to disappoint them, but I can't in good conscience let this continue any longer. I'm hoping you can help me convince them I'm no goddess at all, but a simple, flesh-and-blood person just like them."

Naliki studied her for a long time in silence. Long enough that Karen had a nearly overwhelming urge to squirm under the bright, birdlike stare.

Then Naliki said slowly, heavily, "I'm sorry. I cannot help you. For, you see, you are exactly who they think you are."

Karen stared. Replayed what the woman had just said to make sure she hadn't misheard it. "I beg your pardon?"

"You are Freya. Or at least her reincarnated spirit."

Oh, good Lord. Not this woman, too! "I *so* don't believe in stuff like that," Karen declared.

Naliki shrugged. "You do not have to believe it for it to be true. If you do not believe you are beautiful, and yet everyone who looks at you sees a beautiful woman, what are you? Ugly or beautiful?"

Karen frowned. She'd always focused only on her own self-image. She knew what other people saw when they looked at her. A big, strong, manly woman they wouldn't want to tangle with in a dark alley.

"You are a warrior woman. You have unusual strength. Special skills and powers. Other people who look at you see the Viking goddess within you. Whether you want to admit it or not, Karen Turner, you are the living embodiment of Freya."

The northern coast of Norway, March 5, 10:15 p.m.

Isa scowled as he jumped out of the skiff and onto the gravel shore. A goddamned glacier rose in front of him, blue in the moonlight and partially obscured by drifting whorls of snow.

He'd promised himself the last time he left this godforsaken icebox that he'd never come back to Norway in winter again.

Yet here he was, a scant month later, freezing his ass off. And worse, it was supposed to get even colder over the next few days.

"Okay, men, let's get those snowmobiles on shore. We've got a buttload of hauling to do."

He wanted to get the finished product the hell away from the cabin before anyone else attacked the place. And, he'd brought in enough lab equipment—purchased at his own goddamned expense—to double the lab's output. They had to make that quota. Six hundred kilos of white powder. Enough to bring the whole goddamned western world crashing down upon itself.

Two weeks in this eff-ing refrigerator. Then the drugs would be ready and delivered. After that, he was heading for a beach. A nude one with beautiful western whores lounging all over it.

Lakvik, Norway, March 5, 10:30 p.m.

"You're wrong. I'm no goddess!"

"Child, I am not wrong. I have seen you in my dreams. *You.*"

"It's not possible! We've never met before."

Naliki chortled. "Whether or not you believe it, the truth does not change."

So, maybe the woman was psychic and had dreamed of her. Stranger things had happened. Or maybe Jack had given Naliki information to mess with Karen's head. And as soon as that thought occurred to her, it stuck.

Karen asked sharply, "Has a guy named Jack Scatalone talked to you recently? Or someone from the Norwegian military, maybe?"

Naliki shook her head in the negative. "No, no. Nothing like that. I'm telling you the truth."

Karen's mind whirled, entirely off balance.

Naliki fell into the singsong rhythm of a storyteller. "Freya is one of the most enduring of the old gods. Memory of her has never faded, and many still wait for her return as was promised in the days of old. If she were to come back to earth and walk upon it as a mortal, would it not make sense that she would choose the form of a woman who is sturdy and strong, and that she would guide her mortal footsteps to walk the path of the warrior?"

"But I don't believe in this stuff!"

"It may not be your way to believe in reincarnation. But it is ours. Who is to say which set of beliefs is right and which is wrong? You cannot know for certain that you are *not* a reincarnated spirit any more than I can know for certain that I *am*. According to Sami beliefs, you are who you are. And you *are* Freya's reincarnated spirit."

"Wouldn't I know that about myself if I were?"

"Not necessarily. Our lore has it that when the spirit decides to take form again on Earth, he or she must leave all they knew before behind."

"Even a goddess?"

Naliki shrugged. "I do not know. Apparently. Since you do not remember who you are, I must assume that even gods and goddesses leave behind all their memories."

Karen just shook her head. How could a person argue against crazy logic like that?

"This gathering of the Sami tribes is the first step in restoring our people's heritage. A council of *siida-isits* has convened, and they are drafting a letter to the governments of all the nations who currently hold Sami lands. It is a great step forward for our people. One we have never managed to take until now. It is because of your coming that this thing has happened."

"Yes, but I had nothing to do with them getting together!"

"You had everything to do with this gathering. It was the prophecy of your coming that brought them all here."

Frustration bubbled up very close to the surface and threatened to overflow the seething cauldron of her gut. Karen struggled to contain it. She was a Medusa, dammit. She was disciplined. In control of herself. She would *not* lose her temper!

"*Noaide* Naliki. I have never made any pronouncements or prophecies of any kind regarding your people. It was your dream. Your thought. *You* are the one who made this grand statement that is uniting your people."

Naliki grinned, showing gaps in her teeth. "I am an old woman. In all my years, I have never had any notion of uniting the Sami people. Such thoughts never even occurred to me. It is you who put them into my head. You are the sign. The goddess returned. The one who leads the way."

"Stop it, dammit! I'm not your—"

The door burst open. "*Noaide.* Come quickly! More gods have come!" The Sami man threw a superstitious look in Karen's direction.

Karen leaped to her feet. *Thank God.* Jack and the Norwegians must have gotten tired of waiting to be found and come looking for the Medusas instead. Naliki struggled to unfold her creaky limbs and climb awkwardly to her feet, and Karen reached down to help her. The woman was surprisingly frail. After the force of the diminutive elder's words, it was a shock.

She helped Naliki wrap a fur coat around herself and picked up the large leather sack Naliki pointed at. And then the two women stepped out into the night.

They followed the man back toward the bonfire. And as they drew close, Karen registered two things. First was the awed silence enveloping the crowd. And second was the strange noise coming from somewhere nearby to fill the silence. It sounded like war chants—half screaming, half singing, wild, almost drunken in nature.

Someone in the crowd of Samis standing around wide-eyed and silent looked over his shoulder and spotted her and Naliki. He called out something in Sami and the crowd parted to let the two of them through. Karen stared at the sight that met them.

Three teenaged boys had stripped down to their pants and fur leggings and were dancing, bare-chested and wild, around the bonfire. The unintelligible outbursts she'd heard before were coming from them. Their black ponytails were undone, and hair flew across their faces. The firelight jumped and swayed on their skin as they whirled and flailed their arms like puppets dancing on invisible strings. They did, indeed, look possessed.

Great. Just what she needed to convince the Samis she wasn't Freya. Now other people were starting to speak in tongues and act like reincarnated Vikings.

Anders glided up beside Karen, parking himself at her left shoulder. "The locals think these boys have been possessed by Viking warrior spirits. Traditional berserkers."

"They look drunk to me," Karen muttered back. Then she cursed under her breath. The three boys, until now on the far side of the fire, had spotted her and were jerking and twitching their way over to her, jabbering and howling all the while. How creepy was that? Karen schooled her face to complete implacability.

Anders shrugged. "All these other people have been drinking hard all evening and they're not going whacky. Just those three boys. I've never seen anything like this before among the Samis."

The teen closest to Karen gave a bloodcurdling scream, arched his back and flung his arms wide for a suspended moment of time. His wild gaze caught hers. Froze her immobile for an endless second. Insanity glittered in the kid's eyes. Power. Invincibility. *Rage.*

The youth collapsed dramatically to the ground. The crowd took a step back, oohing and ahhing, their gazes flitting back and forth between her and the prostrate boy.

He began twitching and flopping at her feet. *Oh, for crying out loud.*

"Mamba!" Karen called as she rushed forward. "This kid's having a seizure."

Karen knelt beside the teen and put her hands on his shoulders. She didn't try to stop him from moving altogether, but restrained him just enough to keep him from injuring himself badly by hitting his head on the ground or rolling into the fire.

Aleesha materialized out of the crowd in a matter of seconds. "I can give him a shot of muscle relaxant, or we can let him ride this seizure out."

Karen struggled to protect the youth from himself. He was incredibly strong, tossing and turning powerfully beneath her hands. It took all her formidable strength to hold him down. She grunted, "Naliki said these kids get violent during their seizures. They strike out at anyone around them. Might be best to knock them out."

"While I go get my bag, monitor his breathing and make sure he doesn't swallow his tongue. This seizure seems confined mostly to his large muscle groups."

Karen shrugged off her parka and tucked it under the boy's head to protect it from the rocky, frozen ground. The other Medusas gathered around, laying their hands on the youth's limbs to help restrain and protect him. Karen put her hands on either side of the patient's head to guard it from harm.

Aleesha returned with her bag and dropped to her knees beside Karen. "What's he on?"

"Some sort of drug. Naliki doesn't know what it is. Says it causes seizures, violent outbursts, unconsciousness and death."

Aleesha swore under her breath. "Didn't Anders say something a few days ago about an outbreak of the same sort of symptoms among drug users in Oslo?"

Karen frowned. "Yeah, I think so."

Aleesha was busy for the next couple minutes taking vitals on the unconscious kid and stabilizing him. Eventually, she muttered, "I gotta get access to a phone. This kid is a mess. Whatever he's on is tearing him up from the inside out."

As Aleesha's muscle relaxants and tranquilizers took effect, the rigidity left the boy's body and he relaxed beneath the Medusas' hands. A collective sound of awe went up from the crowd. Karen looked up, and realized everyone was staring at her.

They'd just watched Aleesha administer treatment to this kid. Why in the hell were they all staring at *her?* Karen mumbled, exasperated, "Anders, Naliki, tell them I didn't do anything. He had a seizure and we rendered basic first aid to keep him from hurting himself. Nothing more."

Anders answered dryly, "They won't believe us. They saw you lay your hands on him and take the warrior spirit from him with their own eyes."

She glanced over at the other two boys who were still whooping and whirling, oblivious to their friend's collapse, then glared up at Anders. "These kids are not possessed by Viking warriors! They're high and acting like idiots. Tell your people, Naliki!"

The shaman shrugged. "They will not believe me."

"Try," Karen ground out. She let go of the kid's now-still head and stood up to get out of the way so Aleesha could continue watching him. The crowd actually took a step back as Karen surged to her feet. She scowled even harder. An urge to commit violence washed over her. "I'm *not* a goddess!" she snapped.

The crowd melted out of her path as she stormed away from the fire. And damned if they didn't *bow* as she strode past them.

She was getting out of here and finding Jack Scatalone if she had to walk all the way to Oslo to get the parts to build a homing device to track his happy ass down. She'd had it with all this Viking goddess crap. It was time to put an end to it once and for all and get the hell out of here.

Chapter 11

Lakvik, Norway, March 6, 4:00 a.m.

There. She was done. Karen stared at the awkward jumble of wires and circuit boards on her sleeping bag. She'd worked on it most of the night while Anders slept peacefully on the other side of the fire. As best as she could tell, she'd just cobbled together a working signal detector and crude homing device. Only way to know if it worked would be to take it outside and test it. But she was freezing cold and it was really late. She'd grab a quick nap and then give her gizmo a go. She threw more fuel on the fire, which was doing precious little to stave off the frosty air.

Carefully, she moved her tracking gadget aside and slid gratefully into the quick, light warmth of her down sleeping bag. After roasting near the bonfire for much of the evening, the dark and chill of the hut seemed even more intense than usual. It probably didn't help that she was dead tired either. What a bizarre emotional roller coaster the day had been. Clearly, she needed to take a few hours and get a solid block of sleep to re-center her nervous system and cure the sleep-deprived crazies in her head.

Except when she woke up a couple of hours later, she didn't feel a whole hell of a lot better. When she tried to wake up Anders, he mumbled something about the whole village being hung over and not going anywhere soon. Then he rolled over and went back to sleep.

Karen was jittery. Her nerves jangled and her hands wouldn't stay still. The idea of sleeping held no appeal to her. Her head might say Anders was right, but no way was she going back to sleep.

She lay down. Counted backwards from a hundred. Made it to one. Counted sheep. Counted dead grass roots sticking out of the sod walls. Tried self-hypnosis. Nothing worked. She was wired far too tight to get any more rest. And that was worrisome. Something was wrong with her. She *never* had trouble sleeping. Even on operational missions with tension through the roof, when it was her turn to stand down and rest, she could go unconscious instantly and sleep hard, any time, any place. Not so now.

She tossed and turned for several hours. Eventually, Lakvik began to come to life as people finished sleeping off the effects of the party, or rather the booze that had flowed at the party.

She jumped out of her sleeping bag, relieved beyond words at finally getting to *move*. It was an exercise in sheer torture to wait while Anders and her teammates got up, got dressed, ate breakfast, brushed teeth and donned their gear in what looked like intentional slow motion. It was all she could do not to fling their rifles at them and scream for them to get moving. But finally, the Medusas stood in the middle of the village, surrounded by most of the Sami men of hunting age.

"Okay, here's the deal," Karen explained. "We need to find a Norwegian Army team of about six men who are hiding somewhere in this general vicinity, and we need to find them fast. You know the area and are superb hunters, and we're hoping that some or all of you might be willing to help us."

One of the Sami men spoke up. "This is big country. To find a small group of men who do not want to be found will be like searching for a single blade of grass in a meadow."

Karen let a sharklike grin slide across her face. "That's why I built us a gadget to help." She held up the backpack in which she'd carefully tucked the signal detector. "I've built a homing device that should pick up radio signals from these guys. It won't be exact, but it should lead us in the right direction and put us reasonably close to our targets."

The Samis smiled and nodded at that news, and the spokesman said, "Forgive me. I forgot for a moment with whom I spoke. Of course, you came up with a way to find your prey with ease."

Karen's eyes narrowed. She was about to just declare herself Freya and tell them all to bow to her and call her Your Majesty. It would be less frustrating than continually trying to fight their misconceptions of her. She ground out with scant patience, "I studied engineering in college. It's no big deal. I just wired up a gizmo that detects radio signals. Any first-year student could do it."

Vanessa muttered under her breath, "Give it up. You'll never change these guys' minds."

Karen glared at her boss. And then blinked in surprise. In the first place, Vanessa outranked her. Junior officers didn't throw mutinous glares at their superiors. Ever. It was blatantly unprofessional, particularly in front of outsiders to the team.

Second, she respected Vanessa. Loved her like a sister. The Medusas didn't fight among themselves. Their unity was perhaps their greatest strength. Vanessa stared back, clearly startled, herself.

"I'm sorry," Karen said quickly. "I don't know what's come over me. I've been really out of sorts the past day or two."

Vanessa nodded just a touch tersely. "I noticed. If there's anything you need to get off your chest, I'm always available to listen."

Karen nodded glumly, disgusted with herself. She was turning into such a bitch. She took a deep breath. "Let's turn on this machine and see if it works."

Isabella helped Karen carefully don the backpack without disturbing the jumble of wires. Then, Isabella connected the last wire to the battery. Cautiously, Karen held one earpiece up to her ear. It didn't electrocute her, and even better, she heard faint static. She walked down Lakvik's main street toward the east, and the static didn't change noticeably. She swung north out to the edge of the tent city. The change was miniscule, but perhaps the static got just the tiniest bit fainter. To test her theory, she turned around and headed to the south side of town.

All the while, the Sami men trailed along behind her in expectant silence. And as she strode around the village, she picked up more of an audience. By the time she reached the south end of the village and was sure the static had gotten slightly louder, she had an entire parade trailing along behind her. Children were being shushed in the back of the crowd. Women had stopped their chores and tagged along, and the Medusas brought up the rear of the whole thing, grinning at her over the heads of the shorter Sami people.

Great. She'd gone from Freya to Pied Piper. At least *he* got the satisfaction of killing all the rats who followed him out of towns. She gritted her teeth, seated the headphones more securely on her head and marched south out of Lakvik. They could all come for all she cared. She was going to go find Jack and put an end to this stupidity for good.

What the hell. If you can't stop 'em, run to the front of the parade and act like you're leading it. Whistling "Hi Ho, Hi Ho, It's Off To Work We Go," she marched jauntily out of town.

She stopped about ten minutes out of Lakvik and waved all the Samis behind her to silence. Fortunately, the women and children had mostly peeled off and headed back to town. The remaining Samis were experienced hunters. They knew how to be quiet. She listened to the static again. Yup, definitely louder than in town. She resumed walking south.

About an hour out of Lakvik, it became clear that a course correction was needed. She went through the same routine, walking a bit to the east, then back to the west, and the static definitely got louder when she headed east. East she went.

The good news was the vigorous exercise seemed to burn off the worst of her unreasoning fury.

It was midafternoon and the sun was starting to go down when the static in her ears changed slightly. It took on a pulsing quality.

Karen called out, "Hey, Adder. Come listen to this."

Karen held out the headphones to her teammate, who was the team's communications expert. Isabella listened intently for several seconds. "We must be getting close enough to pick up their actual jamming signal instead of just the background field."

"That's what I was thinking, too."

Vanessa piped up and asked, "Any guesses as to how far we are from our targets?"

Karen looked around. They were near the top of a high ridge facing east. "Well, they're probably sitting on top of a mountain. We definitely know they're in front of us, because the ridge line at our backs would block any direct signals from the west. I'd guess we're no more than three miles away."

The other Medusas groaned. In the three miles stretching away at their feet, there must've been at least twenty mountain peaks. Karen concurred. She didn't relish the idea of scaling every last one of them. Damn that Jack for putting such a difficult task in front of them! Who did he think he was, anyway? What kind of sadistic instructor tortured his students like this? The guy seriously needed taking down a peg or two. A brief, satisfying image flashed into her head of her hands around his throat, his face red-purple, his veins bulging, his eyes panicked. Aggression surged through her. Oh, yeah. They needed to find Jack. The sooner the better. Her palms itched to feel his throat.

"Hey, Python. Slow up there!" It was Vanessa.

Karen started and glanced over her shoulder. She was all but running on her snowshoes, and the only person keeping up with her was Anders. No surprise, there. He wasn't an Olympic cross-country skier for nothing. But everyone else was straggling well behind. She slowed down to a pace mere mortals might be able to keep up with.

At about eight o'clock, the Samis wanted to stop and make camp for the night. Wimps.

Karen had drawn breath to tell them to get a move on and quit whining when Vanessa intervened. "That's a great idea, gentlemen. Is there anywhere near here you'd suggest?"

Karen fumed inwardly. The bitch! This was *her* hunt for Jack, not Vanessa's. And *she* was the one the Samis had asked about stopping, not Vanessa. Her jaw set in fury, she declined an offer by her teammates to share an igloo with them. She'd build her own damn shelter, thank you very much. Adrenaline made hefting the heavy roof blocks into place a piece of cake. She was vaguely aware of the Samis sneaking awed peeks at her as she attacked the snow, but she didn't much care. So she was strong. Big freaking deal.

She endured sitting around the campfire, sharing supper with the Medusas and the Samis, but after a while, the whole kumbayah atmosphere was more than she could stand. Surly, she retired to her igloo to rest. She fiddled with the homing beacon a bit to narrow the signal bandwidth, then she lay down on her sleeping bag, too restless to sleep.

Her head said she needed some real zzz's, but her body disagreed. She was a bundle of nerves and twitchy muscles. She needed to move, dammit! Jack Scatalone was out there some- where, and her gut twisted with the need to cause him pain. To see blood fly. Oh, yes. It was time to move.

She waited until she thought everyone would be tucked in for the night, and then donned her Arctic camo gear and grabbed the signal tracker. She crawled out of her igloo and glanced around the camp. Igloos glowed here and there, low yellow humps in the landscape of moonlit blue-white. But the camp was still. No one moved about. Perfect.

She crept silently out of the site and into night, her killer in- stincts fully and gleefully aroused.

Oslo, Norway, March 6

Jens closed Astrid's bedroom door quietly. Thank God she was finally asleep. She'd lain there for hours, just staring up at the ceiling. It would've been so much easier to comfort her if she'd cried or screamed or had hysterics. Personally, he didn't give a shit if Willie was dead. But his baby girl's pain was doubly his pain.

As he tiptoed down the stairs, he pulled out his cell phone and speed dialed Ivo. "Hey, partner. I got a favor to ask you."

The kid sounded surprised. "Sure. What is it?"

"Will you take my daughter out?"

"*Excuse* me?"

Jens had to smile at the shock vibrating through Ivo's voice. "Astrid's pretty torn up about her boyfriend's murder."

"I don't think rebound dating is going to ease her pain, sir—"

"This isn't about her pain. Willie, the dead boyfriend, was passing her pills to take. She doesn't know what they were, and she's afraid—hell, *I'm* afraid—they were tainted. She says she met the guy Willie got his drugs from once. She thinks she might recognize the dealer if she saw him again."

Ivo swore quietly, then asked quickly, "What do you need me to do?"

"Take her out to some of the clubs Willie and she used to hang out at. See if she can spot his supplier. I'm not going to sleep decently until I've tracked down these pills and know she's going to be okay."

Jens sat in his usual armchair in the living room, pretending to read a newspaper while he eavesdropped. Ivo was actually doing a really good job of talking to Astrid. The kid had gotten her to open up a hell of a lot more than he had in the past twenty-four hours.

"…think you'd recognize him if you saw him again?" Ivo was asking.

"I think so. He looked Mediterranean. You know. Dark hair. Dark eyes. Tanned skin."

"Was he a big guy? Short? How was he built?"

The good news was Astrid had grown up a cop's daughter. Her powers both of observation and description were pretty good. She answered, "Medium height. Slender build. But the guys with him were big. Beefy."

"How many guys?" Ivo asked calmly.

Jens peeked over his paper at Astrid as she considered the question. Man, his partner was doing a great job of keeping her relaxed. Focused. He couldn't have—hadn't—done so well himself. All he'd managed to get out of Astrid were monosyllabic mumbles for answers and red-rimmed eyes that refused to shed their tears.

Ivo was talking again. "Do you think you could work with a sketch artist to come up with a composite of this guy?"

Astrid shrugged. "Maybe. It wouldn't be very detailed."

"Anything's better than nothing," Ivo replied placidly.

"You don't even know if this guy's the one passing the tainted drugs," she retorted.

Ivo shrugged. "Well, you said Nicklaus was getting his stuff from Willie. And Nicklaus obviously got a hold of some of the tainted drugs. It's not a bad guess that Willie's supplier was the source of the stuff. Once we catch the guy you saw, we'll catch the guy he got his drugs from, and the guy he got his drugs from, and so on, until we reach the source."

She released a wobbly breath.

Ivo reached out and took both her hands in his. Gazed deep into her eyes. Totally unprofessional. Said gently, "You're doing great, Astrid."

His daughter flashed a watery, grateful smile at Ivo. The first smile Jens had seen since he broke the news to her yesterday. He was surprised that his protective instincts didn't flare at the exchange. But if his partner could make her smile, Jens was all for it.

"Can you think of anything else that might help us find this guy?" Ivo murmured.

"He had a weird name. Started with a vowel." Astrid frowned, concentrating like something was dangling just out of her reach. Then, suddenly, her face lit up. "Izzy! That's it! I told you it was weird."

Ivo glanced over Jens' way. "I put a call in to the sketch artist before I came over here—just in case. He can see you tomorrow morning."

In that moment, Jens could've hugged Ivo. God, he was such a sap. But hey. Dads are allowed to look out for their daughters.

They were also allowed to find the bastards who fed their daughters tainted drugs and bury them. Very, very deep.

Southeast of Lakvik, March 7, 1:00 a.m.

By narrowing the signal bandwidth even more while she listened to it, she was able to home in fairly accurately on Jack's signal. In fact, she was able to narrow the transmitting site down to one of three mountain peaks. From there, it was simply a matter of choosing the tallest one to try first.

But what a mountain. It was steep, icy and criss-crossed by treacherous crevasses. It was insane to hike it alone. If she slipped and hurt herself or fell down one of the deep cracks in the ice, the odds of anybody finding her alive were absolutely zero.

And she didn't care one bit. Pin pricks of cold and exertion stabbed her eyeballs, and a throbbing ache started right in the center of her head and radiated outward. With every pounding pulse of agony, her fury at Jack Scatalone grew. Arrogant bastard. Tried to mold the Medusas in his image. Didn't care a bit if they were women and could use a break now and then. Never cut them an inch of slack. Parked himself on the highest goddamned mountain in Norway and dared them to come and get him.

Oh, she'd get him all right. He'd be on the lookout for a full frontal assault, or something equally spectacular from the

186 The Medusa Prophecy

Medusas. And why not? They'd learned about grandstanding from the master.

Jack wouldn't be looking for a lone hunter coming in swift and silent on wings of fury. And that was why she'd spill his blood all over the snow. God, it would be a thing of beauty. One foot after another, step after step, closer and closer to vengeance.

She knew from the signal tracker that Jack and the Norwegians had to be on this southern face of the mountain. So, she worked her way gradually around to the north to come in from the opposite side. It put her in the way of even more wind-carved crevasses and deadly drops, but the danger only served to fuel the raging glory running through her.

In the end, it was an easy matter to spot the two low mounds of snow in the lee of a tall rock face. The spot was reasonably protected from the winds howling up here. Karen worked her way down a fissure in the rock face until she was crouched in a deep shadow at its base. One of the mounds was small and round, in the Alaskan Inuit fashion. The other one was longer and much larger, more oblong in shape, along the lines of what Anders had taught her to build. It could hold six guys. A tight fit, maybe, but she'd found their camp.

Exultation roared through her and she nearly laughed aloud. This was going to be so easy. Jack might as well have put a neon sign over his shelter saying, "Jack Scatalone is sleeping here. Come and get me."

And that gave her pause. It was too damned easy. Jack knew better than to make a camp right out in the open like this. She took a closer look at the snow drifting across the two tunnel entrances leading to the shelters. Both openings had accumulated a small drift of snow with a tiny, perfect overhang of crystallized ice. They looked like waves exactly at the moment they break over, but frozen in place, never to crash down to the sea.

Those drifts were *too* perfect. No one had been in or out of those tunnels in a good twenty-four hours, if not more. The igloos in front of her were a trap!

Rage exploded across her brain like a fireworks display, great booming chrysanthemums of fiery red and blazing white. Jerk! Bastard! A roar of fury rose up in her chest, only barely cut off by the need to hunt. To find her prey. And to kill.

Jack had to be close. Her signal detector was pulsing strong and steady. She had to be all but on top of the damned transmitter. She lay down in the snow and began to move. By inches. Which was why she spotted the trip wire nearly buried in the snow as her eyeballs drew level with it.

She didn't have Aleesha's surgeon hands when it came to disarming traps. She'd better go around it. She glanced up. If she stood here in her white camo coat and pants, she'd show up against the black cliff as though a spotlight was on her. Better to go under it. She rolled ever so slowly onto her side, presenting her back to the camp. Her movements thus protected from prying eyes, she dug carefully with her hands, forming a shallow ditch beneath the wire. And then came the difficult limbo-dance maneuver to slide under the trip wire without touching it. No telling how sensitive a switch it was connected to.

The whole exercise took close to a half hour. And with each passing second, her impatience to get to the kill grew. She could almost taste blood on her tongue, and it was sweet and salty and satisfying.

It took another thirty yards of low crawling, which took another twenty minutes, to go around the fake camp. But eventually, she lay at the edge of a tall outcropping of rock, looking down the south face of the mountain. And spotted the second camp. This one was much better concealed, the shelters nearly flush with the snow and dotted unevenly across the mountain-side in between upthrusts of rock and shadow.

She nearly crawled into a couple of more trip wires, but both of these were so placed that she could rise to a crouch and ease over them without showing herself.

The signal detector was now clicking quickly in her ear. "You're getting hot," it seemed to whisper. "Hotter. Burning hot."

She lay in the snow, oblivious to its grasping cold as it greedily sucked the heat from her body. The fire within her replenished everything the snow took and more. She felt as if her coat was strangling her. She eased a hand up to unzip her parka a bit. Fingers of cold wind seeped down her body. Fire and ice collided in her and she reveled in the pain. *God, to feel so alive was breathtaking!*

Her eyes narrowed. Seven shelters. And one held her target. Using every bit of stealth Jack had ever taught her, she glided on her belly into the middle of the camp, like the python she was named for. Now, to figure out which one was his.

It took her two full circuits around the camp over the course of an hour to spot it. A footprint frozen into the snow just outside one of the tunnels. She hadn't grown up hunting with her father for nothing. She was an extremely skilled tracker and read signs with the best of them. The print was the right size and depth for a man of Jack's size.

Only person likely to have been in Jack's shelter was Jack. The hut was too small to accommodate more than one man without the occupants having to get uncomfortably close. And more to the point, the print was an American combat-boot tread pattern. She'd noticed before that when Anders took off his boots and turned them upside down to dry, the tread pattern on Norwegian boots was different than hers.

Bingo. *Houston, we have positive target acquisition.*

She didn't particularly care about being caught after she offed Jack. If he died noisily and the Norwegians came out to investigate, so be it. As long as she spilled his blood all over the snow first like she did that other guy's. Ever so carefully, she buried herself not far from the tunnel entrance to Jack's igloo. She left her eyes and nose above the snow, but that was all.

And now to wait.

Time lost all meaning for her. There was only the cold and the dark and the hunt. The wind blew, and a thin drift of snow accumulated on and around her. And the fire raged on inside her.

Sometime later, in the deepest still of the night, her predator's trance was interrupted by a movement. Someone was coming out of Jack's shelter. If she'd had a tail, its tip would have twitched. Adrenaline ripped through her, and every ounce of bloodlust within her surged forth. She was ready. Jack Scatalone was a dead man.

He rose up out of his tunnel, his foot landing in almost exactly the same spot as the previous footprint she'd found. He glanced at his watch and moved over to an antenna sticking up out of the snow. She'd found it earlier and had probed the snow to verify that the jamming device was, in fact buried in that spot. But that was no longer her target. She was hunting bigger prey, now.

Jack hunched down on his heels, his back turned to her.

Her fingers wrapped tightly around her knife, and she rose up slowly out of the snow, silent and lethal, a living specter of death. It was time.

Every muscle in her body uncoiled at once. She shot forward, too sudden and quick for her prey to escape.

Let fly the wings of fury! I am fate and my name is Death, Jack Scatalone.

Chapter 12

White House living quarters, March 6, 9:00 p.m.

Henry Stanforth propped his feet up on the coffee table in front of the sofa and picked up a file from the stack beside him.

"Don't put your feet up on the table, Henry," his wife reproved mildly. "After all, we don't own it."

"I took my shoes off. My socks won't hurt it."

It was a running argument with them. He insisted on actually living in the White House, and his wife labored under the notion that they'd been locked in a museum for four years and shouldn't touch anything the entire time they were here.

He had some catching up to do from earlier today. A talkative group of farmers lobbying for increased farm subsidies had taken too long in the Oval Office, and his schedule, usually planned down to the last, efficient minute, had been fouled up for the rest of the day. His secretary had been near cardiac arrest for most of the afternoon.

He'd barely had time to dive into a preliminary point paper on next year's budget when a quiet knock sounded on the hallway door. His wife went over to open it.

She smiled a greeting at the Secret Service agent and said dryly over her shoulder, "It's for you, dear."

Wasn't it always? "What can I do for you, John?" Stanforth asked.

"There's a phone call for you, sir. Prime Minister of Norway. Mr. Bjornsen says it's not an emergency, but if you have a moment, he'd appreciate a word with you."

"Transfer it up here, will you?"

"Yes, sir." The man backed out of the room and closed the door behind him.

He wished the Secret Service guys wouldn't wear those stupid white cotton gloves whenever they opened and closed doors. Who'd ever heard of living in a house where the doorknobs were such priceless collectibles you couldn't touch them? If he had his way, he'd take a hammer to every last Lalique-this and Steuben-that doorknob in the place.

The phone rang beside him and he picked it up.

"President Stanforth, thank you for taking my call at this late hour. I recall you saying you're a night owl and I took a chance that you might still be awake."

Stanforth laughed. "Our work is never done, is it? What can I do for you, Tryg?" After they'd spent an afternoon together last summer sailing in a magnificent Norwegian fjord, protocol allowed them to use first names in private like this.

"I'm afraid I have a rather strange question for you, Henry."

"I get lots of strange questions in my line of work."

Bjornsen replied, "I know the feeling. I received a letter a few hours ago. A set of demands, really. It came from a delegation of Sami people from Nordland. You might know them as Laplanders. And in case your Norwegian geography is a little dusty, the county of Nordland is up in the Arctic Circle. Northern tip of mainland Norway."

"I'm with you so far," Stanforth replied.

"The list of demands are predictable for a native people struggling to maintain a separate identity in the face of encroaching modernization and the defection of their youth to the cities."

"And your strange question?"

"Well, it's not the demands that have me puzzled. It's something else. The Sami people follow an old belief system. Polytheistic, nature-based stuff. A little bit of Viking mythology mixed in. And they believe in prophecies. Apparently, the fulfillment of one of their prophecies has led them to approach me now with their list."

Stanforth was lost. What the hell did any of this have to do with him? And why was it important enough to bother him at this hour of the night? It was 3:00 a.m. in Oslo.

The Prime Minister continued. "It seems this prophecy concerns the second coming of a Viking warrior goddess to their people. Freya, to be precise, if you happen to be up on your Norse mythology."

"And?"

"I got in touch with my military to find out who exactly this warrior goddess might be, who has suddenly appeared to the Sami people. My own officers refused to tell me a thing. All they would say is that I must contact you or a General Wittenauer to get the details."

And then it hit Stanforth. *The Medusas.* He burst out laughing. He wouldn't admit the Medusas existed to many world leaders, but Tryg Bjornsen had proven himself time and again to be a man of prudence and great personal honor, not to mention an unswerving ally of the United States through trying times. He'd keep a secret if asked to. Stanforth would bet his life on it. More to the point, he'd bet the Medusas' lives on it. "My girls have become goddesses, have they? What are they up to now?"

"Fomenting rebellion among my native peoples for one thing," Bjornsen answered a bit tartly. "Who are these women? My Special Forces wouldn't tell me a word about them. Just told me to call you."

Stanforth did his best to contain his mirth, but wasn't entirely successful at it. "Well, Tryg, a few months back, we tried an experiment. Trained ourselves an all-female Special Forces team. Turns out they're pretty darned good, and we made them permanent. But, for obvious security and political reasons, we're keeping them a deep, dark secret. Only a handful of people in the entire world know they exist. That's why your people wouldn't talk about them. We swore your Special Forces to complete secrecy before the Medusas were allowed to go to Norway to train with your people."

"Some training they're doing! I've got Samis parked on my steps all but demanding their own country because of your ladies."

"Ahh, Tryg, if it wasn't the Medusas, it would be something else. Your Samis would find another reason to make their demands sooner or later. Have you considered giving the Samis exclusive rights to run casinos in Norway? It's done wonders for the economic plight of the Native American population."

"Thanks for the suggestion," Bjornsen replied dryly, "but gambling's already legal over here."

"Too bad. So, what do you need me to do about the Medusas?"

"Perhaps have them back off of stirring the Sami people to rebellion?"

"I'll pass the message along. You'll be glad to know it's a very short chain of command from me to my snake ladies. Only two men. General Wittenauer and the ladies' direct supervisor, Colonel Jack Scatalone. I expect he's in Norway with them. Last briefing I got, the Medusas were heading for the Arctic Circle to do some winter-survival training."

"We've got plenty of winter up there for them."

"Tryg, I need to ask you for your complete discretion. Their existence is a very closely held secret. It's why they continue to be such an effective weapon for us. Nobody expects a team of women."

"Thank you for your candor, Henry. As always, you know you can trust me. The Medusa secret is safe."

South of Lakvik, Norway, March 7, 4:00 a.m.

The distance between her and Jack Scatalone melted in slow motion. Her hungry blade raised itself high over her shoulder, a serpent's fang, dripping death. She took aim at the back of his neck. The kill zone. The very kill zone he'd taught her how to strike.

Somewhere in the deepest recesses of her mind, a tiny voice forced itself through the red haze, one whispered, barely heard word at a time.

What.

Are.

You.

Doing?

He'd made her the warrior that she was. He'd pushed her to the breaking point and beyond. Had shown her she had no limits at all. Whatever she could imagine, she could achieve if she only worked hard enough and put her mind to it. He'd found her greatest weakness and torn back the layers of her psyche that protected her Achilles' heel—her embarrassment over her size and power. She'd fought against it ever since. Because of *him*.

And in this suspended moment out of time, this critical turning point of student destroying master, something unexpected happened. She was *glad* for her exceptional size, her muscular power. They were the very attributes allowing her to succeed now and kill the man who'd taught her how to harness both. Had it not been for Jack, she'd never have made her peace with either. But he'd forced her to face who she was. To embrace it. He'd given her the final tool that made her invincible.

The little voice pushed through the bloodlust again, a little louder this time. *Why are you killing him?*

A lightning bolt of clarity burst through.

She looked up at her fist, gripping her hungry knife. The blade was ravenous. Eager for the hot, iron taste of life flowing across steel. It urged her fist downward. *Plunge me into flesh. Feed me life's blood!*

She recoiled in horror. Stumbled to a stop. Her fist went slack, her fingers opening one by one. The blade tumbled from her numb fingers into the snow.

"Jack," she rasped.

He whirled around, leaping to his feet.

And then she had to get rid of it all. She pulled out her ankle knife and threw it in the snow. Stripped the MP-5 off her back. Even with rubber bullets, it still represented death. Pulled out the rubber-handled garrote. Absolutely everything she could imagine using as a weapon, she scrambled to get away from herself. Tears flowed freely. She was filthy. Tainted. The hunter had nearly gotten the best of her. *She'd become a monster.* A killer had put on her skin.

"Karen! Are you all right?" Jack asked urgently.

"Take it away. Get it off me," she sobbed, scrubbing at her skin now.

He stepped forward, his brow creased in alarm. "Talk to me. What's happened? Where are the others?"

Another voice came out of the darkness, startling Karen badly. She lurched around. *Anders.* "The Medusas are back at camp. They're safe."

"What the hell's going on here?" Jack demanded.

Karen fell to her knees in the snow, wrapping her arms around herself and rocking back and forth.

"Something's wrong with her. She's been getting more and more irritable the past few days. Has quit sleeping. Is prone to violent outbursts."

Anders' words floated over her head, sound without meaning. She'd almost killed Jack. What had happened to her? Something had snapped, and she'd become the embodiment of evil—death directed at a man she respected. She might not always like him, but he'd certainly done nothing to her that warranted killing him, other than make her long-held dream of being in the Special Forces come true. She owed him gratitude, not murder!

Anders continued somewhere in the distance. "She left camp by herself tonight. I followed her to keep an eye on her. It's incredibly dangerous to travel alone out here."

"No kidding," Jack growled.

"I wouldn't have let her kill you. I'd have shot her first."

Karen vaguely registered the rifle in Anders' hand as he stepped forward. It didn't matter. He could kill her flesh, but the monster would go on. It had no body, no form. It invaded minds and took them over, bending them to its twisted will.

"Kill me?" Jack repeated in shock.

"She had your back. Made a charge at you with her knife raised. She stopped at the last second before I pulled the trigger."

And then Jack was on his knees in front of her. She couldn't look at him. She'd almost killed him. "Talk to me, Karen," he said quietly. "What's happened?"

How was she supposed to tell him about the monster? About how it made a person hunger for blood, how it drove a soul over the edge into madness?

An arm came around her shoulders. Not Jack. Anders. Warmth registered. She must be cold, then. But she felt nothing. She was empty. Had the monster gone?

Anders spoke soberly. "We encountered some Samis the first day out. The Medusas asked if they'd seen any outsiders set up camp in the area. The Samis led us to what we thought would be you and my men. We attacked the cabin. Turned out to be a probable drug lab. We got into a shootout."

Jack frowned. "You're only carrying training rounds."

Anders grunted. "No shit. It was a close thing. Your women are remarkable."

"Go on."

"I was knocked out and Karen hauled me out of there. Saved my life."

"That sounds like the Karen I know."

"We moved the small, nearby Sami encampment to a larger village where they'd be safe from reprisals from the drug makers. Karen came across one of the drug gang's scouts. Killed him. Nice piece of work, actually. Neat. Silent. You taught her well."

Jack nodded at the compliment, and Anders continued. "Not long after that, she started acting funny. Twitchy. It was little things at first. Stuff that should've made her laugh irritated her. She started having trouble sleeping. Got more volatile. Stopped sleeping."

"You think making the kill messed her up?"

Karen felt Anders shake his head beside her. "She handled it just right. Wasn't thrilled to have had to do it, but wasn't bothered by it. I don't know what's done this to her."

"Is that all?" Jack asked.

Anders finished his quick debrief. "We need to call in the location of the drug lab and get a fully armed team to go out and deal with it, but the Samis' cell phones and radios aren't working. The Medusas figured out you're jamming all communications signals in the area. Karen built a nifty little signal tracker and used it to home in on your position. We were going to zero in on you and make a simulated assault tomorrow." He shrugged. "But instead, we have this."

Staring down numbly at the ground, Karen saw when Jack rocked back on his heels. Her brain felt like mush. She was missing something obvious. Something important.

"Let's get her warmed up."

Right. Like that was going to do any good. But she let them lead her over to Jack's igloo. Anders ended up crawling inside with her while Jack stayed outside, which was just as well. She couldn't imagine letting Jack put his arms around her, share his body heat with her. He belonged to Vanessa. And then there was that whole bit about having just come very close to killing him.

Anders wrapped the two of them, parkas and all, in a couple of Mylar blankets and spread Jack's sleeping bag over them. And then he hugged her close, murmuring, "I've got you now. You're safe. I won't let anything bad happen to you."

She wasn't the kind of person who let anything get the best of her. Ever. It was one of the hardest things she'd ever done in her entire life, but she mumbled, "Help me, Anders. I don't know what's happening to me."

His arms tightened around her. Strong. Safe. A shelter from the monster. "Don't worry. We'll figure it out."

"I can't go crazy. It'll ruin everything. The Medusa Project is too new. If a woman cracks up in the field, they'll shut down the whole project. Oh, God. What if I hurt one of my teammates?"

"You're not going to hurt anybody. And you're not going crazy. Maybe sleep-deprived. Overstressed. But the very fact that you can ask such questions tells me you're not crazy. Rest now, Karen. We'll sort this out together."

She subsided. The silence was deep and cold and complete. And for the moment, it quelled the source of her earlier, unreasoning rage. How long they lay together like that she had no idea. But Anders never wavered. He shared whatever warmth, whatever comfort, he had without reservation.

She might even have slept a little.

Some time later, she jerked to full consciousness when Jack appeared in the tunnel opening. His igloo was too small for him to come all the way inside with Anders and her already overfilling the space, but his head and shoulders fitted through. He propped himself up on his elbows to talk to them.

"I just had a very interesting conversation with your headquarters, Larson."

"Do tell," Anders said mildly, not letting go of her. Not shy about embracing her in front of Jack, was he? She couldn't say the same. She was acutely uncomfortable cuddling up with Anders in front of anyone. Her feelings where he was concerned were too new, too deep, to want to expose to others.

"I mentioned that one of my operators had gone through an episode of some kind but was doing better now. And the controller commented that it sounded like what was going on down in Oslo."

Karen closed her eyes as sudden understanding washed over her. Of course. Oslo. The drugs. Seizures followed by violent outbursts. She hadn't had any full-blown seizures, but she'd been twitchy as hell. Unable to sit still long enough to sleep.

"The barrels of powder," she muttered.

Anders nodded. "It has to be."

Karen turned to Jack. "We know where the drug is getting made that's making everyone go nuts in Oslo. It's the same stuff that's making me go nuts—I hope. When you tell the Norwegians about it, could you please give the Medusas the credit for finding the lab so we can stop romping with the reindeer trying to impress these guys?"

Jack laughed. "There's my old Karen back."

"You may have *your* Vanessa, but I'm not *your* Karen."

"Like hell. I trained every one of you women. You've all saved my life and I've saved yours. We're family whether you like it or not."

Karen subsided. *He considered her family?* Her misery over having nearly killed him deepened. Was the attack only a result of the drugs or was it something else? Schizophrenia? A multiple personality disorder, maybe? Except she could remember what the other Karen, the one in the grip of the monster, had thought and felt. She was that other Karen, too.

Jack asked casually, "Do you remember what was in your mind right before you attacked me?"

"I was just thinking about that. I remember it all. How I felt, what I did. I'm not going split personality on you. Crazy, maybe. Possessed, even. But there's only one of me."

Jack shook his head. "You're one of the most level-headed people I've ever met. I've seen guys crack in the field and this isn't it."

Anders chimed in, "Absolutely not. This came on too suddenly. And you showed none of the usual erratic behaviors of an operator losing the edge."

Whether or not they were being truthful or just saying that to make her feel better, she didn't really care. It was reassuring to have two such experienced Special Forces soldiers tell her she wasn't going nuts.

Jack asked, "Is Mamba close by or is she back in the village?"

"All the Medusas are a couple miles from here. We figured it would take the whole team to knock out both you and Anders' team."

"When it gets light, I want to find her. Have her take a look at you."

Karen nodded. "She treated a Sami kid last night who probably ingested the same stuff I did."

Anders commented, "I spoke to the boy's father earlier. He thinks his son has been doing drugs pretty steadily for the past several months. Maybe it takes building up a bunch of this stuff in your system to suffer the full effects."

Yeah, like death. Karen sighed. "I doubt Mamba will be able to tell anything without running tests in a hospital."

The men met that observation with silence. There wasn't much else they could do for now.

She became aware of a new emotion roiling deep in her gut. Not rage this time. Oh, no. This was Fear. Capital *F.*

Did she have it in her to pull back from the precipice a second time? It had been a really close thing to regain her senses before she did something tragic and irreversible. What if next time she didn't stop at the last second? What if Anders wasn't behind her with a rifle next time, ready to take her out?

What if she lost it again, and next time she *killed* someone?

Chapter 13

Oslo, Norway, March 7, 11:00 a.m.

The phone on his desk rang, and Jens set down his cup of coffee a little too hard. It splashed on the latest murder file, which lay open on his desk. Swearing, he brushed the coffee off the paper as he picked up the phone.

"Schumacher," he bit out.

"This is Marta Ogden down at the coroner's office."

He sat up straighter. She was the chemist in charge of analyzing all the tissue and fluid samples taken from all the people who'd gone ballistic in Oslo over the past week. "Do you have something for me?" he asked.

"We've made a positive ID on the unidentified chemical that's showing up in all your murder cases. As we first suspected, it's a variant of lysergic acid diethylamide. One of the ethylamides has been replaced with a methyl benzoate, and a carbon chain rearranged—"

She must have heard his brain glazing over through the phone line because she stopped abruptly. "I bet you want that in lay language, don't you?"

"That would be nice."

"Somebody has tweaked an LSD molecule and come up with a new compound that's never been recorded before."

"LSD? The hallucinogenic?"

"The very same."

"I'll be damned. Good work," he commented. "Okay. So we know what the marker molecule is. Who's making it? What kind of lab facilities would it take to make this stuff?"

"Didn't you hear what I just said?" the chemist retorted. "This stuff is a variant of LSD. It isn't a marker molecule at all. It's a drug in and of itself. As in potentially capable of causing psychotic episodes all on its own."

He frowned. "Yeah, but it's only showing up in miniscule quantities in our perps."

The chemist answered heavily, "I know."

Holy shit. Jens sat bolt upright in his chair and knocked the coffee cup completely over this time with the telephone cord. Fortunately, the hot liquid sailed off the side of his desk harmlessly to the floor. "Are you telling me that a few molecules of this stuff is enough to make people run around randomly attacking and killing before it kills them?"

"We don't know yet. We're running more tests. Problem is, I don't have isolated samples of this stuff that I can feed to lab mice to see what happens."

"Take a guess at what would happen."

"I'm a scientist. I don't guess."

"Indulge me. People are dying out there on the streets."

"LSD is what's known as a psychotomimetic drug. That's a fancy word for mimicking psychosis."

Jens interjected. "In other words, you take LSD, and it makes you temporarily crazy."

"Close enough. The thing is, these types of drugs affect everyone differently. Some people have good trips and some people have bad trips. Some people hear music and others go suicidal—or yes, homicidal. With me so far?"

"Yup."

"What I'm guessing—and it's purely a guess at this point— is someone has synthesized a variant of LSD, either by accident or on purpose, that consistently causes the subject to have a bad trip. A really bad trip. The kind where the subject becomes aggressive and violent."

"When someone takes LSD, how much of it shows up in blood and tissue samples after the fact? Does it dissipate quickly and only leave behind a trace?"

"Oh, no. LSD resides in certain cells, sometimes for years, after the subject takes a single dose."

"So if our marker molecule is some sort of LSD, why isn't more of it showing up in our perps?"

"You're asking me to guess again."

"Go ahead, Marta. Live dangerously."

She laughed at that.

"Okay, Jens. Here goes: I'd *guess* a small quantity of this stuff was cut into some other drug. Maybe it was an attempt to give users a particularly powerful drug experience— perhaps to encourage them to come back to the same supplier for more. Or, for that matter, it could've been a prank. Someone thinks they're getting a little coke—get a quick buzz and a boost of energy—but instead, they get a psychedelic trip. Joke's on them. Worst case guess, someone knows exactly what this stuff does and contaminated the drug supply with it intentionally."

"Talk to me about making this stuff."

"It would take a fairly basic laboratory. Nothing elaborate, but you couldn't do it in your garage. You'd need specific equipment. Given its chemical makeup, it would probably be a white powder. LSD melts at around eighty degrees Celsius, so if our variant acts the same, relatively low cooking temperatures—a normal household stove or even a Bunsen burner would be sufficient. LSD tends to be more stable at cooler temperatures, so I might expect there to be a refrigerator to store it in."

Jens snorted. "It's winter in Norway. All they'd have to do is set it outside."

"True."

"Anything else for me?"

"We're going to try to isolate enough of this stuff to inject it into a mouse and see what happens. Could take a while."

"Hurry, will you?"

"I'm working about twenty hours a day on this."

Geez. "Remind me to take you out to dinner after this is all over to say thanks."

A pause. Crap. Was that good surprise or bad surprise that made the phone go silent like that?

Finally she said in what sounded like a no-kidding fit of shyness, "I'll hold you to that, Jens."

Hot damn!

She continued, "In the meantime, look for a new wholesale supplier. Someone you haven't seen before. Might be passing through town—here to release this stuff and then leave before all hell breaks loose."

He retorted dryly, "Then he's long gone by now. Hell has

most certainly broken loose in Oslo." On that depressing note, he added, "Call me if you get anything else."

"I will."

Jens hung up the phone and stared at it thoughtfully for several seconds.

Ivo interrupted his train of thought. "Did I just hear you invite Marta Ogden out to dinner?"

Jens looked up, scowling. "What of it?"

"Jesus. It's a match made in Heaven. She's as bad a workaholic as you."

"She involved with anyone?" Jens asked casually.

"Not to my knowledge. Good-looking lady, too."

And to stop that glint in his partner's eye from becoming a series of embarrassing questions or comments, he said quickly, "Marta says to look for a new drug supplier in town. Someone looking to release this stuff and then move on."

"Like the elusive Izzy?" Ivo replied.

"Exactly." Jens reached for the phone to call Yurgen in Tromsö. If it took cold conditions to store the drugs, northern Norway was the place for that.

Lakvik, Norway, March 8, 2:00 p.m.

A burst of light accompanied the opening and closing of her hut door. She blinked awake as a dark shape loomed over her.

"How's she doing?" someone murmured. Aleesha.

"Starting to come around." That was Anders. "When you said you were going to knock her on her butt, you weren't kidding. She's been out for twelve hours."

"She needed the rest."

Karen mumbled, "You don't have to talk about me like I'm not here." She squinted into the shadows. There was Anders, sitting on the far side of the fire, watching over her as he had been doing around the clock for the past two days. All through the return trek, first to rejoin the Medusas and their Sami escorts, and then back to Lakvik, he'd never left her side.

As she'd predicted, Aleesha couldn't tell much about the condition of Karen's blood or brain without further tests. She had, however, given Karen a shot when they'd got back to Lakvik last night and knocked her out cold to get some much-needed sleep.

"What time is it?" Karen asked Anders.

"Two o'clock in the afternoon."

Wow. She *had* slept like the dead.

"How're you feeling?" Aleesha asked.

Karen frowned. "Physically, like I've been worked over with a baseball bat. Mentally, exhausted. Emotionally—" She thought about that one for a moment. "Irritable. That underlying anger I told you about is still there."

Aleesha's expression was sober. "I'd sure as hell like to know what was in that powder you went swimming in at the cabin. At least you didn't ingest much of it. All I can tell you right now is to keep talking. Communicate your frame of mind to Anders or whatever Medusa is with you. Okay? No matter how much it pisses you off. We need the feedback so we can help you."

"Yeah, so I don't murder one of you," Karen replied wryly.

Aleesha laughed easily. "Well, there is that."

The door opened again. Great. Her and Anders' hut was turning into Grand Central Station. This time Vanessa blew in on a gust of wind and sunlight.

"Phone call for you, Oberstløytnant."

He put the device to his ear, listened for a moment, and replied in rapid Norwegian.

Karen murmured to Vanessa while Anders engaged in what sounded like a bit of an argument, "How's Jack doing?"

"Fine. Why?"

"He's not too mad at me, is he?"

"Heavens no. He knows you'd never try to kill him if there weren't something seriously wrong with you." Vanessa added lightly, "If anything, he's impressed you got that close to him. He admitted to me that if you hadn't stopped on your own, you'd have had him."

Karen glanced over in Anders' direction as he disconnected the call. Apparently, he hadn't told the Medusas that he'd had a rifle trained on her back and had been on the verge of shooting her. Jack would never have died. She would have, instead.

"Vanessa, there's something you should know—" she started.

Anders interrupted. "That's right. There is something. My headquarters has denied your request to blow up the drug lab. That was my boss's boss, and he insists that we need positive proof of what's going on in that cabin before they'll send out a sortie to blow it up."

Aleesha replied, "As soon as that powder's identified, they'll have their proof. How's that coming along, anyway?"

He shrugged. "They're working on the sample you sent them. Still no identification. They've sent some of the powder down to Oslo for analysis."

"Keep me informed. I want to know the second your people get an ID on that stuff."

Anders nodded. "That's what I told them. They promised to call."

Karen sighed. "So, I'm a ticking time bomb, and we still don't know what's setting me off."

Anders chuckled. "Go ahead. Blow up. You can't take me."

Karen scowled at him. "I took you once. I can do it again."

"Hah. I bet you twenty krone you can't."

She planted her hands on her hips. "You're on. If I try to kill you and I fail, I owe you twenty krone. If I succeed, I'm taking it out of your wallet."

He laughed. "Deal."

Karen couldn't help but laugh back.

Aleesha put a hand on her shoulder. "Keep laughing, sister. That may be the best medicine of all for what ails you."

Aw geez. Now she was going to cry. After what she'd nearly done, the support of her teammates was a gift she hadn't expected, let alone their understanding and forgiveness.

Aleesha and Vanessa, likely sensing her need to be alone and collect herself, ducked out of the hut. But Anders, being a man, showed no such finely honed sensitivity and prodded the tender spot. "How are you feeling?" he asked.

She sighed. "I'm not generally one of those women who spends my life wearing my heart on my sleeve. It's not my style to run around announcing what particular emotion I'm experiencing at any given moment."

He replied quietly. "I'm sorry to have to pry into your privacy like this. For what it's worth, anything you say is safe with me."

"Thanks." A pause. "And thanks for not telling the others about how you nearly had to kill me. Why didn't you, by the way?"

He shrugged. "It seemed like something personal. Between the two of us. You'd have cared enough for me to do the same. You wouldn't have let me live with killing a comrade in cold blood on my conscience."

She studied him for a long time. She had to think about that one. Would she have killed him? Because she *cared* for him? She grasped what he was getting at, but it was a strange way of looking at it. He would have killed her precisely because he cared for her enough not to let her descend into the hell of having killed Jack.

Quietly, she said, "Honestly, I'm an emotional wreck right

now. I'm experiencing everything too strongly. I'm too guilty and too grateful and too teary-eyed."

"In other words, you're feeling hormonal."

She laughed. "Norwegian women get that way, too, huh?"

He grinned. "I don't have much time for women, but in my experience, yes, they do."

Karen scoffed. "A good-looking guy like you? An Olympic skier? Surely you're a big celebrity in Norway. Women must flock to you."

He shrugged. "I don't pay much attention to them. They don't understand who I am or what I do."

"Aren't the two one and the same? A special operator is who you are, and it's what you do."

He smiled. "See? You get it. But most women don't."

She wasn't most women. She was a killer. One who'd come a hair from losing the edge.

"Quit beating yourself up."

She glanced up at Anders. "I beg your pardon?"

"I know that look. You're feeling bad about what almost happened. But, it didn't happen. You pulled back from the abyss and stopped yourself. I can't imagine the strength of will that took. Jack doesn't blame you and I don't blame you and your teammates don't blame you. So stop blaming yourself."

"Easier said than done."

"Understood. But try." He added, "For me?"

One corner of her mouth quirked up ruefully. "How can I say no to that?"

"You can't. I'm a big celebrity who's irresistible to women, remember?"

She snorted. "Yeah. And modest, too."

"How about a bite to eat and then a little exercise?"

"Doctor's orders?" she asked.

He nodded. "Mamba thinks it may help even out the chemicals in your body."

"What did you have in mind?"

His eyes twinkled. "Have you ever cross-country skied?"

"No. I hear it's grueling. Uses every muscle in the body and hurts like hell."

"That's what I hear, too."

She laughed at that one. "You're going to kick my butt, aren't you?"

"'Fraid so. I'm going to ski you into the ground, and I'll just be getting warmed up."

Still laughing, she said, "Let's go, medal boy. Let's see what you're made of."

Lakvik, Norway, March 9, 3:00 a.m.

Karen jerked awake. It was cold and still and dark. The fire was nothing more than a few glowing embers. But heat rolled up and out of her gut. The inferno was back. Why in the hell did they think something was wrong with her anyway? She was in complete control. She owned the power, knew how to ride the wave. They were just jealous. They didn't know how to harness the rage—

"Anders," she ground out between clenched teeth.

He sat up immediately. Smart boy. He'd slept fully dressed.

"It's back."

He didn't have to ask what "it" was. "Fight it, Karen. Stay with me." He moved around the fire pit to kneel in front of her.

"I need to hit something."

Anders picked up his sleeping bag. Wrapped it around his right hand and forearm. "Have at it."

Karen stared. "Really?" The rage leapt and whirled in delight.

He gave her a challenging look. *Challenging?* Did he have no idea what he was *doing,* provoking her like that? She hauled off and slugged his hand. Her fist plowed through the layers of padding and found bone with a satisfying thud. She felt no pain.

He snorted. "You hit like a girl."

The rage flared, white-hot. *Arrogant jerk!* She hauled off and slugged the light-gray mass of fabric and down feathers again.

"Harder."

She glared. They didn't call her She-man for nothing! She pounded on the sleeping bag again. And again. She pummeled it with both fists like a punching bag. God, that felt good. The crunch of bone on yielding tissue, the impact up her arms. Faceless and nameless, that blob took on a life of its own, and she was going to kill it dead. She attacked it until sweat rolled freely down her face.

Finally, she drew back panting. Man, it felt good to have that out of her system. The beast was not finished, but it was appeased for the moment. Silent, Anders handed her a towel. She mopped off her face. He passed her a bottle of water. She slugged down the whole thing. He sat down beside the fire and she followed suit.

She broke the silence first. "Are you sure you want to sit this close to me? I could hurt you, you know. You'd never see it coming. I'd lunge, and then I'd have you by the throat—" she broke off. "I can picture the blood that would spray all over them. It's so beautiful—"

Strong hands gripped her shoulders. "Look at me!" The voice was sharp. Commanding.

She glared up at him, fighting the fury with all her might. She reached desperately for her sense of humor. "Don't tell me what to do! I killed that sleeping bag with my bare hands, after all. Didn't you know I'm a goddess?"

He chuckled. "Sorry. I didn't get that memo. Tell me your name."

"Karen. Karen Turner."

"Where are you from?"

"Who cares?" she shot back, losing the hold on her humor. She fought to regain it.

"Tell me about the farm you grew up on. How many pigs did your father have?"

Startled, she spat out the answer.

"What did your bedroom look like?"

She described the cast-iron bed, the pink-and-white gingham-check curtains and lace bedspread she'd secretly loved, the picture of her mother over her bed, looking down on her like an angel from Heaven. And the rage began to waver.

"Tell me about going fishing with your father. Where was your favorite fishing hole?"

Her father loved her deeply. Didn't know what to do with a girl, so he did what he knew how to do with her anyway. He taught her to fly fish. To tie lures.

"Tell me about your favorite lure," Anders prompted.

"No."

"Do it." His words lashed at her. Flayed back every defense she erected against him. Invaded her mind and dragged out memories she didn't want to think about by main force.

She answered that question. And the next, and the next. His words broke down every wall she tried to build to keep him out of her mind. Inch by inch, her rage gave way before the onslaught.

How long he made her talk about all the humble, mundane, everyday details of growing up, she didn't know. Long enough so her throat felt raw and dry. A couple of hours, maybe. Anders' interrogation left no detail of her life alone. The thought made her squirm in shame. But there was no help for it. He demanded answers, and she clung to the sanity his questions pulled from her.

And somewhere in there, the worst of the madness loosed its chokehold on her mind. The rage receded, taking with it the strange sense of invincibility. Arrogance was a foreign state of mind to her, and it left a sour taste in her mouth.

Finally, her shoulders slumped. Sudden exhaustion swept over her. She stared down at her hands, red from where she'd clenched them desperately to keep from wrapping them around Anders' throat. Fingers touched her cheek lightly, and she jerked away, startled. Looked up. Anders was studying her intently. After a moment, his mouth curved up in a gentle smile. "Welcome back."

"How do you know it's me?"

"The real Karen is looking back at me now. You have such beautiful eyes."

She had no defenses left against him. Not after what they'd just been through. She said aloud exactly what was in her heart, with no will to stop the words from coming. "So do you. Everything about you is beautiful."

"I can't say that's something I've been called much, but thank you."

"Handsome, then. Attractive. Movie-star gorgeous."

He shrugged as though she'd embarrassed him. He looked away, then seemed to force his gaze back to her. "I'm sorry for what I just put you through."

"Why are you apologizing? I'm the one who just spilled her entire life story on you. You know what they say. Familiarity breeds contempt."

He frowned. "I admire your family. They gave you wholesome values. Taught you to stand up for yourself but still think of others. They pulled together through good and bad times. I wish my own family had been so close."

Karen smiled. "You realize that it's only fair you tell me all the deep dark secrets of your childhood now."

"All in good time. For now, do you feel like you could get some sleep?"

"I don't know. I suppose so."

He stood up with that easy, athlete's power of his and went around the fire. He laid out his mangled sleeping bag on his air mattress and dragged both around to her side of the fire.

Alarm coursed through her. "What are you doing?"

"A little enlightened self-protection. I need to get some sleep, but I want to feel if you move." And then he grinned. "That's my story and I'm sticking to it. This has nothing to do with any desire to hold you in my arms."

"Hold me in your—" Karen spluttered.

He plopped his bed gear down beside hers and stretched out next to her, his arms opened invitingly. "Come. Join me. We'll share body heat and get some rest."

He had to be kidding.

"After all," he added, "you did kill my sleeping bag."

"Did I really?" She sat up to look at the fluffy nylon and down mass. It looked okay to her.

"It's fine. I'm just making excuses to get you to sleep with me. Please?"

Stunned, she scooted over beside him and lay down with her back to him. He wrapped his arms around her, and she lay there as stiff as a board. What in the hell was she supposed to do now?

Almost as if he'd picked the thought out of her brain, he murmured, "Relax. I won't bite."

Easy for him to say! She lay there for several agonizing minutes. She'd give anything to be able to roll over and wrap her arms around him, to bury her face in his shoulder, to tell him how grateful she was that he was there and she wasn't alone.

His voice came out of the darkness. "I suppose now's not the best time to tell you I've been attracted to you ever since I first saw you."

Yeah, right, she thought skeptically. "You mean when I was lying on top of you holding a knife to your neck?"

His chest vibrated with a chuckle against her back. "Yup. I was a goner. How could I resist a woman who could do that?"

Her thoughts locked up, frozen solid. Anders was attracted to her?

She half rolled in his arms to stare up at him. "Are you serious, or are you just saying that to make me feel better about all the stuff you ripped out of me with your merciless interrogation methods?"

He propped himself up on an elbow and grinned down at her. "That's me. The cruel, sadistic Norwegian."

The very idea of steady, solid Anders actually being sadistic made her laugh. "Yup, you Norwegians are hard-core."

His face was all shadows and dark planes. "I am serious about being attracted to you. I wouldn't joke about something like that."

Well, okay, then. She frowned up at him. "I really want to believe you. But…"

"Who put it in your head that you're not attractive or feminine or lovable?"

"It's little comments I've gotten here and there. Getting dumped over and over for petite, fragile girls. Heck, even Jack takes his potshots at me. Did you know he calls me She-man?"

Anders' eyes narrowed to irritated slits of blackness. "I should have let you kill him."

"No, no. You did the right thing." Then she added reflectively, "The knife was too fast a way to go. Next time, let me strangle him. Slowly."

He chuckled. "You've got yourself a deal. Maybe that's why you fixated on him in the first place. Because he called you names."

"But, I'm a Special Forces soldier, for God's sake. I have a tougher hide than that. So what if he calls me names?"

Anders shrugged. "There's the job, and then there's the personal stuff. Sometimes it's hard to separate the two when so much of your life revolves around your work. I know I'm not very good at it. Otherwise I'd be enjoying more of those groupies you seem to think hang out around me all the time."

She tilted her head to study him. "To be honest, you don't strike me as a womanizer. You seem more like the kind to find one woman and be loyal to her forever."

He nodded slowly. "You're right. And I happen to have found one."

Karen shook her head. "But I'm a nutcase."

"No, you're not," he retorted forcefully.

She sighed. "Face it, Anders. Any way you slice it, I'm a menace. You're taking your life in your hands to be around me."

"I'm still here, aren't I?"

Chapter 14

Lakvik, Norway, March 9, 7:00 a.m.

And he was still there when she woke up. Sometime in the night fatigue had finally overcome her wonder and she'd drifted off to sleep. The two of them had cuddled together through the night—out of no need whatsoever to share warmth. It had been more than nice. It had been pure bliss. It was amazing to let down her physical guard to go along with the emotional guard she'd lost to him. For the first time, she felt really comfortable with him.

Maybe some of it was the fact that by sleeping with him, she got a true sense of him being bigger and stronger than her. Maybe some of it was the fact that he'd volunteered to be there with her. Or maybe it was his mostly unconscious—but very real—sigh of contentment when she rolled over in the wee hours and succumbed to the urge to wrap her arms around him and find the crook of his shoulder with her cheek. Heck, maybe it was all of the above.

With the sounds of the village beginning to stir outside came a knock on their door that pulled her the rest of the way to full consciousness. Karen sat up guiltily, but Anders showed no such trepidation about someone finding them wrapped in each other's arms. He remained lying down, spooned around her.

"Come in," he called.

She threw an exasperated look down at him, but he smiled back with that bland smugness only a guy or a cat can summon at the most inconvenient possible moment.

Vanessa ducked inside. And froze in place where she stood. *Please God, let that be her eyes adjusting to the dark and not shock over finding us all snuggled up like this.*

All Vanessa said was, "Phone for you, Anders."

He sat up and took the cell phone. At least he was fully dressed. Karen hated to think what Vanessa would've thought if he'd been shirtless when he sat up. Karen stood up and moved away from him, too uncomfortable snuggling with some guy in front of her boss to stay beside him any longer.

"Larson here." He listened for a long time. Frowned. Glanced over at Karen as if he was startled and frowned some more. And then he said the last thing Karen expected to hear. "Roger, I copy. We are green-lighted for the operation."

He disconnected the call, and she and Vanessa said in unison, "What operation?"

"Looks like we've got a job to do, ladies."

"Another training mission?" Karen asked, frowning.

"No. The real deal. Let's get the team together and I'll brief all of you."

Vanessa nodded briskly. "I'll be back in five with everyone."

Anders stood up quickly and began stripping off layers of clothes. Karen blinked, startled. "Any particular reason you're getting naked?"

He looked up from where he was rummaging in his pack. And grinned. Wolfishly. "Why? Wanna go for a quickie before they all get here?"

Her eyes narrowed. "Don't mock me. I'm a homicidal maniac."

He laughed, completely unconcerned, as he came up with a clean shirt. "I need a dry shirt. I'm afraid spending the night so close to you made me sweat." He added, "And not in fear, I might add."

She stepped behind the curtain that hid the chamber pot to don new clothes herself and called out, "I kicked your butt once, smart aleck. I can do it again."

"That twenty-krone bet is still on," he called back. "Any time, Turner."

She'd just stepped around the curtain when the door opened and Misty, Kat and Aleesha stepped in.

"How's my patient this morning?" Aleesha asked, coming over to Karen to check her vital signs.

Karen shrugged. "I had a rough night."

Anders added, "But we got through it. The exercise yesterday seemed to make things worse, not better, though. And I have some new information for you, Doctor."

The door opened again, and Isabella, Vanessa and Jack walked in. The gang was all here. And the atmosphere in the hut was electric. But then, it was always like that before a mission brief. As soon as they knew what they had to do, everyone would calm down and get to business. But until then, you could cut the adrenaline with a knife.

Aleesha looked up from where she was unwrapping the cuff from around Karen's arm. "You blood pressure's reasonable under the circumstances," she murmured to Karen. To Anders she said, "Well, laddie, don' keep me hangin'. What's de word up?"

"My headquarters said to tell you the Oslo Police have identified the powder from those barrels. It's made up of an engineered molecule similar to LSD."

Into the heavy silence that greeted that announcement, Karen said, "Gee. That explains a lot. I'm tripping on LSD."

Meanwhile Aleesha was nodding. "Of course. LSD resides in fat. That's why exercising hard made you worse last night. You burned some fat cells that released more of the drug. What quantity of this stuff are people ingesting to induce these episodes, and how long does it take to clear their systems?"

"Ops didn't say. But if you call them, they can probably patch you through to someone who knows."

Karen blinked. This was a side of Anders she hadn't seen so far—the brisk, no-nonsense team leader. And it was sexy as hell. Especially when combined with the intimate, gentle side of him she'd seen last night.

Anders continued, "Given the contents of those barrels, my superiors feel comfortable authorizing the destruction of the drug lab and the apprehension of all persons associated with it. But the storm everyone's been forecasting is finally moving in. Everything from Bodo to Tromsö is already socked in and we should get hit by tonight. The army can't send up anything airborne to knock out the lab for a couple of days."

A general groan went up.

"Here's the kicker," he said grimly. "Satellite imagery shows heavy activity at the lab. Seems they're moving barrels away from the lab on snowmobiles at a steady and continuous rate. They're ferrying the barrels to a small cargo vessel moored off the coast. The Norwegian Coast Guard is steaming in that direction, but they're being hampered by heavy seas. It may be another couple of days before they can reach the ship."

"Any estimate from your headquarters on how long it'll take the bad guys to finish moving out the barrels?" Vanessa asked.

"Less time than it'll take the storm to pass and the airport to open back up."

"In other words," Karen interjected, "we get to go in on foot and eliminate the problem."

Anders nodded. "That's the idea."

"Any chance we can get your people to drop off some weapons and ammo for us before we have to do this?" Vanessa asked.

"Nope. Everything the army has is already grounded. It's pretty common in the winter. A combination of ice and fog shuts down everything even before the main storm arrives. We're stuck with what we've got." There was a brief pause while everyone absorbed the implications of that.

Karen shrugged. "The good news is we're in a substantial village. We ought to be able to improvise with what's on hand around town."

Misty added wryly, "Terrorists do it all the time. We can, too."

The next hour was spent getting Jack up to speed on the layout of the drug lab and brainstorming different methods to take it out with the supplies they had at hand. And then it was time to act.

As the Medusas stood up to scatter to their various tasks, Karen asked quietly, "What should I do?"

They all looked at her. Oh. Yeah. The psychopath. What could she be trusted to do? They'd already removed everything she could conceivably use as a weapon from her hut.

Anders said readily, "Come with me. I could use some help cooking up the ammonium nitrate."

They'd settled on making an improvised diesel fuel and fertilizer bomb, and the first step was to wet down and shape the ammonium nitrate fertilizer into cakes. She looked at him uncertainly. "Are you sure?"

He shrugged. "Yeah. It's not like you can fertilize me to death."

She grinned. "It's your neck on the line."

He looked her square in the eye and said candidly, "I'd feel better if you're where I can keep an eye on you. Besides," he added lightly, "I enjoy your company."

The other Medusas looked away hastily, but not before she saw Jack's eyebrows shoot straight up to his hairline. Crap. New fodder for him to harass her about. Mirth twinkled in his eyes as Jack turned back to her. He opened his mouth to speak, but she cut him off before he could utter a word.

"Don't get started with me, Jack. I already tried to kill you once. Don't make me do it again. Besides, who are you to talk?" She gave a significant glance in Vanessa's direction. To Karen's immense gratification, both Jack and Vanessa colored up. Uh-huh. That's what she thought. They'd gotten their own hut last night and hadn't been talking business.

The Medusas chuckled as a group and Jack subsided with a bow of the head. "Touché, Python. I shall hereby shut the fuck up."

"Thank you," she said loftily. "C'mon, Anders. Let's go make us a bomb."

Oslo, Norway, March 9, 4:00 p.m.

Jens stared down at two more fresh murder files. He rubbed a hand down his exhausted, whisker-stubbled face. He didn't go much for all that the-world-is-coming-to-an-end stuff, but be damned if he wasn't starting to believe he'd lived to see the end of days. His phone rang, startling him badly. Damn, he had to get some sleep soon.

"Schumacher," he said irritably.

"Are you always this grouchy when you answer your phone?" a female voice asked pleasantly.

"Marta. I'm sorry. Long day. What do you have for me?"

"You'll never guess what just came in to the lab."

"A four-headed gargoyle wearing a yellow polka-dot bikini?"

She laughed that wonderful laugh of hers again. "Close. But no. A package from Tromsö."

"Okay. And what's so exciting about that?"

"It's an entire bag of our LSD variant."

Jens' chair rocked forward with a thump. "A *bag* of it? Pure? Where the hell'd somebody get that much of it?"

"They can't tell me. It's some big military secret. But now we can test it on some mice and get an exact idea of how this stuff works. Maybe figure out how to counteract it."

"That's great news. Lemme give the folks in Tromsö a try and see if I can get any more information for you."

It took him an hour of fast talking and flat-out bullying to finally work his way far enough up the military chain of command to reach someone who seemed to have the authority to give him actual answers to his questions.

But finally, he was told to stand by one more time while his call was patched through to someone else. Sheesh. What a headache this military red tape was!

And then the officer he'd been talking to said tersely in English, "Go ahead, Python. This is Detective Schumacher from the Oslo Police."

Jens started as a female voice replied in American-accented English, "I have you loud and clear. Go ahead."

"You're a woman!" he exclaimed.

"Thanks for clearing that up for me," the voice replied dryly. "I wasn't sure."

Laughter burst out of him before he could bite it back. "Sorry. No offense meant."

"None taken. What can I do for you, Detective?"

"Who am I speaking to?"

The American woman ignored the question. "Headquarters thinks I might be able to answer some of your questions. I understand you're having an outburst of violence in Oslo that you think might be drug-related."

"That's correct. We're looking for the dealers who are passing this stuff. Do you have any idea who the suppliers might be?"

The woman's reply startled him. "HQ. Are you still up?"

A male voice—sounded like the last guy who'd patched Jens through to this woman—answered, "Affirmative, Python."

"Am I cleared to respond?"

Jens frowned. *Who in the hell were these people?* "We've got folks dying down here. We need whatever you've got."

A pause. And then the male voice said, "You are cleared to answer, Python, but are prohibited from revealing any exact locations."

"Copy." That was the anonymous woman again. "Sorry about that, Detective. Had to make sure I had permission to speak."

So. She was military. A woman out on exercises with the Special Forces? Interesting.

She continued, "We have located a laboratory that appears to be producing a dangerous chemical substance. We believe it may be the same substance that's causing the problems in Oslo."

"Are you responsible for the bag of powder our chemists received earlier today?"

"Affirmative."

"That is, indeed, the same drug we've been spotting in the blood toxicology workups of our perpetrators down here. What can you tell me about the guys making the stuff?"

The woman replied, "Approximately twelve men. Working in shifts around the clock to make and transport the substance to a small cargo vessel. All dark-haired, olive-skinned. Ages range from early twenties to late thirties. Generally medium heights, slender builds. Minimal paramilitary training. Reasonably disciplined. Well-armed. Unfamiliar with Arctic operations. I do not have photo intelligence on them at this time."

This chick sounded like a Special Forces operator herself! He asked, "What's your best guess as to their nationality?"

No hesitation. "Middle Eastern, sir."

"Are we looking at a terrorist cell?"

"That is our working assumption."

Jens frowned. "How much of the chemical are they making?"

"Our current estimate of their stockpile is four hundred kilos of the powder. Blowing snow is impeding satellite imagery, however, so that number may be somewhat low."

Jens lurched. "Four hundred *kilos?* Do you realize that miniscule dosages of this stuff are enough to send people around the bend? We're talking twenty micrograms or less!"

Grim silence met his outburst.

"Are you still there?" Jens asked.

"Yes." The woman sounded tense. "Can you tell me exactly how much of this chemical must be ingested to cause death?"

"Our chemists don't know yet. They think some of that may have to do with how it's ingested. They think swallowing it or injecting it would deliver it most effectively to the blood stream."

"What about breathing it?" the woman blurted.

"Now that our chemists have a large sample of it, they should be able to tell more soon. But my understanding is that it needs to reach the bloodstream directly. I should think inhaling it wouldn't be nearly as effective."

"Thank God," the woman muttered.

"Anything else you can tell me about who's selling this stuff?" Jens asked.

"Given the amounts of the drug we're seeing in production, our guess is that Oslo is only the tip of the iceberg when it comes to the target of this terrorist cell."

Jens absorbed that one for a moment. "Do you think it might be prudent to put all the police in Norway on alert?"

"I think it might be prudent to put all the police in Europe on alert."

Jens swallowed hard at that one. "Any chance you can take these guys out and their drugs with them before they turn this stuff loose on Europe?"

"We're working on it, Detective."

"Thanks for the help, ma'am."

"No problem." A short pause and then, "Could you do me a favor?"

"Sure," he replied.

"Call me when your chemists figure out how much of this stuff will kill a person."

"I will."

Jens hung up the phone. Young Middle Eastern men. A possible terrorist cell. Hundreds of kilos of this stuff being released all over Europe?

To nobody in particular, he breathed, "Holy shit."

Lakvik, Norway, March 9, 8:00 p.m.

The Samis threw the Medusas a traditional feast that evening. As Karen understood it, the party was a send-off to wish the hunters good luck and a safe return. It was sweet of the Samis really. Especially with a big storm moving in.

At least she'd gotten fairly good at ignoring the Samis continual bowing and scraping in her direction. If they wanted to believe she was a goddess, who was she to stop them?

But she could've done without the chanted *loiks* and that godawful rotgut. Jack, Anders and the Medusas all declined the liquor since they were heading out later. But the locals indulged freely, and the drunken smell of it on their clothes and breath was enough to make Karen faintly ill.

What she wouldn't give for a hamburger and fries right about now. She was roundly sick of reindeer this and reindeer that. Didn't these people ever get tired of the same old diet day in and day out? The reasonable side of her brain said they were probably grateful to have food at all. But the other part was still disgusted.

She leaned over and murmured to Anders, "I'm getting a tad bit pissy, here. Perhaps it's time for me to make a graceful exit."

He murmured back, "If it makes you feel better, I'm a little pissy myself. Let's get out of here."

He said something in Sami that made the natives all roar with laughter, then he helped her to her feet. As he led her away from the fire into the darkness, she said accusingly, "You told them you're taking me out behind a hut to have your way with me again, didn't you?"

He laughed. "What if I did?"

"You rat!" she exclaimed. "What happened to the whole, 'you shouldn't lie to the natives' bit?"

"You're absolutely right. We'd better correct that lapse on my part." His arms swept around her and he did, indeed, pull her into the deep shadow behind a hut. His mouth closed on hers, and she couldn't have spoken, even if they weren't kissing.

He came up for air and she gasped, "Where did you learn how to do that so well?"

He laughed quietly. "Do you want me to stop doing it and answer that question?"

"Heck, no." She threw a hand behind his head and pulled him down to her again. "You taste awesome."

"Like reindeer stew?"

"No." She laughed. "Like fruit. Berries maybe."

"Ahh," he said between light, easy kisses. "The dried lingonberries one of the Sami women gave me. Good, aren't they?"

She kissed him again and then licked her lips. "Mmm. Delicious."

He backed her up against the wall of a hut. She giggled against his neck. "I hope we're not showering whoever's inside with dirt."

"I don't care," he breathed, kissing her with mouth and hands and body. "I want more of you."

She strained into him as desperately as he did for her. She'd wanted him since she'd landed on top of him that first day.

"God, I hate all these clothes," he muttered against her lips.

"That's why there are only five million people in Norway. You all wear far too many clothes to procreate frequently."

He laughed then, drawing her close against him and burying his face in her hair. "God, I think I'm falling in love," he chortled.

She froze. And then he froze.

"I'm sorry," he said hastily. "I didn't mean to—"

She put her fingers across his mouth, stilled his lips. "It's okay. No apologies necessary. It just slipped out in the moment. It's all right."

"No. You don't understand. I'm not retracting what I said. That's what I've been feeling. I'm just apologizing for saying it in that way. I should've waited until there were candles and roses and…and we were warm."

She stared, stunned all the way down to her toes. And then, for lack of anything else to say, she stammered, "I'm okay with reindeer dung and dead grass as a romantic backdrop. And I've gotten so used to being cold I hardly notice it anymore."

He brushed his fingertips along her cheek. "Ahh, you're my kind of girl. A true romantic at heart. It's not the gifts but the gesture that matters to you, isn't it?"

She nodded slowly. "I don't need much out of life. But I do want loyalty. And honesty. And genuine concern for me."

He shocked her by dropping to one knee, right there in the snow. "Karen Turner, I swear on the stars above that you have all three from me."

Holy cow. She reached down and tugged on his hands. "Stand up, you big oaf. You're embarrassing me."

"I'll take that as acceptance of my declaration, then."

She smiled shyly at him, peeking up through her eyelashes. She couldn't believe that Karen Turner, commando and killer, was receiving romantic declarations from this guy. But then, she'd never have believed he'd go down on one knee and say something like that to her, either.

She gathered the moment close to her heart. And then a blast of bitter wind caught her parka hood and blew it back, exposing her head. She snatched at it hastily and pulled it back up. She glanced up at the sky.

"Those stars you just swore on are disappearing fast. I'd say our blizzard's about here."

He glanced up as well. "I'd say you're right. We'd better get back to the hut and batten down the hatches before the brunt of it hits."

They hustled back toward their dwelling, pushed toward it by the sudden and powerful wind. Man, *that* had blown up fast. As they hurried across the village, the locals scurried to put out the last of the bonfire and head for their homes.

And then a scream cut through the air, barely louder than

the rising howl of the wind, but a scream nonetheless. Karen and Anders exchanged alarmed glances with each other—just long enough to verify that they'd both heard what the other one had. They took off running in the general direction of the noise.

"Any idea where that came from?" Anders grunted.

"Off to our left, I think," Karen replied.

They veered toward the double row of permanent houses. Karen wasn't surprised to see Aleesha, Jack and Vanessa racing toward them from the other end of the street. A woman in a doorway screamed again.

Karen and Anders got there first. Anders bit out something fast in Sami. "What's wrong?" no doubt.

The woman jabbered something over her shoulder as she turned and hurried through the tiny living room and into the even tinier kitchen. The source of her panic was immediately visible. A teenage boy lay on the floor with a middle-aged Sami man sprawled on top of him. The older man was trying with no success to keep the youth from flopping around in the throes of a violent seizure.

Karen recognized the boy. He was one of the kids who'd been "possessed" by the Viking warrior spirits a few days ago at the big bonfire. The ones she'd thought had been drunk. The ones she now knew to be infected with the same chemical she was.

Karen and Anders helped the older man hold the teen down, but the boy's strength was unbelievable. He arched up off the floor, lifting all three of them with him. Aleesha raced into the now-crowded space, took one look, and took over immediately, barking out commands like the emergency room physician she'd once been.

In short order, they had the kid's arm pinned down, his sleeve pushed up, and a hypodermic needle buried in a vein. Aleesha pushed in a chunking dose of an anticonvulsant. It took about a minute, but gradually, the youth's body went flaccid. Everybody climbed off the kid.

And then, just like that, the boy clutched at his chest and his face contorted.

"He's crashing," Aleesha announced urgently. "Break out the cardiac kit."

They worked frantically on the kid for upwards of twenty minutes, ventilating him, performing CPR, and eventually getting his heart beating regularly again.

Finally, Aleesha sat back on her heels. "If we hadn't been sitting right beside him when his heart stopped, he'd have died."

Karen stared down at the kid. Damn, that had been close! Aleesha was a hell of a fighter, though. She didn't give in easily to death with any patient of hers. Warily, Karen continued to watch the teen's chest rise and fall—when had the simple act of breathing become such an incredibly fragile thing? Was this what she had to look forward to? Seizures leading up to heart failure and death?

Chapter 15

Lakvik, Norway, March 9, 11:30 p.m.

Anders held their hut door for Karen, which was no small feat in the gale force winds. She helped him wrestle the wood panel shut, and threw the bar that served as a latch into its slots. The door rattled its protest. The storm was upon them.

The sudden stillness of the thick-walled hut surrounded Karen like a blanket. It stood in sharp contrast to the turmoil inside her. That Sami kid had nearly died, and she was loaded up with the same lethal drug he was.

Oh, sure, Aleesha had tried to reassure her. Had reminded Karen that she had only rolled around in the stuff, fully clothed. She hadn't swallowed it or injected it, and that potentially made a huge difference in how her body reacted to it and whether or not it would affect her the same way it had this kid.

Aleesha had also reminded Karen that everyone reacts differently to different medications, LSD in particular.

Not one bit of it made her feel any better. The drug inside her could still kill her.

Yet again, Anders seemed to pluck the thought right out of her head. "It won't kill you," he said quietly. "You're strong."

"I wasn't strong enough to fight its effects when I went after Jack."

"But you didn't kill him. You overcame the drug's effects. Besides, I'm not going to let you be alone for a second. You're not in this fight alone anymore."

"My own knight in shining armor, huh?"

He shrugged. "I prefer to think in terms of your own fur-clad Viking warrior conquering all your demons."

"I'll just call you Beowulf."

He smiled at her, and her insides reacted with their usual twist of attraction. "We've still got several hours before we have to leave. You want to try to lie down and catch a nap?"

She sighed. "We ought to."

Skipping a fire since they were due to leave on their op in a few hours, they duly crawled into their sleeping bags. Karen stared up into the dark, her eyes wide open. Whether it was the insomniac effect of the drug or her disquiet over the idea of dying, she couldn't tell. But either way, sleep was *not* happening.

"You asleep?" Anders whispered after nearly a half hour.

"Not even close," she replied, surprised. "Why aren't you out cold?"

His voice floated out of the darkness. "Can't get past the idea of losing you, I guess."

Karen jolted upright. "You'd have to *have* me first in order to lose me."

A rustle of nylon indicated he'd sat up, too, but he didn't

say anything. A flashlight flared, and Karen squinted into the sudden glare. She watched in silence as he got up and lit an oil lantern the Samis had provided. Her breath hung in the air in front of her, its fog obscuring the details of his expression. But she could still see he was dead serious as he turned to face her, his fists planted on his hips. Actually, he looked annoyed.

"Let's get one thing straight, Karen Turner. I intend to have a relationship with you."

Her mouth flapped open and shut a couple times. What in the bloody hell was she supposed to say in response to that? She blurted the only thing that came to mind. "I can't possibly have a relationship with a guy I can beat in a fight."

He studied her intently for several seconds. His eyes narrowed. "Fair enough, then. A fight it is. You owe me a rematch on that ambush, anyway. And I'm happy to take your twenty krone."

She felt a smile hovering at the edges of her mouth. "Hah! Who says you're going to win?"

"Only one way to find out."

She stared over at him speculatively. "You're on."

He stared back for a long moment, then sighed. "I'd take you up on that, except I don't want to trigger another episode in you."

"I'm willing to risk it."

"I'm not," he retorted.

His words were a kick in the gut. He was afraid of her. She was so strong and so violent when the drug had her in its grip that he wouldn't risk sparring with her.

"Shit," Anders muttered. He stood up. Walked over to where she sat glumly and held a hand down to help her up. "C'mon. Let's do it."

Her gaze jerked up to him.

"I wasn't worried about my own safety. I was worried about

yours. I have no doubt that I can take you, drug-induced rage or not. I just didn't want you to hurt yourself. If you have a seizure, I'll go get Aleesha. I'm game to settle this thing between us if you are."

She stared at his hand for a moment. She ought to be smart. Do the cautious thing and not chance losing control. Except she trusted Anders. He'd take care of her if she lost it.

"But what if I win? If I go nuts then, you could be in real danger."

He shrugged, his hand still extended to her. "I'm willing to take that chance."

She hesitated a moment longer, then reached out and took his hand. Their palms grasped, warmth to warmth, easy strength to easy strength. He gave a tug and she rose to her feet. She looked up the few inches into his ice-blue gaze and was startled by the intensity she saw there. Without releasing her hand, he pulled her closer until they stood chest to chest with only their clasped hands separating them.

"I *will* win, Karen," he said quietly.

"How can you be so sure?" Damned if she wasn't feeling a little…*sheesh*…breathless. She didn't *do* breathless. But here she was, panting like a dog after a rabbit chase on a hot summer day.

"I'll win because I've got so much riding on it. And I'm not talking about my health. I'm talking about *us*."

A slow smile unfolded on his lips that tempted her to reach up and kiss it. So distracted was she by the urge to taste that choco-late-and-roses smile, that she almost didn't catch his next words.

"You'll lose because you want me, too."

Her eyebrows shot straight up. "Of all the nerve!" she exclaimed.

He laughed. "And you love it."

She stripped off her outer sweater and pushed her sleeping bag against the wall. "So, what are the rules of engagement here?"

He considered her for a moment. "Hand-to-hand. No weapons."

She snorted. "Good call."

He continued, "Yield the fight on a move that would incapacitate or kill, otherwise, no holds barred. We go until one of us cries Uncle."

In other words, this would be a free-for-all, just like the last time they'd fought. This would be a test of strength on strength, skill on skill. And this time she wouldn't have surprise on her side. Her natural desire to win surged to the fore. Except…he had a point. Wouldn't it be lovely if he *could* beat her? Regardless, she wasn't about to hand this to him. If he won, he'd have to do it fair and square.

"I'm not throwing the fight for you," she warned him.

He raised an eyebrow. "I'd be tremendously disappointed if you did. I want to settle this once and for all. Here and now. And if you threw the fight, you still wouldn't know if I could take you. We'd have to do it again."

She laughed. "Okay, now that might just be the argument that makes me give this fight away."

He took a step closer, invading her personal space, and glared down at her. He pronounced each word succinctly as he said, "Don't you dare tank this on me."

Ahh, there it was. Now she had him good and riled up. In her experience, special operators didn't scream when they got well and truly pissed off. They went quiet. Got real still and focused. Like a tiger about to pounce and kill. Pretty much like he was doing right now.

Sparks flew as their gazes collided. "I wouldn't dream of giving this to you," she replied, her voice dripping with silky threat. "If you want it, you're going to have to come and take it."

He stepped back, and his gaze raked down her, stripping off every stitch of clothing she had on. His eyes blazed with silver fire. And her body tingled from head to foot. The fight. She was talking about the fight when she told him to come and take it.

Yeah, right.

A hum of need started vibrating low in her belly. A need to lay her hands on him, to have him do the same to her, pricked her palms until they tingled.

He nodded slowly, maybe in approval at what he saw as he blatantly ogled her, maybe in affirmation that he was, indeed, going to come and take everything she had—by force if necessary.

Fair enough. After all, she was the one who'd put him up to this fight. A fight she was going to get.

The two of them moved all their gear to one end of the hut and pushed aside the rocks that formed the fire pit. The whole center of the space was bare dirt now.

"Ready?" Anders asked, all business.

"Yup. Any time. Take your best shot."

She stared in dismay when, instead of attacking, he shrugged out of his shirt. Now that was a hell of an unfair tactic. How was she supposed to fight with all that gorgeous, bare-skinned guy standing in front of her? Good grief, she could stare at his chest forever. It was all smooth skin, rippled bulges of bronze muscle and no body fat. None. The vibration of need low in her gut ratcheted up a notch to an insistent tickle.

"How in the heck do you manage to have a tan in this country at this time of year?" she demanded.

He grinned at her. "Thanks for noticing. After the Olympics, I spent a few weeks in the Caribbean. Remind me to take you there after this is all over. I know the most gorgeous beach.

Totally deserted. You can strip down to your skin and sleep in the sun for hours."

Oh, Lord. What an image that called to mind! Her and Anders naked together. No tan lines. Turquoise and emerald waves lapping up on soft, white sand. Just the two of them and a beach towel with the sun and the heat—

Holy cow.

"Shall we get started, then?" he asked politely.

Norway. Hut. Dark and cold. She grasped at her fragmented thoughts, pulling them away reluctantly from her island fantasy. At least Anders remained. And he was the only part that mattered.

He stepped forward, his hands held out in front of him, relaxed, but clearly at the ready.

"Is that a Krav Maga stance?" she asked conversationally as she circled him, relaxing into her own fighting stance. She pushed him to the left and what she knew to be his weaker side. Not that either side of an Olympic athlete would be all that weak at the end of the day.

"Yes, it is. I spent a year in Israel training with one of their counter-terrorism teams," Anders answered casually as he jumped forward.

She jumped back fast from the feint. He didn't follow it up with an attack. Measuring her reflexes, apparently.

"You're quick," he commented on cue.

"Thanks."

They circled once more around the hut in silence, each watching how the other moved, their balance, how they shifted weight, the way they used their eyes. He was superbly coordinated. Totally aware of where his body was at all times. She could only imagine what making love with someone like that would be like. Someone who was aware of every millimeter of their own body and hers...damned if

that tickle in her gut didn't kick up to a rather uncomfortable tingle.

The fight, dammit!

Anders was giving her precious little by way of openings to
exploit. But then, Krav Maga—the street-fighting technique developed by the Israeli Defense Forces for quick, effective take-
downs—wasn't about giving your opponent openings.

"You look lovely in this light," Anders remarked, his voice
sliding across her skin like velvet.

"Do you make love as smoothly as you talk?" she replied.

A dark smile was all the answer she needed. "Only one way
to find out. Shall we take a rain check on that?"

Okay, the tingle had just become a shiver that shot up her
spine. "You'll have to beat me, first."

"We have a plan, then. Win the fight; ravish the girl." A
pause while he forced her to reverse directions in their circling
dance of stalk and retreat. Then he added, "Remind me to drive
you out of your mind with pleasure before I'm done with you."

She arched an eyebrow. "You need a reminder of that?"

He laughed, sounding genuinely amused. "Hardly. I'm no
inexperienced boy."

That made her gulp. Knew his way around a woman, did he?
And didn't that just send the shiver shooting out to the tips of
her fingers! And then he leaped in on the attack.

The move was designed to hit her off center and knock her off
balance. He was too fast for her to dodge completely, so she
stepped into the lunge and met him head-on. She grunted as his
body slammed into hers. He tried to grab her wrists, but she
evaded him with a nifty wrist slip. She jerked hard and spun,
dragging his hand across her belly, electrifying her with
the intimacy of it…and she was free! She jumped back, breathing hard.

He lunged again.

This time she dropped low, slipping under his attack and reaching for his legs as he went past. Her hands slid across his thighs. Registered rock-solid muscles. He'd have the capacity to make love hard and deep with all that muscle to back him up. She could just feel his thighs flexing against hers as he pounded into her. And given his cross-country skiing training, she'd bet he could keep the rhythm going for hours. He did a slick, midair direction reversal within her grasp and leaped clear.

The leg strength and agility it had taken for him to do that and not go sprawling was incredible. "Nice move," she managed to force past the raging lust closing down her throat.

He grinned back at her. "I have lots of good moves. I can't wait to show them all to you."

She gulped. Did having an orgasm while in a half-Nelson constitute winning or losing this particular fight? It was getting hard to tell. Although two could play that game.

She gave as good as she got. "You know, pretty soon you're going to break a sweat. And with all those gorgeous acres of glistening muscles to look at, I'll be a goner. I'll pack in the fight and ravish you instead."

"Just so long as we understand that counts as a loss for you and a win for me," he retorted. He tossed off the thumb lock she tried and added, "It remains to be seen who ravishes whom, however. After all, I'm the Viking."

"Yeah, but I'm the reincarnated Viking goddess." And she jumped. She feinted for his head, and as he ducked the grab, she plowed into his gut with her left fist. He grunted and spun away before she could grab him in a bear hug. Man, he was fast!

"Good shot," he said, a little breathless himself.

"Need a break?" she asked.

He threw her a withering glare. "Do you actually ask hostiles that in the middle of a fight?"

"No," she retorted scornfully.

"Then don't ask it of me," he bit out as he slid fast to her right and came in from the strong side. The move surprised her. Very few people ever attacked her strong side. She stumbled as he slammed his shoulder into hers, and was stunned to trip backwards over his right heel. How in the heck had he gotten that leg hooked behind hers without her noticing? She crashed to the dirt floor. At the last second, she partially tucked and rolled, enough to absorb the worst of the impact.

But Anders was on top of her before she could even draw a full breath.

She tossed her body weight from side to side and he partially lost his grasp on her, but he pursued her relentlessly.

"Oh, no you don't," he grunted. "I'm not letting you get away. I've waited my whole life for a woman like you."

His whole life? Whoa. Distracted, she barely got an elbow wedged between them in time to stop him from putting a smothering, full-body hold on her.

"No fair distracting me," she protested.

"Who said anything about playing fair? I want you."

His forearm landed across her collarbones with his full body weight behind it. He'd pinned down her shoulders with bruising effectiveness. She lifted her right leg, struggling to wedge a knee between the two of them. Although why she should want to do that, she had no earthly idea. His body, sprawled across hers with only minimal clothing between them, felt absolutely delicious. An insidious, weakening warmth began to steal through her muscles. Instead, she wrapped her leg around his waist—oh, man, that felt amazing, having the right parts of him pressed against her core like that—and squeezed for all she was worth. It was probably futile to try to rob him of oxygen given his level of aerobic fitness, but it was the only move she had left.

She lurched against his arm, nonetheless, testing its strength. He rocked his weight forward to put more pressure on her shoulders, and in the process, ground his hips squarely against parts of her that needed no encouragement. Her leg tightened convulsively around his waist, pulling him even tighter against her. Heat scalded her feminine flesh.

A groan of bliss escaped her lips, and he jolted, raising himself up on his arm to stare down at her. Nope, she hadn't gotten lucky. He hadn't misinterpreted that sound.

His eyes blazed with raw desire. He rocked his hips against hers again. No matter that they weren't actually having sex. Her blood pounded and her body throbbed until she could hardly breathe.

She heaved up, trying to toss him off her. His forearm slipped slightly, and she redoubled her efforts.

"I'm…going to…win. I want…all of you," he grunted.

Straining just as hard, she retorted, "You…make me…sound like…a bowl of…ice cream."

"No ice cream…is going to…taste as…sweet…as you," he answered through clenched teeth.

She finally yanked her right arm free from where it had been trapped beneath her and wedged her own elbow under his chin. She pushed for all she was worth. He shifted his hold, entangling their arms as they struggled for purchase, she to toss him off, and he to subdue her once more. Her biceps began to fatigue. Burned under the strain of holding him off. Then trembled under it.

Millimeter by millimeter, Anders pushed her arm aside. His free arm rested on the floor beside her, nestled intimately against the side of her breast. Ever so slowly, he was forcing her right arm down to her side, approaching completing a bear hug on her ribcage that would finally immobilize her. She had no doubt he was strong enough to prevent her ribs from expanding enough for her to breathe.

His grasp wrapped more tightly around her. She flailed back and forth, but his superior body weight was to his advantage. He spread his legs wide, tripod fashion, and used them to prevent her from rolling over. Damn, he was strong!

Too winded for wordplay now, they grappled in silence.

And ever so slowly, he got the best of her. How long it took, she had no idea. But eventually, blessedly, he forced her arms down to her sides. His own arms wrapped tightly around her upper torso. He planted one leg wide on either side of her body, his powerful skier's legs making it impossible for her to roll out from under him. His face was inches from hers, his eyes glowing with victory—and sexual anticipation that stole away what little breath she could draw in his iron grasp.

"Ready to surrender?" he gritted out from between his clenched teeth.

She looked up into his beautiful, blazing eyes. Time stood still around them as they strained against one another, nearly identically matched adversaries. *Nearly.* All her major muscle groups were near their limit. And for once, the trembling fatigue and burning pain felt amazing.

She'd done it. She'd found a man she couldn't beat. At least, not every time. And that was good enough for her.

She smiled up at him brilliantly. "Uncle."

Chapter 16

Northern Norway, March 11, 7:00 p.m.

Karen lay on her stomach in the snow at the top of the ridge, peering down through her night-vision goggles on maximum magnification at Point X-Ray, which they'd dubbed the cabin. As in X marks the spot.

The cabin looked much the same as it had the last time, with a few minor changes. Where once a pile of twenty or more fifty-five-gallon steel drums had stood, now the pile was down to three drums. A wide, packed trail led from the cabin door off to the east—left to right in her field of vision. It looked to have been made by a small, tracked vehicle. A snowmobile to judge from those small, horizontal ridges in the snow.

The cabin was surprisingly active. Lights were on in several rooms. She'd spotted outside floodlights mounted on each corner of the cabin, but they were blessedly turned off at the moment. Those exterior lights were both good and bad. On the plus side, if they got flipped on, they'd illuminate any human targets like ducks in a shooting gallery. On the minus side, the lights would negate the Medusas' night-vision gear and any advantage they'd have of operating in the dark. The bad guys would be blind, however, to anything and anyone beyond the range of the floodlights. The Medusas could use that to their advantage.

Well, the Medusas minus her. She didn't get to play with the other children because she couldn't be trusted not to flip out with a rifle in her hands. That, and Aleesha was concerned that too much exertion might release more of the drug stored in fat cells into her blood. She had to sit in the principal's office and watch the other kids have recess out on the playground, dammit.

Irritation flared in her gut. And it *didn't* have anything to do with the drugs coursing through her system! It was just plain annoying to be cut out of the action.

"Any movement, Python?" Vanessa asked from over where everyone else was huddled, a few yards away, well below the ridge line. They got to plan out the attack while she played harmless spotter.

"Three men are moving around the main room. Looks like they're setting up more lab gear."

"Anyone outside?" her boss followed up.

"I would have told you if there was," Karen snapped. "I mean it's not like I don't know how important it would be to announce that they have a sentry posted."

"Riigghht," Vanessa drawled. "Thanks."

Karen scowled. And now they were going to accuse her of going crazy again. She was just feeling a little testy. She had complete control over it.

"...so Anders will plant the explosives in and around the cabin with Aleesha and Misty helping him. The rest of us will move around front and create a shooting diversion. If they retreat inside and refuse to come out, we warn them verbally to surrender. If they refuse, we blow up the place with them in it. If they do surrender, Anders, Jack and I will go inside and clear the cabin. Because we haven't practiced room clearing with Anders, we'll go into each room solo. I don't want us to kill each other because the Norwegians and the Americans manage their fields of fire differently."

No kidding. That would suck to have one of your own team-mates rake his weapon fire across your position and cut you in half. Although a tiny part of Karen's brain was amused at the idea of jumping into a room with a half-dozen other Special Forces operators and mowing them all down where they stood. She could just imagine the looks of surprise on their faces as they went down.

Vanessa continued, "When we go through the front door into the main room, we'll do a standard wedge field of fire. I'll spin in and take the left third of the room, Jack will spin in and take the right third, and you go in straight and take the middle, Anders."

Karen frowned. That put Anders in the most vulnerable position. What was Vanessa trying to do? Get him killed?

Her boss continued, blithely unaware of Karen's fury beside her. "After the main room is clear, I'll take the southeast bedroom. Jack, you take the northeast bedroom and the bathroom. Anders, you take the kitchen. When the three of us have reported an all-clear, we'll retreat outside, and Anders will blow it."

"Everybody clear on the plan?"

Karen couldn't resist being pissy. In a fake perky voice, she announced, "And I'll knit everyone scarves so we'll all be cozy and color-coordinated when this mission is over."

Vanessa replied evenly, without breaking her briefing tone of voice, "I need you to act as the spotter for both teams. Take up a position two hundred yards east of the cabin where you can keep an eye on that snowmobile trail for movement and watch both the group setting the explosives and the group picking the fight."

It was a sop. A fake job to make her feel like she was part of it while they kept her out of the way. But let her do a real job? No way. Her eyes narrowed and her gaze clashed with Vanessa's.

Viper said quietly, "I realize you don't like being left out of the fight, Python. But if you were in my place, would you put a weapon in your hands?"

Karen scowled, but a tiny part of her appreciated Vanessa's blunt honesty.

Viper continued, "I don't have the manpower to spare to put someone on you to watch you and make sure you don't lose control. I need you to watch our backs and hold it together. Those are important jobs and I need your full concentration on both of them. I'm trusting you, here."

Karen sighed. Her boss was right, but that didn't mean she had to like sitting out here with only binoculars for a weapon.

Vanessa announced, "I want one more equipment check and a radio check. Then we head out."

When it was her turn to come up on frequency and report how much ammo she was carrying and indicate that she could hear everyone else loud and clear, Karen responded blithely, "Two knitting needles locked and loaded, and I hear you five by five." Meaning, on a scale from one to five, her radio reception strength and clarity were both at maximum.

Anders moved over beside her and murmured off microphone, "You okay?"

"Yeah. Why?"

"You sound a bit…belligerent."

"Wouldn't you be belligerent if all you got to do was watch the damned operation?"

He shrugged, although his parka masked much of the movement. "I suppose so. But we both know why it has to be that way."

She glared back in silence.

"I'd kiss you if I didn't think our lips would freeze together," he murmured. "Be safe. I don't want to lose you now that I've found you."

Okay, so that punctured her belligerence a little. Still. *Go over there and watch us, Karen. Be a good little girl and let us know if anyone is coming. Oh, and you don't get to carry any weapons. You can't be trusted...*

Yada, yada, yada.

"Let's head out," Vanessa transmitted.

Oslo, Norway, March 11, 8:00 p.m.

Jens opened the front door. "Come on in, Ivo. She's almost ready."

Ivo came inside, brushing off his coat. The snow was coming down hard out there. Or rather, it was blowing sideways hard. Jens doubted much of it was reaching the ground in these winds.

Ivo commented, "I'm hoping that with the clubs more crowded on a Friday our boy will show up to push his pills."

"Let's hope so. We could really use a break, since we've had no luck stopping the stuff from hitting the street."

"Well, maybe the military operation up north can shut down the lab making it."

Jens snorted. "Can you imagine what would happen if this stuff got distributed all over Europe?"

The two men traded grim looks. It didn't even bear thinking

about. Fortunately, Astrid chose that moment to stroll down the stairs wearing a dress that was too tight and too short for a father's taste, but seemed just right for Ivo's.

Ivo held her coat for her while Jens bit back an urge to tell the two of them to be careful. They knew that. And besides, an entire team of undercover cops was accompanying them everywhere they went. It would be okay. He hoped.

Northern Norway, March 11, 9:00 p.m.

Karen slogged down the ridge line to her left and lay down in the snow to tunnel below the crest so her passing wouldn't be visible from a distance. It was just like their first day of training when they'd done this little maneuver. Except this time she felt no pain from pulling herself forward on her elbows, and the cold and snow down her jacket felt good. She was burning up all of a sudden.

It was slow going pulling herself along on her belly in the snow. She stopped now and then to turn her head and check out the cabin through her NVGs. Still no movement outside. But the guys inside were scurrying around like rats in a cage. In a big hurry, apparently. What had their knickers in such a twist?

The wind howled around her like a moaning ghost. The storm's fury had lessened to a dull roar for the moment, but new snow still whirled and danced like a dervish. Visibility sucked. She was two hundred yards from the cabin at the moment and couldn't see a blessed thing but white. She'd have to move in closer. To hell with Vanessa's instructions.

She angled toward the cabin, crawling until she reached the snowmobile trail. She supposed she ought to treat it like a stealthy road crossing and do it fast and low when the coast was clear. But, hell's bells... In this weather, she could park in the middle of it and do a jig, and no one would see her! As tempting as that was, she rolled her eyes and did it the old-fashioned way by scooting across on her belly. She hoped that, wherever Vanessa and Jack were lurking right now, they were satisfied.

She turned around, which was a pain in the ass flat on her stomach, reached out, and used one finger to repair the snow-mobile tread marks as best she could. It wasn't perfect, but she highly doubted the bad guys would be coming through here with a fine-tooth comb to notice the hastily repaired track. When the wind settled down and actually let snow fall to the ground, new snow would cover it anyway.

She crawled for another fifteen minutes in fits and starts, keeping her movements arrhythmic and slow. She stopped about fifty yards from the cabin when she could actually make out the building and the shadows around it. Yup, just as she'd thought, having a spotter out here in these low-visibility conditions was a complete waste of time. Incoherent anger choked her at being set aside like this.

She dared not get much closer or she'd end up in someone's field of fire and get hit by a stray bullet. But much farther away and she couldn't see anything at all. She refused to sit off by herself in the middle of a freaking blizzard while the others did this op.

She burrowed carefully, digging a shallow depression for herself to lie in. Then she propped her NVGs on the edge of it and commenced watching the snow go by.

Her palms itched for a weapon. Any weapon. A damned knitting needle would be better than this!

And then she saw a movement. On the snowy slope right behind the cabin. A white shape low to the ground. No way to tell if it was Anders, Misty or Aleesha. But at least she had a fix on Team One. She turned her attention to spotting the other Medusa team. They were impossible to pick out. They'd probably already moved into position while she made her way to this little garden spot. Without them moving or firing, there was no way she'd pick them out of the amorphous blob that was the night and blowing snow. Which was good. The name of the game was to be invisible. She went back to watching Anders and friends.

It was textbook. They crept down to the back of the cabin and laid several blocks of explosives along the wall. That must be Anders in the front setting the explosives. For legal reasons, a Norwegian needed to do the actual work. He'd also be the guy to push the little red button.

A second white form was crawling along behind Anders, checking the wiring. That must be Aleesha, the Medusas' explosive ordinance expert. Which meant the third figure, the one passing Anders the bricks of go-boom must be Misty. Anders disappeared around the far end of the cabin for several minutes, then made his way back down to the end nearest Karen and the remaining barrels of psychedelic powder.

Ideally, they'd enter the cabin to drop the bulk of the improvised explosive. ANFO, ammonium nitrate/fuel oil, performed best when set off in a confined space, like, oh, a bedroom. The next part of the op was for Anders to enter the cabin and set the majority of the ANFO under one of the beds. To that end, Karen concentrated hard on the two bedrooms, both of which had a window facing this direction.

"Both rooms clear," she murmured. "Neither lit but ambient light is entering both from the hallway. The door to the southeast one is about halfway closed, the other door's wide open. Neither appears occupied, but the top bunks in both rooms are obstructed from my view."

Which sucked for Anders. He'd have to go in on the assumption that the bed was occupied. And that meant he'd have to go in quickly. In this weather, an open window would be discovered within seconds.

Anders was too close to the cabin to respond aloud. But Karen didn't need him to tell her what he was up to. He stopped under the southeast bedroom window. Aleesha and Misty crouched on either side of it. Aleesha would jimmy the window open, Anders would dive in, Misty would pass him the duffel of ANFO and det cord, and Aleesha would close the window behind him. Done right, a silent, five-second maneuver.

It took four seconds.

Karen held her breath for too long, waiting for Anders to show up again. Her lungs burned, and then her entire chest ached with the suspense. He would've rolled under the bed, out of plain sight, to set up his toys. When the bag of ANFO was all wired to blow, he'd click his throat mike once. Aleesha and Misty would open the window at the same time he dived for it, and he'd be out of there in two seconds. Three tops.

Two minutes passed. Three. Five. He ought to be more than ready to get out of there. Tension mounted in Karen's gut, coiling tighter and tighter. It felt as though a python was wrapping around her chest, constricting by inches. With every breath she took, it got harder and harder to suck air into her lungs. *Where was he?*

Something was wrong. He ought to have clicked by now. She couldn't see anything that would stop him from leaving. What was he hearing?

Vanessa murmured, "Python, report."

"All clear. No movement in the bedrooms or hallway. Anders is still in place, however. He's been inside—" a quick glance at her watch "—six minutes."

Which was to say, since Anders was monitoring this frequency, too, get the hell out of there already!

So focused on Anders was she that it took her a while to register the ever-so-faint vibration in the ground beneath her. At first, she put it down to her wildly pounding heart. But it got heavier, and then an almost subliminal noise began to accompany it.

Shit! She rolled over on her back and looked behind her, down the snowmobile track. She peered between gusts of snow and made out a dark shape. Coming toward her fast.

"Incoming!" she announced urgently.

Oslo, Norway, Midnight Sun Lounge, March 11, 11:00 p.m.

Astrid looked around the disco. They were all starting to blur together in her head. She and Ivo had been in and out of so many that she could hardly keep them straight. But the routine was always the same. They went in, staked out a place at the bar, sipped a soda, did a little dancing so she could have a look around at the patrons, and got friendly with the bartender and whoever looked like regulars in the place. Then Ivo casually dropped the name Izzy to see if he got any response.

She still was intimidated by Ivo. And the more she got to know him, the more intimidated she got. He was just such a decent guy. A white-hat type all the way. So out of her league. She couldn't help feeling like an immature teenager when she was with him. He talked about things like politics and theater—stuff she was interested in but had never talked about with guys before.

"The usual?" he shouted in her ear over the pounding music.

She smiled and nodded at him. Ginger ale with a twist of lemon. It looked like an alcoholic drink, but she could have a dozen and not be the worse for it.

"I need to go to the toilet," he shouted. "Will you be okay here for a few minutes?"

She grinned back at him. "What would you do if I said no? Hold it or take me with you?"

He laughed. "Tough choice. I think I'd take you with me. I like being with you."

Her toes curled into tight little knots of pleasure. "Go on. I'll be fine by myself. And the rest of the team is still watching me."

She watched his tall, lean form weave around the edge of the dance floor toward the neon sign pointing to the restrooms. And, as her eyes followed him around the room, she noticed a cluster of people at tables in the back corner. She and Ivo hadn't scoped out that area yet. She peered through the dim light. And started. For a second there, a man had waved his hand in the air sort of like Izzy did it.

She squinted harder at the guy. She couldn't be sure from this distance. A dark-haired man, maybe in his late thirties or early forties, sat at a table with several other people. Three girls and two more guys. A crowd of empty glasses filled the table in front of them. Even though the guy was dressed plainly, he had a vague air of, 'I'm a rich guy who can afford to pay for all my friends, and the women hang all over me.' Sort of like Izzy. Although the pimpish vibe had been much more pronounced in the drug dealer she recalled.

Had she spotted their guy? How cool would it be if, when Ivo got back, she could tell him she'd found his man for him? It would go a long way toward proving that she could handle herself like an adult.

She leaned forward to shout at the bartender, "Do you know that group at the fourth table from the back wall over there?"

The bartender looked where she indicated. "Nope. But they've been in here a couple times before. Met a few weeks back with some guys from a medical supply company. I overheard a couple of the salesmen talking about closing a deal for some lab equipment."

"What are they drinking?" she shouted across the bar.

"Absolut Citron."

"Give me a bottle of it. Put it on the tab of the guy I'm with."

The bartender nodded and passed her a fresh bottle of the Swedish vodka. She grabbed it by the neck and headed out across the dance floor. She wasn't a half-bad looking blonde herself, and with the vodka in hand, she had confidence she could get close enough to have a good look at the dark-haired guy.

She pasted on what she hoped was a seductive smile and walked up to the big table. "Where's the party?" she shouted.

Everyone at the table turned to stare at her. The blondes looked stoned out of their heads already. The two beefy guys on the ends of the booth—bodyguard/thug types—looked up at her much more alertly, however. But the dark-haired man was the one who answered.

"Who's asking?" he shouted back.

"My name's Astrid. My boyfriend—make that my *ex*-boyfriend—is a jerk, and I want to have some fun." He definitely looked like the guy she remembered. Although this guy looked thinner. Older. Maybe she'd been wrong about him.

Her target flicked a wrist swathed in a gaudy gold-and-diamond watch. "Make room for our new friend."

Okay, now that did look familiar.

One of the thugs stood up and let her slide into the booth. To her chagrin, the guy sat back down, effectively trapping her. Drat. She'd been hoping to sit on the end where she could make a quick exit if she had to. Ivo was going to come back and spot her over here. Then, he'd either kill her or let her drown in her own stupidity. Neither option was appealing, and either way, he'd never want to date her again.

She turned quickly to her host and held up the bottle of vodka. "Can I interest you in a little of my favorite poison?"

Surprise showed in the guy's eyes for a millisecond, then he said smoothly, "Next round's on Astrid."

The other blondes murmured vague thanks at her. Creepy. She looked the dark-haired guy in the eye and asked boldly, "What's your name?"

"Call me Ingmar," he replied.

Ingmar? The guy looked more like an Ahmed. And his choice of words had been interesting. The guy didn't say, "My name is…" He said, "Call me…" And then there was the fact that Ingmar started with an *I* like Izzy.

"You been in town long, Ingmar? I don't remember seeing you around."

He downed the double shot of vodka she'd poured for him and grimaced as its fire hit his throat. "I'm passing through."

"Where are you headed, sailor?" she asked with a hint of seduction in her voice. She leaned forward so the neck of her dress gapped open.

The guy was sharp. He didn't miss her tone or her invitation. He tossed her a sharklike grin and then took a slow, thorough look down her dress. She might not be model-thin, but she was stacked. She let him ogle to his heart's content. Men never equated boobs with brains. The longer he looked, the dumber he'd think she was.

After nearly a minute she sat up straight. He hadn't answered her question, dammit. She prodded again. "Traveling's tough in this weather. You gonna be in town a few days while the blizzard clears?"

He frowned. "I gotta get north. Got a pick-up to make. I fucking hate snow."

She laughed easily. "Then you're in the wrong place, Ingmar."

"No shit." He cursed liberally through the next few minutes of desultory conversation and dodged any more of her efforts to get him to divulge anything about himself.

But the longer she sat here, the more sure she was that this was her guy. Except he never talked about dealing drugs or having any business in Oslo. In fact, the only business he talked about was getting his delivery up north. That was the one thing that wasn't adding up. The man she'd remembered had been pushing his little pills hard. Wanted to move as many as possible as soon as possible. Yet this guy never even hinted at having a stash of pills to move.

She eyed the hallway from which Ivo should emerge any second. She needed to get out of here. Soon. She'd probably learned all she could about this Ingmar fellow. And it was plenty to know the police should definitely have a little chat with this guy.

She picked up the vodka bottle and poured another round of drinks. By grossly overfilling everyone's glasses, she was able to empty the bottle. She'd use the excuse of getting up to fetch another one as soon as everyone finished this round. But darned if Ingmar didn't decide to sip at his glass.

A lean, familiar form appeared in the entrance to the hallway leading to the bathrooms. Crud. Time was up. She had to go. Now.

To the thug beside her she shouted over the music, "Let me out. I'll go get us another bottle of vodka."

The guy shrugged. "That's what waitresses are for."

She glanced to her right. Ivo had spotted her. He was frowning and making his way through dancers toward her. She glared at him and tried to warn him off silently, but to no avail. She even frowned and shook her head slightly at him. Not going to take a hint. Now what?

"Hey, Ingmar," she said brightly. "Wanna dance?"

The guy lolled on his bench. "Do I look like a dancer?" He laughed.

She smiled brilliantly. "Sure, you do. C'mon. I'll show

you some steps. It'll be fun. I can move my package like nobody's business."

The thug beside her interrupted. "We got a problem, Mr. U. We got a cop incoming. And he looks pissed."

The change in "Mr. U." was immediate and startling. He lurched upright, his arms yanking away from the blondes, one of whom whined in protest. His gaze narrowed, darting left and right. "You said there'd be no cops in here," he snarled at the talking thug.

"They don't usually come in here."

"Usually isn't good enough. *No cops,*" Ingmar hissed.

Okay, then. So even if this guy wasn't Izzy the drug dealer, he was definitely a criminal. No law-abiding citizen was that freaked out by the idea of a cop approaching his table.

The thug beside Astrid stood up. Thank God. She slid to the edge of the booth. As soon as the big man took a step forward, she could slip out of here. But the thug didn't move. Instead, he said gruffly, "Can I help you, Officer Dahl?"

Astrid couldn't see around the bodyguard type, which was probably just as well. Ivo must be royally torqued off that she'd gone fishing for Izzy on her own like this.

"Jaeger. Long time no see. They finally let you out of jail, huh?" Ivo said from the other side of the mountain of man in front of her.

"Yeah. I'm out."

"So, introduce me to your new friends."

"They ain't your friends, Dahl. Unless you got some business with me, why don't you just move along now?"

"Ah, but they are my friends."

Astrid noticed Jaeger's hands flexing into fists inside his jacket pockets as he drawled, "Dahl, you're off duty. Go away before I gotta do something…like this!"

Astrid gasped as the man lunged forward, for she'd seen

something from her low angle directly behind Jaeger that Ivo undoubtedly could not. Jaeger's right hand wasn't empty as he pulled it out of his pocket.

"Ivo!" she screamed. *"Gun!"*

Northern Norway, March 11, 11:15 p.m.

Karen reported tersely, "Two snowmobiles. One rider each. Anders, hold your position."

She drew breath to tell Aleesha and Misty to make like snow-flakes, but as she turned back their way, they'd already melted away into white nothingness. Anders and his men had taught them well. Time for her to do the same. Her adrenaline scream-ing, she pulled the snow she'd pushed aside earlier over her legs. Awkwardly, flapping her arms like seal flippers, she tossed snow over her back. Jeez. Her heart felt as though it was going to pound its way right out of her chest. Her breathing came light and fast and there wasn't a damned thing she could do about it.

How in the hell did Jack and Vanessa operate together on missions? She was so worried about Anders she couldn't even draw a full breath.

The first snowmobile drew level with her, the chainsaw scream of its engine deafening as it roared past. It was towing some sort of long, crude sled behind it. So much for anyone noticing her tracks. A second snowmobile passed her. It was towing a sled, too. The vehicles neared the front of the cabin.

Now would be the perfect time for the Medusas out front to start shooting. Except they dared not start a fight until Anders was back outside. Odds were somebody would rush into a bedroom to grab gear or hide, and he had to be gone before that happened.

"Get out, Anders," Karen ground out. "The show's about to start out front."

Infuriatingly, he didn't respond. The first snowmobile parked in front of the cabin. The front door opened.

"Come *on,* golden boy!" she urged.

The second snowmobile pulled to a stop. Any second it would cut its engine.

"A bunch of the hostiles are out front being social with each other. Let's *go!*" Karen whispered furiously.

Finally. A single click.

Misty rose up out of the snow beside the cabin instantly, a snow-covered Sasquatch. The window sash was barely halfway up when a white form half-dived, half-slithered through it. Misty yanked the window back down.

"He's out," Karen announced tersely.

"Fire," Vanessa ordered.

The idea was for Katrina, the team's sniper, to knock out a window. A non-lethal shot that would startle the bad guys and shake them up without killing anyone. An announcement that armed forces were outside the cabin. A rifle report rang out, its sharp noise distorted by the storm into a tremendously loud crack. Karen barely heard the tinkling shatter of the kitchen window over its echoes off the mountains around them.

The bad guys reacted all right. Before they'd barely flinched, they'd all leaped for the cabin door. Four of the five men hit the opening simultaneously. They looked like a bad cartoon, all trying to shove through it at once. They popped through to the interior. The fifth guy crouched—a slightly more military reaction, took a quick look around, appeared to realize how exposed his position was, and dived for the cabin, too.

As they'd predicted, the outside floodlights went on. Karen had already pulled up her night-vision goggles just in case. No need to fry her retinas tonight, thanks. She squinted into the abrupt and blinding light.

And then tinkling noises sounded all around the building. All the remaining windows were being broken out…from the inside!

The bastards were planning on shooting back!

"They've taken firing positions in all the windows I can see," Karen panted. God, her chest hurt. And she didn't have a damned thing to fire back at the guys looking out the bedroom windows in her direction except insults. And now, with them looking out, she couldn't move either, lest she be spotted.

Shots started ringing out. Undoubtedly the tangos. The Medusas wouldn't waste their limited ammo in such wanton fashion. Besides, the clunky, bolt-action rifles the Medusas were stuck with didn't allow for the rapid fire she was hearing.

With the weird acoustics out here, Karen couldn't tell where the shots were going, but it sounded like it was mostly aimed out the front of the cabin toward Medusa Team Two. Dang, the noise was loud! It rang in her head, one crack stacking on top of another until she was sure her skull was going to split. The pain was excruciating. Her eyeballs were going to explode! *Make it stop.*

It was all she could do not to scream.

Stop. Rewind. Since when did she scream in the middle of a firefight? She'd lain on more firing ranges than she could count, for hours on end, and they'd been a hell of a lot louder than this.

Why it hadn't dawned on her earlier that she was losing it again, she had no idea. But sudden awareness of the encroaching madness did burst across her brain. Crap. Not now!

The cabin in front of her fuzzed out. She blinked hard a couple times to clear her vision. And what she saw when it came back into focus chilled her to the bone. Anders and her teammates were sitting against the side of the cabin, not three feet from the guys peering out the windows over their heads.

"Don't move, Team One," she whispered urgently. "One tango in each window above your position. Armed. Can't tell for sure, but they look like AK-47s."

There was a momentary lull in the firing. And another sound intruded upon the scene. A voice. Speaking in slow, deliberate Norwegian through a megaphone. Jack. Reading off the sheet Anders had given him. It translated roughly to, "Come out with your hands up. Surrender now and we will let you live." The alternative if they failed to surrender went unspoken.

A voice shouted back at them from inside the house. And Karen's jaw literally dropped. That sounded like…

"Arabic," Isabella, the Medusas' resident linguist bit out. "He more or less told us to go to hell."

"Repeat the message in Arabic," Vanessa ordered.

Jack, fluent in that tongue, complied.

More shouted Arabic that translated to a rather ruder version of "go to hell" than before.

"So be it," Vanessa bit out. "Blow it."

"No!" Karen retorted. "Team One is pinned down against the side of Point X-Ray."

No transmission answered that, but in her head, Karen could just picture Vanessa swearing under her breath.

Karen squeezed her eyes shut, but the haze of red wouldn't go away. Knives stabbed into her head from all sides. Needles of pain pierced her eyeballs until her eyes watered and she couldn't see a thing.

"We need to draw these bastards outside," Jack growled between shots.

"Cobra and Adder only, return fire," Vanessa replied. "Maybe that'll do it. If they hear only two weapons, maybe they'll think they outnumber us."

It wouldn't work, but who was Karen to argue? She was

going to be blind by then anyway. An urge to roll around in the snow, to scour her face in its icy cold nearly overwhelmed her.

How long the standoff continued, she had no idea. The tangos must've had a boatload of ammo in there, though, because they continued to shoot with complete abandon. Either that or they were completely undisciplined amateurs. She felt an overwhelming need to move. To get up and run around, to shake all her limbs and fall down in the snow and roll around. And she could only lie there in the snow staring at Anders and her teammates, trapped beside the building.

And then a new movement off to her right caught her attention. Somebody, one of the gang on Team One, poked their head up above a drift of snow.

"You're exposed, Team One!" Karen called urgently.

Vanessa came up behind her on the radio. "Jack, what are you doing?"

"Drawing fire."

"Yeah, well it's working. Get down! I'm not having you stick your neck out and getting killed on my watch. There's got to be another way to draw them to the front of the cabin so Team One can egress away from the building."

For indeed, the hostiles seemed content to hunker down in their thick-walled cabin that was largely impervious to bullet fire and sit this thing out. Karen frowned. What if, instead of drawing the two snipers in the windows in front of her to the front of the cabin, they merely drove the hostiles away from the windows?

She transmitted, "If I had a weapon, I could shoot at these jokers and extract Team One myself."

Vanessa replied, "I can send Cobra over. It'll take a while, though."

Karen reviewed the supplies in the team's backpacks, which

lay in the little hollow beside her. "Mamba, do you have any alcohol in your crash kit?"

"Yeah. You need some?"

"High-grade pharmaceutical stuff?"

"Yeah. Why?"

"I have an idea."

Moving at the necessary snail's pace not to attract the attention of the men peering through their weapon sights in her general direction, she pulled out an aluminum canister used to store one of the tents. She slid the tent out of it. Rummaging in the medical crash kit she found a scalpel—Hah! They hadn't succeeded in removing all weapons from her proximity, the bottle of nearly pure alcohol and a big wad of cotton.

Slowly, she turned so her back faced the window. That way she could work quickly with her hands without being seen. She shredded the cotton into a light, airy mass. Then, using the scalpel, she poked a hole in the side of the tube very near the closed end. Using a tent pole, she lightly stuffed the cotton wad down the tube. And then she poured in some alcohol. She was completely guessing as to the amount. She hadn't made a potato cannon since she was a kid, and she and her cousins had used liquid propane, not high-grade alcohol.

Then she looked around for a nice, sharp chunk of ice about the same diameter as the tube. It took a little carving on the ice ball with the scalpel, but she achieved a smooth fit. She shaped several more ice bullets and laid them beside her. She aimed her improvised cannon at the cabin. Now the trick would be not to kill Team One with this thing. She propped it on the front lip of her hollow and did her best to sight down the length of the tube at the northeast window. She estimated windage and sinkage and made the necessary corrections.

No telling if the thin aluminum would blow up and kill her

or if it would hold under the pressure of rapid gas expansion as the alcohol burned. To improve her chances, she packed the cylinder tightly in snow and ice, leaving only a tiny tunnel down to the hole in the tube. She twisted the cotton's paper wrapping into a wick of sorts and stuffed it into the opening.

Then Karen transmitted, "Team One. Get down as low as you can."

"What are you doing?" Vanessa demanded.

"I'm gonna throw a snowball at the bad guys."

"A snowball?" Vanessa repeated, shocked. "Are you nuts?"

Karen grinned. "I'm certifiable. Thing is, I'm lobbing that sucker with a potato cannon."

A moment of silence met that announcement. And then, with a hint of laughter in her voice, Vanessa replied, "Fire at will, Python."

Chapter 17

Oslo, Norway, March 11, 11:30 p.m.

Everything happened in slow motion. The thug raised his pistol to fire at Ivo. Astrid bolted up and out of her seat and rammed into the guy's right arm from below, knocking the weapon upward. Ivo dived. Rolled toward the thug. The bad guy turned toward Astrid and backhanded her viciously. She staggered back, falling across the table and sending liquor and glasses flying everywhere.

Ingmar half stood, clawing his way backward from the table. Thug number two pulled out a weapon.

Screams erupted but were a vague, distant noise. Ingmar climbed over the table beside her and landed on his feet.

Shots rang out as both thugs shot at Ivo and the undercover cops commenced shooting back.

"No!" she screamed, rolling off the table. Mid roll, she vaguely noticed Ingmar sidling to the left behind his beefy bodyguards. He was eyeing the fire exit not far away. The jerk was going to escape!

She slammed into thug number two. God, the guy was a rock! He barely budged as her full body weight impacted him. It felt like she bounced more than anything else as she careened off him and toward the first thug.

"Izzy's getting away!" she shouted over the chaotic din of screaming and gunshots.

Who knew if Ivo could hear her or not. She saw he'd come up onto his knees, his pistol held in front of him at eye level with both hands.

Thug number one's pistol tracked Ivo's movement. And then slowly, deliberately, in exaggerated time-stop motion, he fired. A spit of orange flame came out of the barrel as her mouth opened to scream.

Ivo toppled over, crashing to the floor. Still, the pistol tracked him, pointing this time at Ivo's head. She saw the hammer draw back again as the thug's finger started through another trigger pull. The bastard was going to kill Ivo!

Astrid jumped.

Northern Norway, March 11, 11:31 p.m.

Karen's hand shook almost uncontrollably as she held a lighter to the piece of paper. By dint of intense concentration, she suppressed the tremor and lit the fuse. The flame took a couple of maddeningly slow seconds to devour its way down the twisted paper.

And then there was a loud whump.

It sounded just like a tear gas launcher. Good Lord willing

and the creek don't rise, that's what the bad guys would think, too.

She peeked up over the edge of her hollow. There was no splat of white on the dark wood wall, so she'd either missed the cabin completely or sailed her snowball through the broken window. She would assume the latter.

Neither bad guy was visible in the bedroom window at the moment. Well, it had made them duck at any rate. With fumbling fingers, she reloaded her cannon as quickly as she could with another wad of cotton, some more alcohol and another snowball. She aimed at the other window. Sure enough, that guy poked his head up first to have a look outside. She'd forgotten to make another fuse, so she held the lighter directly to the hole.

The whump was immediate this time.

"Both windows are clear," she stuttered between chattering teeth. She glimpsed Team One rising to a crouch and sprinting away from the window. Or more accurately, floundering as fast as they could through the snow away from the window. She turned to the task of reloading. It was getting harder each time. Her whole body was twitching now, and it was nearly impossible to control her movements. By dint of incredible concentration and sheer force of will, she loaded again.

And fired again. This time there was a big, white spray of snow on the wall between the windows. No matter. It was all about keeping those hostiles out of sight. Just another few seconds and Team One would be clear.

She tried to reload again with her last snowball. She spilled nearly half the alcohol in the snow and dropped the snowball twice before she managed to get the cannon reloaded. It was taking so long that she kept having to pause and check the windows for returning hostiles.

The third time she did so, she bit out, "Get down!" The top

of a head was emerging above the window ledge in the right-hand window.

She aimed the cannon carefully. This was her last shot. She had to make it count. A burst of gunfire erupted from the window. Crap! There were two guys there now, both firing. Thankfully, Team One had hit the snow, and their white camo gear made them nearly invisible a few yards beyond the circle of bright light falling on the ground near the cabin.

She lit the fuse.

Whump.

A man screamed.

Sweet! She'd hit one of the jerks! She hoped the ice had put his eye out.

"Clear," she managed to force past her chattering teeth.

Anders, Aleesha and Misty jumped up and took off running again toward her position. Anders flopped into the tiny hollow beside her while Misty and Aleesha commenced widening the hollow to accommodate themselves.

"How's it looking?" Anders panted.

Karen scowled and enunciated carefully, "You have a grenade?"

"No, but I've got a flash-bang."

Flash-bangs were grenades loaded with a minimal amount of black powder, just enough to make a bright flash of light and a loud bang, but not do any real damage.

"Let's shoot it at them."

Anders eyed her improvised cannon. "You gonna lob it in the house with that?"

Karen nodded, since she didn't trust her mouth muscles to continue cooperating.

Anders reached for a pocket in his coat while Misty transmitted, "Team One is clear. We've joined Python."

"Blow it up, Anders," Vanessa ordered.

"No can do. I overheard these guys talking earlier. They're terrorists. The powder they made is part of some larger plan. An attack of some kind. I got the impression they're planning to lace their psychedelic powder into something unexpected that'll reach the general population of Europe and North America. They were gleeful about the target. We need to take one of these guys alive for questioning."

Karen swore under her breath and had no doubt all the other Medusas were doing the same. This *was* a simple, straightforward mission. It had just gotten significantly more complicated.

Concentrating ferociously, Karen loaded the cannon one more time. Anders held the grenade's handle down and pulled the pin. "This has a five-second delay," he murmured.

Karen nodded. After he let go of the grenade's handle and rolled it down the cannon, she'd have five seconds to light the cannon, blow the load, and get the grenade through the window. No sweat. Assuming her cannon didn't disintegrate under the pressure of this heavier missile. Assuming her luck held and she actually hit the window one more time. Assuming she didn't collapse into a full-blown convulsion in the next few seconds.

Carefully, she aimed her potato cannon one last time—at the right-hand window. The room without the giant bag of explosives hidden in it. She moved deliberately, not only to get this shot right, but also to hide the way her whole body wanted to twitch. She poured all the remaining alcohol down the barrel.

"I'm ready," she said.

Holding the tent pole in one hand and the grenade in the other, Anders said, "Here we go, then. On my mark. Go!" Working fast, he shoved the live grenade into the mouth of the cannon and quickly pushed it down with the tent pole. He yanked the pole free and dived to the side. "Fire!"

Karen touched the fuse with her lighter.

Snow flew in all directions as the aluminum tube finally gave up the ghost. The whump was a deafening boom this time. Karen looked around frantically to see if the grenade had been spat out somewhere in their foxhole. A flash-bang might be small, but if a person was sitting on it, they'd still get messed up bad. No sign of the fist-sized gray metal.

And then a second explosion flattened her in the snow again. That one had come from inside the front bedroom. Yes! The flash-bang had found its target.

The front door slammed open and six men poured out pell-mell.

Jack got on the megaphone again and called out something in Arabic. The men dropped their weapons instantly and followed the weapons down to the ground. Damn, that was easy! One flash-bang and the whole gang wilted. Amazing, given that the bad guys had them severely outgunned.

Anders climbed to his feet cautiously, his rifle held shoulder-high in firing position. It was an awkward way to have to advance, but the old-fashioned rifle didn't leave any other option. Misty and Aleesha went with him, advancing in similar fashion, alert for any tricks from the men now lying face-down in the snow.

Jack and Vanessa materialized out of the darkness and met Anders at the front door. A quick hand signal from Vanessa, and the three of them disappeared into the cabin. Isabella and Kat stayed under cover for now just in case something went wrong. Karen also stayed put. Not only was she unarmed, but she honestly didn't know if her shaking legs would support her body weight.

Karen couldn't be of any help to the team inside, so she turned her field glasses on the prisoners. They wore bulky, bright-colored, nylon parkas that should keep them warm and dry even though they were literally lying in the snow. Misty was patting them down one by one while Aleesha watched cautiously.

What a bunch of wimps. If she were any one of those six guys and they were only being guarded by one woman while another rendered herself combat-ineffective by having to search them, she'd jump her captors so fast her head would spin!

One of the bad guys turned his head so his face was toward her. She zoomed in on him to see if she could recognize him from any international wanted lists.

His face came into focus in her lenses. Olive skin. A little dark hair sticking out of his hood. Black eyes. And…Karen frowned. The guy looked…

…smug.

What the hell was up with that? He'd just been busted, his operation uncovered and stopped. What did he have to be smug about?

She pushed aside the bubbling rage in encroaching red haze. Something was seriously wrong here. She had to keep her head in the game. She blinked her eyes hard to clear the stabbing pain from her temples. Please, just a second's relief so she could think! That was all she needed. Her body gave a particularly hard twitch, and her back muscles spasmed. She furiously fought the need to arch backward. *Think, Karen!*

Why was that guy so pleased with himself?

These guys made the drug ripping up her system right now. That made them chemists or lab techs. Smart boys, then. And…what? Come *on,* brain!

A moment of clarity broke over her. Where it came from, she didn't ask. Maybe it was a gift from the gods, or maybe a few of her brain cells broke free of the fog of fury enveloping her. But suddenly the problem was as clear as a bell.

These guys *made* the drug that was messing her up. Lived in the same building with it day and night. Moved it around, packaging it into barrels.

Karen reached for her throat mike button. It took her several tries to land a finger on it. "V…Viper, is th…there a negative p…pressure ventilation system in th…there? Click if yes. S…silence if no."

Silence stretched out in response to that.

Yup. As she'd thought. These guys must have ingested the same stuff she had—breathed it, swallowed it, gotten it on their skin, *some*thing. So why weren't they twitching around on the ground having seizures and psychotic episodes?

More to the point, if she'd just been defeated in battle, she'd be so mad, no way could she contain the rage she was barely staying on top of now. How could that guy lie there and be *smug?* These guys had just been in a gunfight. They'd been shooting wildly and taken incoming fire. Their adrenaline alone should be sky-high. And with the effects of the drug stacked on top of that—

"Something's wrong," she announced over the radios. "Cobra, Adder, get your weapons pointed at those guys on the ground."

"Talk to me," Misty grunted as she patted down the last guy.

"They're not upset enough about being captured."

Aleesha came up on frequency. "How upset should they be?" she asked reasonably.

Fury at Aleesha's tone shot out of Karen like lava from an erupting volcano. *And that was the point.* She took a deep breath. Focus. Say the words. Make herself understood. Beat back the rage just a little bit longer. "I got exposed to the stuff in the barrels one time. These guys have been living with it. You guys say boo to me and I'm ready to kill you. Why aren't these guys completely insane? If I lost a gun battle, was forced to surrender, failed in my mission, I'd go berserk."

Anders, Jack and Vanessa emerged from the cabin just then. "Clear," Vanessa announced tersely.

Jack used his toe to roll one of the men over. Said something forceful in Arabic. No response. "Not talking," he announced.

None of them were. Out here in the snow with all the prisoners together wasn't the ideal way to get any of them to talk, either. They needed to be divided and separated in rooms by themselves, and then tricked into talking or mentally worked over by a good, hard interrogation.

"Okay, let's get them away from the cabin so we can blow it up," Vanessa said after a couple minutes. "We won't get anything out of them out here. Cobra, Adder, come on out."

Given that there were six hostages, the order made sense. That way there'd be a weapon trained on every hostage as the dangerous maneuver of getting them up and moving was accomplished.

"Let's cuff them before we move them," Vanessa ordered.

Jack pulled out plastic, disposable restraints and passed several to Isabella as she came forward. Both he and Isabella spoke fluent Arabic, and appeared to use it to instruct the prisoners to put their hands behind their backs. The handcuffing procedure went smoothly.

And Karen's disquiet continued to climb. Was this no more than misplaced paranoia? A new symptom of the drug that she was experiencing for the first time? The twitchiness in her limbs started to feel suspiciously like panic. It rattled through her, shaking her from head to foot. Or maybe she was just having a panic attack on top of a seizure.

She tried to stand, and collapsed in an unceremonious heap, rolling down into the bottom of the depression, facing away from her teammates. Tried to reach her mike button to call for help. Couldn't control her hand well enough to make that happen. Only ended up slapping herself in the face a couple times. *Gotta love the irony of that.* Now what? They'd figure out she wasn't joining them, eventually. Someone would come looking for her.

And then a great, fist-like vise closed around her heart, squeezing it mercilessly until she couldn't breathe. *Oh. God. That. Hurt.*

She opened her mouth. Tried to call for help. Nothing. Not a whisper of breath escaped her seizing throat muscles.

Holy crap.

She was going to die.

Oslo, Norway, March 11, 11:32 p.m.

The bullet ripped into Astrid's gut like a hot knife slashing through soft butter. So instant and intense was the agony of it that she barely noticed slamming into the floor shoulder-first. A gush of hot and wet rushed over her belly. And with it came a sense of calm. Wow. She must be bleeding like a stuck pig.

More shots rang out in quick succession then, one right after another. A dozen in all. Something heavy fell beside her, jostling her. New shards of agony seared through her. She heard a long, low moan. Was that her making that awful noise?

There was so much shouting. She wished it would go away. Her head was throbbing from it. At least the throb was slowing down. If only it would stop.

The floor and shoes and darkness swirled around her. She felt as if she was going to puke. But the idea of contracting her stomach muscles to push anything out of her body caused mild panic to swim somewhere in the back of her head.

Something white and round and blurry appeared in front of her. A voice floated down. Said her name. Repeated it louder. Insistently. She just wanted to go to sleep.

"Astrid, honey, it's me. Talk to me."

"Ivo?" she breathed. Lord, what was that raspy sound? Surely not her.

"Stay with me, honey. You gotta fight. Stay conscious. Look at me. The ambulance is on the way."

He was up. Talking. That was good. "You...'kay?" she wheezed. She coughed and the taste of blood filled her mouth.

"I'm fine. I have on my vest."

"Vest—guess I look...dumb...but he aimed for...head..." Her voice trailed off, the rest of the thought lost. Cotton candy filled her brain.

"You dived in front of that bullet for me?" he asked. Sounded shocked.

"Well...yeah..."

"Aww, honey—" But then he disappeared from the narrow, dark tunnel of vision she had left. Another blurry white blob that looked like a face.

Voices started barking out medical stuff over her head. They sounded like they had things well in hand. Finally, blessedly, she let go. And slid into the warm, dark abyss that beckoned.

Northern Norway, March 11, 11:34 p.m.

Karen gazed straight ahead, into the teeth of the storm. What a hell of a place, a hell of a way, to die. She'd envisioned herself going out in a blaze of glory, saving her team from disaster. Maybe saving the world. Something noble at any rate. Not this. Not succumbing to some damned drug.

As whatever was happening to her got even worse, her lungs screamed for oxygen first. And then every cell in her body screamed for it. A hot flush rushed over her, and then intense pain as her muscles shouted for air.

And then something began to materialize in front of her. A

gray shape in the darker gray of the snow. A gust of wind swirled snow more thickly for a moment and she squinted into the blizzard. Was that an angel or something coming to fetch her?

But as she watched, it materialized into a more human shape. Carrying a machine gun. And running.

Some angel.

And then he got close enough for her to make out his face. He was grinning ear to ear. Maniacally. In the full grip of the rage she knew so well. He was crazy as she was. And he was bent on killing. She knew exactly what he was feeling. The way blood surged through his head, how red filled his eyes, how thirst for violence was driving him mad with need.

And he was charging straight at the cluster of people in front of the cabin.

Of course.

The guys inside surrendered at the first opportunity. Laid around a while. Drew out the entire Spec Ops team staging the attack. And then, when all the special operators had come out of hiding, this guy would ambush them. She bet he'd shout a warning. All the bad guys would drop to the ground, and this joker would mow down all the Medusas where they stood.

Slick plan, actually.

Unless she stood her sorry self up this very second and stopped him.

Her body dragged in a sobbing breath. Where it came from, she had no idea. She focused every ounce of her being on doing that again. And painfully dragged in another breath. She had to roll over. Onto her belly. The guy was nearly even with her now, maybe ten yards away. She flopped like a fish on a dock, but managed to get onto her stomach.

Elbows bent. Hands by her shoulders. Jeez, her chest was

killing her! Her left arm was completely numb. A one-handed push-up, then. She slid her right hand by jerky degrees under the center of her body. Pushed. Nothing. Pushed again.

She managed to wedge a knee under her gut. Thank God the snow was soft and she was able to drag her leg through it.

Another push, leg and arm this time. Better. She made it to her hands and knees. The guy was slightly in front of her now. His weapon was coming up into a firing position. And sure enough, he shouted.

The Medusas lurched, whirling to face this new threat. But standing in the light as they were and looking out into the blackness of night and white swirl of snow and fog and wind, they wouldn't be able to see him. But she could. He was a black silhouette between her and the light. Somehow, she managed to hoist herself up to a standing position. She staggered a couple of steps on unsteady legs toward the ambusher.

As one, the prisoners dropped to the snow.

Run!

Karen's brain screamed the command at every muscle in her body. Her teammates were going to die!

How she covered the distance between herself and the gunman, she had no idea. But the machine gun settled against its harness and into firing position as she neared him. A burst of gunfire erupted from the weapon, spraying bullets at her teammates.

Jump!

Out of the corner of her eye, she saw Vanessa fly backward. Aleesha went down in slightly less dramatic fashion, but clearly, she was hit, too.

Karen slammed into the gunman. The two of them crashed to the ground, the guy cursing and screaming at her.

Oh, she knew the feeling. Knew it very well, indeed. This bastard had just *shot* her teammates! Without a moment's hesitation, she unleashed the rage. All of it. Every vicious, violent, *savage* impulse she'd ever amassed.

The pain in her chest was nothing compared to the glory of wrapping her hands around this guy's throat. He tried to fight back, but she swatted his efforts aside like a fly. Thank God for every ounce of power in her big, muscular body that she was able to use to tear this asshole limb from limb! She squeezed the guy's neck tighter and tighter, the same way the vise in her chest was constricting around her heart.

The abyss beckoned, and this time she flung herself into it headlong, sinking down, down, into the enveloping blackness. Everything went silent and dark.

Chapter 18

Northern Norway, March 11, 11:47p.m.

"Karen."

The voice, from far away, sounded vaguely familiar.

"Come back to me, Karen."

There it was again. She blinked up at the voice. What was she doing lying on her back? A face came into focus. *Anders.*

He was kneeling beside her. Plugging her nose. She turned her head away weakly from the annoying pinching sensation. She became aware of a weight on her chest. Glanced down.

"Why are you lying on me, Misty?" she rasped.

"I'm listening to your heartbeat. No time to get a stethoscope."

"What about my heartbeat?"

Anders answered quietly. "You had a heart attack."

Ahh. That explained a lot. He and Misty must've done CPR on her. Hence the plugged nose. "Hell of a way to steal a kiss," she mumbled up at him. "Next time, just ask."

He grinned down at her in obvious relief.

"Vanessa and Aleesha?" she asked, lurching in sudden alarm.

Anders clapped a strong hand on her shoulder, pushing her back down. "Aleesha's wound is superficial. She and Jack have Vanessa pretty much stabilized, and Misty and I got you going again. So it's all good."

He said it lightly, but a certain haggard look in his eyes said both she and Vanessa had come through close calls.

He glanced over his shoulder at where the others must be and then back at her. "You ladies are good. Everybody had the medical training to know exactly what to do. And that Aleesha—she's tough. Got up from her own gunshot wounds to work on Vanessa."

Karen smiled, startled at how much effort it took. "That's Mamba. She mother-hens the whole team."

"You rest. Your heart just had a big shock."

Now *there* was an understatement. Seeing her teammates shot was about the worst thing she'd ever witnessed. And something she sincerely hoped never to see again in her entire life. She frowned. She couldn't remember what had happened right before she had apparently collapsed. "The gunman?"

Anders snorted. "Oh, he's dead. Your ticker didn't give out completely until you'd all but separated his head from his shoulders with your bare hands."

She nodded once. No guilt there. Maybe a little embarrassment over the degree of violence with which she'd killed him, but no guilt. She was thankful that, for the moment, the fire-breathing dragon inside her was sleeping. "Now what?"

He shrugged. "Now we all go inside the nice warm cabin and wait for the storm to break. As soon as we can get a helicopter in here to airlift you and Viper out, we'll blow the place to smithereens."

And that was exactly what they did. It took about twelve hours for the storm to finally abate. Karen slept most of that time. The prisoners were kept in one corner of the main room under heavy guard. No more gloating for them. They glowered sullenly now that their clever ambush had failed.

At one point, Karen woke up to the sound of somebody babbling. She registered Jack leaning down over one of the men and murmuring quietly in his ear. Whatever Jack was saying apparently was scaring the guy half to death. The prisoner was talking as fast as his mouth would go, almost sobbing with fear. The other prisoners were scowling at the hysterical one.

After a few moments, Jack straightened. Nodded at Anders in satisfaction. What was that all about? It looked like he'd been interrogating the guy. She fell back asleep before she could get an answer.

Oslo, Norway, March 12, 4:00 p.m.

Astrid blinked awake into a world of white. White walls, white curtains, white sheets. She turned her head and gasped as pain exploded across her lower abdomen. She felt a need to cough, but the idea of it nearly made her faint with apprehension.

Someone stepped into view. Two someones. Her father—and Ivo.

"You two look like hell," she sighed.

Her father snorted. "You don't look ready to spring up and run for Miss Norway yourself, kiddo."

Ivo just smiled. "You look great."

Jens sighed. "I still can't believe you dragged my baby into the middle of a shootout!"

Astrid protested, "He didn't drag me into anything. I'm the one who approached Izzy. At least I think that's who he was."

Ivo nodded. "He was our guy all right."

"Did he get away?" she asked anxiously.

"Nope. He died in the shootout. Turns out he was a wanted terrorist. Was in Norway illegally. Usually operated in Indonesia but was of Middle Eastern origin."

"What was he doing here?"

Her father interjected, "Besides distributing tainted drugs that turned people into psychopaths? We've gotten information from military sources indicating he was the cell leader of the group making the powder and planning to make a major international attack with it."

There was a commotion out in the hallway, and Astrid glanced out through the open door. A group of a half dozen women and a couple of men in white Arctic parkas rushed past. The hospital staff seemed to be arguing with them about something. And losing.

Jens cleared his throat. "Yes, well. Speaking of investigations, I have a ton of paperwork stacking up on my desk back at the office."

He kissed her forehead and then gazed down at her fondly for a moment. He might be an overprotective pain in the rear sometimes, but he was a great dad. "I love you, Daddy," she murmured.

"I love you, too, sweetheart."

Oslo, Norway, March 12, 11:00 p.m.

Karen's door opened and someone slipped into the room quietly. Hopeful that it was Anders, she turned her head to look. Jack. Looking grim. What was *he* doing here?

Oh, God. Vanessa. She tried to sit up, but the tangle of tubes and wires they had her hooked to held her down.

"Is she—" Karen asked breathlessly.

"She's fine. She's just waking up now. Still pretty groggy. But they got the bleeding stopped."

Karen sagged back against the mattress. Thank God. She would never have forgiven herself if she hadn't dived for that gunman in time. As it was, it had been a close thing. Way too close. She was the spotter. She'd been the one responsible for watching the team's flanks. And she'd let them down. That gunman never should've gotten close.

"I'm sorry I didn't see him coming sooner—" she started.

But Jack waved her to silence. "Give it up. Visibility sucked out there. You couldn't have seen him coming any sooner if you'd have been looking for him. As it was, it was remarkable that you picked him up as fast as you did."

Karen stared as Jack pulled up a tall stool and perched on it beside her. "I didn't come here to chastise you. If anything, I'm impressed as hell that you managed to move in the condition you were in. The docs tell me you must've been in a full-blown seizure and heart failure at the point when you stood up, ran over to that asshole, jumped him and strangled him with your bare hands."

She didn't quite know what to say to that. "Ain't adrenaline grand?" she murmured.

He snorted in disbelief. "That's not adrenaline. That's heart. Pure and simple. Your teammates were going to die and you did whatever it took to save them."

He looked down at her with something suspiciously akin to respect lurking in his gaze. "I owe you an apology, Python. I've hassled you and ridden you hard for a long time. I knew there was a hero hiding in there, but I just couldn't get her to step up and show herself. But what you did—that went beyond heroic. That's the stuff the great ones are made of."

Okay. Now she was embarrassed. She managed a shrug beneath all the electrodes and said lightly, "Hey. What did you expect of Freya?"

He laughed quietly. "You may have to change your field handle after this."

"Never. I'm a Medusa. We're the snake ladies. I'll never give up being Python."

"Fair enough." He stood up. Looked down at the floor. Looked back up at her. "Are we all square?"

She nodded slowly. "Yeah. We're square."

He reached out and laid a hand lightly on her shoulder. "Good. Now I gotta go get square with another Medusa."

Karen looked at him askance. Something in his voice, an odd vibe coming from him, made her ask, "What are you up to, Jack?"

A smile played at the corners of his mouth. "I guess since you can't be there to share the moment it won't hurt to give you a sneak preview." He reached into his pants pocket and pulled out a little black box. He opened it and tilted it down to show her a beautiful diamond solitaire ring nestled in black velvet.

Shock dropped her jaw. "Are you finally going to make an honest woman out of Vanessa?" Swear to God, that was a blush climbing his neck and spreading across his cheeks.

"If she'll have me," he replied.

Karen laughed. "Oh, she'll have you, all right. Go propose, you big lout."

Jack pivoted and all but ran from the room. In the process, he nearly knocked over Anders, who was on his way in.

"Hey, beautiful," he said quietly. "How are you feeling?"

"Quiet," she answered solemnly. And then she added, "For now." The doctors had told her they had no way of knowing how long it would take or if this drug would ever work its way out of her system. They also had no way of predicting when her next psychotic episode, or seizure or heart attack would strike. For now, they planned to keep her hooked up to all these machines and monitor her.

He looked at all the machines surrounding her and grimaced. She knew the feeling.

"What was Jack so hot and bothered about?"

"He's on his way to propose to Vanessa."

Anders grinned. "They're a good pair. But they shouldn't be out in the field together. I thought Jack was gonna kill those guys with his bare hands after he almost lost her."

Karen sighed. "No, that's my job. I'm the homicidal maniac in the outfit."

"No, you're not. It's just the drug and you know it. Oslo's had people going crazy and attacking and killing each other all over the place. You're far from the only one affected by this stuff. Nobody blames you for anything you've done."

"Maybe I blame me."

He perched on the stool Jack had lately vacated. "I believe that rage is what saved you. Saved your teammates. It gave you the strength to overcome your body against all odds, to stand up and take that gunman out before he killed us all. We all owe you—and your rage and your physical strength and your mental fortitude—our lives."

When he put it like that, it didn't sound half-bad. She replied slowly, "Maybe you're right."

He grinned. "Maybe I am at that. Here's something else I'm right about. You and I were made for one another. It's fate that we were brought together like this."

She smiled back at him. "Hey. You're on a roll. Who am I to argue with you?"

Someone cleared her throat in the doorway. Karen glanced over Anders' shoulder to see Aleesha standing beside someone very short while a couple of nurses and a doctor or two hovered in the background.

Aleesha asked, "Mind if we interrupt you two lovebirds?"

For once, being called that didn't drive Karen crazy. She rolled her eyes at Anders. "Come in, Mamba. How're you feeling?"

"Me danced a leetle limbo 'round doz bullets and dey only tickled me ribs."

Karen grinned. It was still too painful to laugh much. She ached from head to foot in spite of the painkillers they were pumping into her.

Aleesha gestured to the diminutive person standing partly behind her. "You have a guest, Python. She's been sitting on the floor outside your door almost since you got here. She says it's time to come in now."

Karen peered around her teammate—and broke into a wide smile. "Naliki! What in the world are you doing here?" She'd been sitting outside the door all day? Karen was humbled by the thought—and amused at how the hospital staff must've reacted to that.

The elderly women threw an arch glare at the medical staff clustered in the doorway. "See? I told you she'd want to see me. And it's bad luck to deny the goddess."

Karen glanced over at Anders. "Yeah. You remember that."

He chuckled as the *noaide* stepped up to the bed, eyeing all the high-tech medical equipment askance. "Bah. All these fancy toys are not necessary."

Aleesha looked amused and the medical staff scowled. Aleesha explained, "Naliki claims to have a cure for what ails you, girlfriend. She's already tried it on the kids in the village and it seems to be working. There's this salt the Samis distill from the ocean. They mix it with what appears to be a local clay of some kind and have been feeding it to the kids who ingested tainted drugs like you did."

Naliki interrupted. "There are healing herbs in it, too. That boy whose heart stopped? He's fine. Drove me to the airport to fly down here. No more episodes."

Karen stared. What the woman had just said was incredible on several levels. First, the kid was okay? And second, Naliki got on an *airplane?* "You came down here in a plane?" Karen repeated, astonished. "Have you ever been on one before?"

Naliki drew herself up to her entire five-foot height. "It was my first flight. But these are extraordinary times. Freya tells me to speak for my people, and so I shall. Here I am in Norway's capital to do just that."

Karen frowned. She didn't remember telling Naliki that exactly, but if that's how the woman wanted to interpret it, okay.

Aleesha commented, "This remedy of hers is a paste you eat. Foul-smelling stuff."

Karen winced. She'd had some of Aleesha's home remedies from Jamaica before, and they were hideous. For Aleesha to think this stuff was foul, it must be truly lethal.

Aleesha continued. "The docs here don't want you to try it until they've run tests on it."

Karen looked up at her. "What do *you* think?"

"I think the medicine is sound. Salts tend to bind to heavy metals. Your body either sweats out the salt and its attached metal, or the salt and its piggybacking metal are washed into your intestines, where something like the clay would readily absorb it and carry it out of your system. It's a crude form of chelation, in fact."

"What's chelation for us non-doctors?" Karen asked.

"In non-doctor language, it's cleaning out heavy metals from your system. We use certain chemicals to bind metal molecules into chelate rings, which are then flushed out of the body, taking the metal with them—"

Karen held up a hand. "Enough. You've lost me." She looked back and forth between Naliki and Aleesha. "So, Naliki says this stuff has cured the boys back in Lakvik, and you say it might just work. I say let's try it. It can't be worse than lying here hooked up to all these machines waiting to have another attack."

A grumble rose up from the doctors. Aleesha rolled her eyes at Karen, who grinned back.

Karen glanced over at Anders. "What do you think?"

"I think you should try it. I've always believed Sami knowledge of the land has been overlooked. If that stuff fixes you and reverses the effects of that drug, all of Norway will owe the Samis one. I'll go with Naliki myself to plead the case of the Sami people to the king and the prime minister."

Aleesha piped up. "I think I can safely say that people at the highest levels of the American government will also want to show their gratitude to the Samis, regardless of whether or not this remedy works."

Naliki gifted them both with a smile. "With the Golden One's help, we shall change the course of history for my people."

Karen retorted, "Yeah, well, let's get the Golden One healthy first. I can't do much saving if I'm stuck here." She had to give the shaman credit. Naliki wasted no time getting down to business. She reached into a leather pouch hanging from her belt, pulled out a recycled tin can whose label declared its original contents to have been pink salmon and passed it over to Karen. "Eat a large spoon of this every two hours until it's all gone."

A nurse bustled forward. "How much, exactly, is a large spoon? In milliliters?"

Aleesha traded amused looks with the elderly Sami woman. "Oh, go on. Live dangerously, nurse. Just plop some goop on a spoon and slop it into the patient's mouth. Medicine isn't always an exact science."

While they waited for a soup spoon to be fetched, Karen reflected that *life* wasn't always an exact science. When she'd gotten comfortable in her own skin—for the first time in her life—she couldn't pinpoint. Exactly when she'd made peace in her heart with Jack, she couldn't tell. And exactly when she'd had fallen in love with Anders, she had no earthly idea.

But there it was. She looked back and forth between Anders, the Olympic athlete and trained commando, and Naliki, the tiny, wrinkled shaman. Between the two of them, they'd already healed her soul. Now all they had to do was get her body to do the same.

Karen took the spoon Aleesha passed her. She scooped up a big glob of the gray paste and shoved it in her mouth. It was the consistency of peanut butter and tasted like dirt. Salty dirt.

Grimacing, she choked, "Water."

Laughing, Anders passed her a glass, which she gulped down. She glared up at him. "Sheesh. The things I do for love."

Anders froze. Stared down at her. And then threw his head back and laughed.

Her laughter floated up to mingle with his, and she didn't feel even a hint of the raging dragon within. She was going to be just fine. They both were.

* * * *

Don't miss the next Medusa story!
The Medusa Affair, *coming September 2008.*

*Mills & Boon® Intrigue brings you a sneak
preview of Caridad Piñeiro's
Secret Agent Reunion…*

*A mysterious betrayal led super spy Danielle
Moore to fake her own death. Now she is ready
to re-emerge and seek vengeance. But things
get complicated when she realises a mole in her
agency is still leaking vital information – and her
new partner is an ex-lover she thought was dead.*

*Don't miss the fantastic second story
in the thrilling*
MISSION: IMPASSIONED
*series, available next month in
Mills & Boon® Intrigue!*

Secret Agent Reunion

by

Caridad Piñeiro

Only someone who had come back from the dead truly knew how deadly distractions could be.

Danielle Moore had let personal feelings get in the way of a top-secret mission over a year ago and had nearly lost her life. So she kept her eyes glued to the man—six feet two inches of thick muscle—as he charged at her like a linebacker after a quarterback, arms outstretched to trap her in his embrace.

Dani used his momentum against him, sweeping him aside with a matador like step. Turning quickly as he stumbled by, she snapped an elbow to the back of his neck and dropped him to the ground. Before she could totally incapacitate him, another more compact man charged at her from the opposite side of the room.

She pushed off the first man's fallen body and came up ready for action, but as she did so, something pulled along her midsection. A twinge of pain followed, but she tamped it down. She couldn't allow physical discomfort or weakness to divert her attention.

As the smaller man shoved past his rising friend, she released a sharp dropkick, catching him squarely in the chest and rocking him backward, where he immediately tripped over the larger man. Both men sprawled to the ground in a messy heap.

Dani stopped, placed her hands on her hips and laughed as they tried to untangle themselves and resume their attack.

"Come on, boys. Is that the best you can do?" she teased in fluent French.

After months of training together, the three of them had developed an easy camaraderie. Even now, when the men couldn't seem to contain Dani as her physical strength and martial arts prowess returned rapidly, they accepted her superior abilities good-naturedly.

Her current physical state was quite different from what it had been nearly three months ago, Dani thought.

After being shot and lingering in a coma off and on, she had emerged long enough to approve the removal of the bullet that had lodged precariously close to her spine. Three months after that, she had finally been well enough to begin physical therapy and try to get back into shape.

She had a new mission waiting for her, after all. At least, that's what the enigmatic man by her bedside had intimated to her so many months ago.

Dani now knew who that mysterious angel was—Corbett Lazlo, the elusive powerhouse behind the Lazlo Group, a private agency known for handling the most discreet and sometimes dangerous of missions. A group well known to her from her time with the Secret Intelligence Service, or SIS, the British equivalent of the CIA and the agency at which she had worked as the Sparrow, a world-renowned assassin.

Caridad Piñeiro

Only she hadn't really been an assassin. All her supposed "kills" had been taken into SIS custody so that SIS might find out more information about an elusive crime organization they called SNAKE, which they suspected of being responsible for a number of illegal operations.

She had let her last mission get personal. Her actions had resulted in the death of the prince of Silvershire and had nearly caused her death and that of her twin sister. SIS had been less than pleased that, in her quest to find her parents' killers, she had messed up the mission in Silvershire, the small European island kingdom she had called home at one time. With her cover as the Sparrow possibly blown and an international incident brewing, SIS had tossed her out.

Lazlo, who had also been thrown out of SIS many years earlier, was the man she had to thank for keeping her alive. He was the one responsible for the medical treatment that had worked a miracle and brought her back from the dead.

He had taken her into his agency and told her that he would let her know when the time was right for her to be reborn and go out on another mission.

She felt mission-ready now and sensed that somehow Lazlo would know that.

He seemed to know everything about everyone while she, like most of the people she had met within his group, knew little about him. To her surprise, few had even seen the elusive Mr. Lazlo.

After thanking her two sparring partners for the training session, she walked to the gym to finish her workout. She took a place at the first station and lifted the weights, evenly pushing up the bars on the bench press and enjoying the strength she had regained in her arms. Satisfied, she finished her reps and moved on to the next station and then the next.

By the time she finished, her muscles trembled from her exertions, but it was a good feeling. The kind of sore that said she was getting stronger.

The kind of pain that confirmed she was still alive.

In the locker room, she peeled off her clothes and grabbed a towel, ready for a long soak in the Jacuzzi. As she passed a mirror, she stopped short, surprised by what stared back at her.

The image of a hard-bodied woman of average height was reflected in the mirror. Shoulder-length hair in need of a trim. Fine-boned shoulders leading to full breasts above a long, barely pink scar that ran down her middle. Beside the scar was the ragged, stellar-shaped wound where she had been shot during her last mission.

The physical wounds of the past year were alive in her vision, much like those in her heart, which had been there far longer. The scar of her parents' murder. The ragged and still unhealed wound from her lover's death barely three years ago.

Dani ran her hand down the long scar, but it was numb. Just as she was numb inside. Paralyzed. Yet she still had things to do so that might make her feel alive again.

So that she could finally go home. Go and see her twin sister, Elizabeth.

Only, as she'd heard before, she suspected that she could never truly go home again.

Lazlo agent Mitch Lama watched as Dani sparred with the two men in the gym.

Was she ready? he wondered tapping his lips with his index finger as Dani deftly handled the two much larger men.

The frailness from her injuries was gone, as was the pallor that had colored her skin for the many months she had been unconscious and battling for life. Months during which he had come to sit by her bedside, urging her to keep up the fight. Reading to her in hopes that she might hear his voice and return because they had things to settle between them.

Now she was back from the dead and he didn't know what to do with her. What to do about the lies she had told him for so long. Lies that had nearly cost him his life and hers.

She looked strong now. Presumably ready for action.

He had always admired Dani's physicality. Been intrigued by the strength beneath the seemingly fragile and feminine surface.

She was a warrior. A champion who was forever prepared to take up a cause and fight a wrong.

He both loved and hated her for being a hero.

For nearly three years, he had been waiting to see her. To talk to her again. To be able to touch her and have her know it was him.

To ask her why she had lied to him about who she was, even as he'd lain dying.

A loud beep came from his computer, notifying him that he had an urgent message from Corbett Lazlo. A second later, his phone rang and he had no doubt who would be on the line.

He shut down his access to the camera trained on Dani, immediately regretting the loss of her.

"Lama," he said, a tinge of annoyance in his voice that he had been pulled away from his surveillance.

Corbett Lazlo identified himself. "Did you get my message?"

"Hold on just one second, sir, while I open it," he said, the cadence and tone from his days in the military coloring his speech. He double-clicked to open the e-mail message Lazlo had forwarded and held his breath as he read it.

The message threatened with its simplicity.

Ready for Round 2?

"I'm assuming Cordez couldn't track the source of this message either?" He wondered why their top computer person was having such difficulty tracing the mysterious missives.

"You're correct. Plus, I have some other news."

He knew the news would be bad so he preempted Lazlo's report. "Another operative is down. I'm assuming the same MO as before?"

"Unfortunately, yes. His body was discovered not far from our Prague offices. Close-range shot to the head, just above the left ear. Hollow-point bullet. I've asked our various contacts to see if they have a record of any assassins with a similar MO but I suspect there may be quite a few."

Mitch considered the facts and sensed that the moment for waiting and watching had ended. Time for him and the Sparrow to join forces and discover who was behind the messages and attacks.

"I'm assuming that you want me to activate the Lazarus Liaison now, Mr. Lazlo."

Silence came across the line before Lazlo asked, "Do you think she's ready?"

He recalled the sight of Dani as she sparred. "I think she's physically ready, sir."

"Quite the political answer. And you? Are you ready? Physically? Emotionally?"

He'd be a liar if he said "yes," and so he provided the only answer he could.

"That remains to be seen, sir."

FREE

4 BOOKS AND A SURPRISE GIFT!

We would like to take this opportunity to thank you for reading this Mills & Boon® book by offering you the chance to take FOUR more specially selected titles from the Intrigue series absolutely FREE! We're also making this offer to introduce you to the benefits of the Mills & Boon® Book Club™—

- ★ **FREE home delivery**
- ★ **FREE gifts and competitions**
- ★ **FREE monthly Newsletter**
- ★ **Books available before they're in the shops**
- ★ **Exclusive Mills & Boon Book Club offers**

Accepting these FREE books and gift places you under no obligation to buy; you may cancel at any time, even after receiving your free shipment. Simply complete your details below and return the entire page to the address below. You don't even need a stamp!

YES! Please send me 4 free Intrigue books and a surprise gift. I understand that unless you hear from me, I will receive 6 superb new titles every month for just £3.15 each, postage and packing free. I am under no obligation to purchase any books and may cancel my subscription at any time. The free books and gift will be mine to keep in any case.

I8ZEE

Ms/Mrs/Miss/Mr...Initials ....
BLOCK CAPITALS PLEASE

Surname ....

Address ....

....

....Postcode ....

Send this whole page to:

The Mills & Boon Book Club, FREEPOST CN81, Croydon, CR9 3WZ